PLAYING WITH FIRE

Michaela Sawyer

This book is dedicated to:

My amazing husband. This dream wouldn't have been possible without you!

To my parents and my friends who have all supported me on this crazy journey.

TRIGGER WARNING

CONTENTS

CHAPTER 1

Harper

Turtling into my body, I tried to make myself invisible on the old, worn couch surrounded by Villa Boys. Being unseen was better than being broken, and that's what my stepbrother, Noah, chose to do—break me.

Glancing up through my lashes, I watched him pace the old trailer's floor. His fist clenched at his side and his nostrils flared; I winced every time his massive boots hit the wooden floor, shaking the trailer. When Noah was in a rage, he usually took his anger out on me. My chest rose and fell with deep, rapid breaths as I tried to control the fear wrapping tightly around my lungs. Noah was unpredictable when angry.

His mortal enemies took something that belonged to him. Even though it was only a dime bag of weed, they were the ones who took it. They would have been furious if anyone took it, but those rich assholes dug a little deeper for Noah and his pack of mutts. I wasn't part of Noah's gang of thugs. I had no involvement in the incident, but I would pay for it.

"Those stupid fucking Valley Boys stole the weed out of my locker." Parker, Noah's second in command, groaned. Parker handled all drug sales within the high school since Noah was too old to get onto the campus grounds. "If I find out which asshole did it, I will break his face open."

The Valley Boys didn't need to steal the weed; they did it to set a fire on the south side of the tracks in the Villas.

The war between the Valley and the Villas went far beyond my eighteen years of life. I'd heard stories about how it started, and it was always different depending on who you asked. Not that it mattered. There would never be peace between the two.

Noah's dark eyes flicked from Parker to me. Squeezing my eyes shut, I said a silent prayer as fear constricted my lungs so tightly it was hard to breathe.

Shit!

Easing my eyes open, I avoided eye contact.

Do not incite the beast.

Noah was a beast, but it wasn't only his size that gave him the nickname; his bad temper and unpredictability were a deadly combination.

Tall, thick, and tatted, Noah wore his long dark hair slicked back into a greasy man bun, and his beard was thick and bushy. A few years older, several inches taller, and about one hundred and fifty pounds heavier than me, I knew I didn't stand a chance against him; at this point, I was trying to survive.

"Harper will go get it," he fumed, never taking his dark eyes off me. I cringed as my name left his lips. It meant I would have to do something I didn't want to. "Right, Harper?"

I wanted to argue, to tell him no, but I knew what would happen if I did.

Blowing out a heavy sigh, I caved. "I'm not sure who has it," I whispered, my pulse racing and pounding in my ears.

Noah was fast.

Before I had time to wince, he had me by my shirt. His fingers tangled into the thin material, lifting me off the couch. "Noah, please." My fingers curled around his wrist to steady myself. It was pointless to fight. He enjoyed it, and I usually ended up in more pain if I struggled.

"I don't give a fuck." His fist tightened as he pressed his face into my cheek. The heat from his breath burned against my skin as the smell of stale beer and weed hit my nose, making my stomach roll. "Get it back, or I'll make you regret breathing." His black combat boots pounded across the floor as he dragged me through the rundown trailer. Throwing the front door open, he shoved me out before tossing me down the broken front steps. A sadistic grin spread across his face as I lay in the dirt, trying to catch my breath for several long seconds before he disappeared inside and slammed the door behind him.

Closing my eyes tightly, I fought back the tears. I wanted to run away, disappear and never come back. I was eighteen, and no one could stop me, but where would I go? I had no car. No one would hire me in this shitty town because of my association with Noah and Levi, my stepfather. I had no money and no family to fall back on. My drug-addicted mom disappeared years ago. I was stuck, so I did the only thing I could. I pulled myself off the ground, brushed myself off, and devised a plan as I took the long walk from the Villas to the Valley.

I wasn't great at being bad, and I never seemed to get better at it, but I continued trying every time Noah forced me to do something I didn't want to do.

"Okay, Harper," I muttered, giving myself a pep talk. "You can do this. You just have to figure out who has the weed."

Rumors around the school were that Lincoln Elliott stole it from Parker's locker. Lincoln didn't bother to hide it because he wanted Parker to know. Thanks to Lincoln, I had a fresh bruise on my shoulder where it hit the porch when I was thrown off it. It wasn't like Lincoln couldn't afford to buy it. The Elliott family was one of the wealthiest in the Valley. Lincoln had two luxury cars, a sports car, and a motorcycle, but he still needed to piss off the Southside by stealing a bag of weed he could have bought.

"Okay." I slipped through the large security gate that protected the Valley homes from the trash of the Southside. "Where would the weed be?" Thinking, I nervously chewed on my bottom lip as my gaze darted around the entrance to the dark community. Even though it was a weekday, I knew the Valley Boys partied most nights at the Chandlers' house.

I would start there.

The likelihood of getting the weed back was slim, and I would take a beating for it, but I would try anyway.

Sucking in a deep breath, I walked the winding roads leading through the gorgeous mansions. If caught wandering the streets of the Valley, I'd be arrested and charged with loitering. No one would question what a Southside Villa girl was doing in the Valley because girls like me didn't belong on this side of the gates. Those gates were meant to keep out trash like me.

Trying to hide in the shadows, I walked the long asphalt path, trying to figure out where I was going. I wasn't sure which was the Chandlers' house. I'd never been in the Valley before.

The houses were spread wide apart, with tons of acres between each piece of property, but I lucked out after a short walk when I found a driveway with a massive rod-iron gate that read "Chandler" over the entrance; even better, the gate was open.

Standing at the entrance, my hands shaking, I attempted to brush off the nerves as my pulse raced and my heart pounded. I went to school with the Valley Boys, rich high school bullies. They partied too much, fucked almost anything with two legs, and got away with everything. In this small town, money talked. It also got you out of virtually any kind of trouble you could find yourself in.

I tried to stay in the shadows as I crept down the narrow driveway. I'd never spoken to a Valley Boy, and I didn't know what they would do to me if they caught me breaking in, but it couldn't be worse than what Noah would do if I didn't find that weed.

CHAPTER 2

Christian

The bass of the loud music vibrated the walls of the pool house. The smell of sweat, weed, and booze filled the air as friends scattered around the house and property partying like we did most nights.

"Here you go, baby," Cassidy purred, handing me a beer before sliding onto my lap, straddling me. My gaze raked over her naked tits and perky nipples as I twisted open my beer. "You wanna have some fun?" I tossed my beer back, taking a deep swig before dropping the bottle. "Dance for me."

Cassidy was a college freshman, but she and her friends were always at our parties. She rolled her hips, flicking her long blonde hair off her shoulder. Cassidy knew exactly what kind of dance I wanted. Her perfect tits bounced up and down as she ground herself against me.

Leaning in, she pressed her breasts to my bare chest as she brushed her lips across the shell of my ear. The heat from her breath made my cock twitch against the denim of my jeans. "We should go to your room."

I didn't fuck girls in my room. If she wanted to fuck, we'd fuck but not in my bed. We could do it in the hot tub, pool, shower, down by the lake, here on the couch, but she would never see my bed.

"Look what I found nosing around where she doesn't belong." My gaze flicked up to see my younger brother Aiden, carrying a dark-haired girl over his shoulder as she thrashed wildly against him.

"Put me down," she demanded, bouncing her fists off his back. "You big dumb jerk." I recognized the girl from school. She was from the Villas.

"Harper," I said dryly, shoving Cassidy to the side and pushing off the couch. Cassidy would have to wait; it wasn't every day a Villa whore broke into your house.

Aiden let the thin brunette slide down until her feet hit the floor but kept a tight grip on her arm. She growled, and he laughed when she jerked against his hold, trying to pull free, but Aiden was twice her size. Hell, everyone was twice her size.

Harper was from the south side of the tracks. She had zero business being here, not just in my house but on the north side, unless it was dirty. "Take her to my room." The music was too loud, and too many people were around to interrogate her in the living room. "There's a pair of handcuffs in the nightstand's top drawer." I kept a pair handy. You would be surprised how many girls liked being restrained during sex.

I wasn't going to hurt her, just scare her a little.

Harper's threats were broadcasted through the bedroom door, demanding she was released or else.

"For being so small, she's strong," Maverick whined, stepping out of the room, gripping and adjusting his jaw like she may have broken it. Considering where she came from, I imagined she had no choice but to be tough. "She has one hell of a right hook."

"I got this," I said, dismissing my boys and stepping into the darkness of my room. Her demands stopped, and she went silent. Her jaw clenched tightly as she adverted her gaze.

Sitting on the edge of my bed with one hand cuffed to the headboard, she refused to make eye contact. I'd had this fantasy before, except she was naked. Of course, she wasn't naked now; but dressed like every other villa slut. Her light pink low-cut top sat dangerously low on her full tits. Her short, tight cutoff shorts defined the perfect curves of her heart-shaped ass, dark hair pulled up into a neat bun on top of her head.

Wondering what her hair looked like down, I reached up and released the clip, letting her long, straight hair unravel down her back. I breathed in the smell of her sweet shampoo. Fuck, she was hot! Valley Boys rarely fucked with Villa whores, but I'd make an exception for her this one time.

"Hey," she yelled, swatting at my hand.

"Why are you in my house," I asked, sinking onto the bed next to her.

"I came for the party." She shrugged.

"Your side of town wasn't invited?" My hand gripped her face, forcing her to look me in the eye. "Did you take something?"

"No." She jerked her face out of my grasp, and I let her. Trailing my knuckle down her neck, my gaze followed, taking in the dust of freckles scattered over her thin, tanned shoulders. The same faint freckle pattern across her nose and cheeks. She flinched away from my touch, and I dropped my hand.

Only criminals lived in the Villas. Harper was the stepdaughter of the largest drug pusher in town, not to mention her stepbrother's gang. We were constantly at war with the Villa Boys, and it only got worse when they forced us to share a school with them.

They didn't like us, and we didn't like them.

"I could have my boys come in and hold you down while I strip-search you."

"Wh—what?" she stammered, her cold blue eyes snapping up to meet mine. "No. I didn't take anything. I swear."

"Then tell me, why are you in my house," I growled, annoyance coloring my tone. I was done with this game.

Blowing out a breath, her shoulders sank in defeat. "I need the bag of weed Lincoln stole from Parker back."

"This bag?" I asked, pulling the small clear bag out of my pocket and holding it up. I knew they'd come for it. Link practically took it right in front of Parker's face.

I hadn't anticipated they'd send *her*, though.

"Yes, please, I'll pay you for it."

I didn't want her money, but I did wonder why she wanted it so badly. I considered asking her, but I knew she wouldn't tell me.

Why would they send her to do their dirty work? I wasn't sure what kind of man threw a 5-foot-nothing girl into the fire. They had no idea what we would do to her if she were caught. Maybe they didn't care. But, of course, if it had been one of them, we wouldn't be having this conversation; there would have been a battle.

"I don't want your money," I finally said, cocking my head to the side, my gaze raking over her.

"Christian, what do you want for it?"

"You could suck my dick."

I gripped my growing erection, stroking it through my pants. Harper's gaze flicked to my hand before quickly darting up to meet mine. Her cheeks flushed a perfect shade of pink. I couldn't deny it turned me on seeing her handcuffed to my bed. Harper had been one of the first girls I'd noticed after Valley View Prep closed, and we were forced to drive forty-five minutes to the closest private school or attend their rundown public high school.

"I'm not sucking your dick, and I'm not having sex with you either."

That's what they all say, but I'll play along. Every girl I'd ever fucked always started with, "I'm not..." And usually ended with me filling their throat or sliding between their thighs. Harper was no different.

The only thing better than fucking her would be owning her. Nothing would piss off the Villa Boys more than claiming their golden girl as mine.

"You want the weed?" I asked again. Harper nodded, flashing me a hopeful look. "You're mine for a month." Her mouth dropped open as her eyes widened.

"I'm not—"

"If we fuck," I cut her off, swiftly grabbing her waist and pinning her beneath me, situating myself between her thighs. My mouth hovered over hers, close enough for her to feel my words against her slightly parted lips. "It will be because you beg me to fuck you." I brushed my lips against hers. "And you *will* beg me."

She rolled her eyes, but I could feel her body reacting to mine beneath me. Like every other girl, she'd be naked and begging for my cock within a week, tops.

"What do I have to do?" she muttered, using her free hand to attempt to shove me off.

"Whatever I tell you to," I answered, rolling over onto my back. "If I say jump, you say how high." She quickly flung her legs over the side of the bed, sitting back up. "If I tell you to do something, you say 'yes, sir.'"

"If I agree, you'll give me the weed and let me go?" I nodded, and the corners of my lips curved up. "Fine, but this has to be between us. Nobody can know."

"Wear your hair down from now on."

I was completely aware that she planned to bail on this agreement, but if she did, I would make her regret it. I handed her the baggy of weed, wondering what was so special about it that she was willing to sell her soul to the devil. Sliding off the bed and walking around to her, I took in one last long look, memorizing every curve of her perfect body handcuffed to my bed for later use, then released her and sent her on her way.

This was going to be fun.

CHAPTER 3

Christian

Skipping third period, I pushed through the door to the girl's locker room. I stopped, letting it slam behind me, when my phone vibrated.

Daisy - I'm in the shower.

"Fuck yeah," I grunted, storming towards the showers in the back of the locker room and ripping my clothes off.

Water pounding against the tile wall echoed through the silent, steamy locker room. Hopping out of my pants, I stumbled around the corner. Daisy Peterson was new to the school. It took two days for me to talk her out of her clothes. That was a record.

Daisy twisted under the shower's spray, and I let my gaze rake over her naked, glistening body. Closing her eyes, she let the hot water run over her face and through her short blonde hair. I followed the trailing water down over her heart-shaped ass.

"I was starting to think you weren't going to show." She smiled, twisting around to see me, running her hands over her full, perky tits. I stepped into the shower, and she moved forward.

"Get on your knees," I ordered, wrapping my hand around the base of my thick cock and stroking myself as my eyes trailed over her.

Licking her lips as she dropped to her knees before me, her eyes locked with mine, a cocky sparkle in them. Daisy thought she was special, and right now, she was, but after I came all over her face, she'd be just another name in a long list of women I didn't remember.

A rush of heat spread over me as she leaned in, brushing her full lips across the wide head of my cock. She thought she was in control, and she was for now. The corners of my mouth curled as I watched her tongue slip out and roll over me.

Sliding my hand up her head, I fisted the short blonde hair, and she yelped when I tangled my fingers tightly, jerking her head back.

"Open," I grunted, wrapping my other hand around the base of my cock. Daisy's lips parted, and I fed her my cock as she peered up through dark lashes; her mouth stretching as I pushed to the back of her throat.

"Fuck," I groaned, my head falling back as my hips thrust forward. Her throat tightened as she gagged hard. My gaze flicked down as her hands reached up, gripping my thighs. Drool slid down her chin as her tears streaked her face. I jerked out of her, and she gasped for air.

"Open," I ordered again, and she did. One hand in her hair, I used the other to brace myself on the wall. My abs tightened as I pumped in and out of her mouth fucking her face.

"Oh shit," someone cried out. It wasn't me, and it couldn't have been Daisy. My head snapped up to see Harper stumbling backward, slipping on the water and landing on her ass.

Daisy shoved me off her. "Omigod!" Daisy rushed to cover herself.

"Fuck," I groaned, my tone laced with annoyance.

Still naked, I strolled over and jerked Harper up to her feet.

"Shit," she muttered, squeezing her eyes shut.

"You should go," I said dryly. "Unless you want a turn." She jerked her arm out of my grasp, storming out of the locker room.

Twisting around, I realized I was alone. Daisy bailed too.

"Fuck."

Throwing on my clothes, I stormed out of the locker room, spotting Julian across the hall, sucking face with a redhead, and Bash, Link, Maverick, and Aiden huddled around Aiden's locker a few feet from them.

"What the fuck, man?"

He pulled out of the kiss. "What?" Julian panted, his wide eyes meeting mine.

"Get lost, Shelby," I told the tall redhead. Rolling her eyes, she twisted and strolled off.

"No," he groaned. "What the fuck, man? She was gonna suck my dick under the bleachers."

"You were supposed to be my lookout." I clenched my teeth.

"I am." He shrugged.

"Yeah?" I forced a sarcastic smile. "Then why did Harper barge in." In a strange way, I wasn't mad about Harper interrupting. My balls were irritated Daisy didn't finish, but I wasn't angry.

"My bad," he scowled.

"It's not his fault," Aiden laughed. "Shelby has an amazing ass. It's distracting."

I rolled my eyes. "Come on; I'm hungry."

I strolled into the lunchroom with my boys in tow, searching for Harper. She usually sat with her friend or alone. Never with the Villa Boys, but it was obvious who controlled her.

Spotting her across the cafeteria, I strolled towards her. She was wearing a grey tank and the tightest pair of ripped-up blue jeans I'd ever seen, and her hair was wrapped up neatly into a bun. Her goth friend hadn't joined her yet, so we slid into the table around her. I threw one leg over the bench seat, straddling her side. She went rigid as her eyes grew wide.

"What's up, Harper?" Lincoln asked, snatching the apple off her tray. Her eyes blinked wide from me to the Villa Boys' table, all watching intently. Good, I had their attention.

"Fuck off," she snarled, snatching the apple back.

"Ohh, shit." Maverick smirked. "She's feisty today."

"I told you to wear your hair down," I whispered against her ear, reaching up and releasing the clip. "I don't like saying something twice." She shoved me away, but I didn't move. "Be waiting at my Jeep after dismissal."

"And if I'm not?"

"Fuck around and find out." I gripped her thigh tightly, digging my fingers into her skin through her denim jeans. "I gave you your one free pass today with your hair. Next time, you won't be so lucky." Her jaw flexed as she stared straight ahead.

Reaching out, I twisted a tendril of her straight dark hair around my finger. Leaning in, I brushed my lips across the shell of her ear. "Oh, and you owe me a blow job," I breathed so only she could hear me.

"I don't owe you shit," she hissed, jerking her ear away.

My lips twitched in amusement. "Oh, but you do." Wrapping my hand around her arm, holding her in place, I brushed her hair off her delicate throat. My gaze traced over every curve, my mouth watering to taste her and twitching like it was drawn to her. "And I always get what I want."

Releasing her, I twisted around, kicking my leg over the table, pushing up, and strolling out. Making sure to flash the Villa Boys a shit-eating smirk on my way out.

CHAPTER 4

Harper

My heart pounded as my gaze followed the Valley Boys out of the cafeteria. My gaze flicked from the door once the Valley Boys were gone to the table full of Noah's guard dogs. Every eye was focused on me as they whispered amongst themselves, and it only made me hate Christian and his rich friends more.

My life had never been easy, but it had also never been this complicated. Why was Christian so set on destroying me?

"Omigod, what was that about," Chloe whisper-yelled, sliding into the seat across from me. "That was Christian Chandler." She fanned herself dramatically.

No doubt Christian was hot. He was 6 foot plus of chiseled muscle, sharp jawline, dark hair and eyes, with a smile that could melt a girl's panties off with a quirk of his full lips and perfect all-white teeth, but he was also 6 foot plus of all asshole who was not only from the Northside of the tracks but from the Valley.

"I'm aware," I rolled my eyes. "It's a long story."

"I got time." She rested her chin on both her fists and batted her eyes dramatically. Chloe was also from the Valley but was an outcast. She didn't fit the typical Valley girl look; she rocked the grunge style. Her hair color changed weekly, usually consisting of dark colors like black, red, or even green, which was her current color of choice. She was covered in tattoos and piercings, most of which were real. She mostly wore black but sometimes added red or other dark colors to the mix. She wasn't typically attracted to rich assholes either, but I couldn't blame her. Christian and his friend were on a different level of hot.

"Actually, I need a favor." She nodded, taking a bite of the disgusting slop the lunchroom called food. "Can you slip out of 7th period early so we can pull out right at dismissal?"

Christian hadn't kept his end of the deal, so I had no intention of keeping mine. I rolled my hair back up into my clip. I hated that I'd had to beg him for the weed in the first place, but Christian couldn't do any worse to me than Noah already did.

"Are you going to tell me what's going on?"

"Yes."

"Then, yes." She was a pain in the ass, but I loved her. She was not just my best friend but my only female friend.

The bell rang, dismissing lunch, and we gathered our stuff. "Do you think they're going to tell Noah?"

"Yep." And there was no telling how Noah would react to that information. I guess it depended on which personality I was dealing with when he found out. Noah hated everyone from the Northside of the tracks, especially the Chandler brothers. They weren't only dangerous; they had money to back them up, making them a threat to Noah, and if Noah thought I was fraternizing with the enemy, he would beat me ten shades of black and blue.

"I'll meet you in the parking lot early." Chloe waved me off as she disappeared into her class.

My class was on the opposite end of campus. The warning bell sounded, and the halls cleared as everyone piled into their classrooms. The familiar sound of boots pounding against the tile floor sounded behind me. Flicking a glance over my shoulder, I picked up my pace. Parker and Mason were hot on my heels.

Shit!

They saw Christian with me.

"Come on, Harper," Mason chanted. "Don't make me chase you."

"Fuck," I mouthed. I couldn't outrun them. There were two of them and one of me. I needed to make a decision quickly. I could run and end up in a place without witnesses, or I could stop here in the middle of senior hall surrounded by classrooms full of students and teachers. The chances of them hurting me here with so many onlookers was slim. They didn't have the same luxury the Valley Boys had. Money meant power and freedom in this town, and the Villa Boys had neither. The Valley Boys could get away with murder because everyone would turn their cheek, especially if they were eliminating the Villa trash. The Villa Boys didn't have the same opportunities.

"What do you want?" I halted, whipping around to face them. Parker and Mason Davis were fraternal twins. Both had dark hair and eyes with fair skin. Parker was a few inches taller than Mason, but what Mason lacked in height, he made up for in weight. Parker's long hair was down, and Mason wore his pulled back.

They both looked too old to be in high school, which was technically true since they were getting close to twenty because they weren't smart enough to actually pass their classes, but that's not why they came to school anyway. They came to sell and distribute drugs to students on campus. The only place Noah couldn't get to. It was only a matter of time before they would be kicked out and told to continue their education at an adult school.

"Is that any way to talk to your future husband?" Mason snarled, his gaze raking over me like I was his next meal as he licked his lips. He grabbed my arm, jerking me into him. I hissed as the pain of his fingertips digging into the sensitive skin of my arm sank in.

Mason believed I was his and that he had a right to me because he was Noah's second in command and I was a Villa whore.

"Get off me," I snarled, fighting against his grip, but it only tightened. "I will never marry you." Mason didn't really want to marry me. He wanted to fuck me.

"Don't try me, little girl," he growled, leaning down so we were at eye level. Drawing in a deep breath, I tried to calm my racing heart. "You fraternizing with the enemy?"

"No," I muttered, jerking my arm, and he released me.

"You better hope not, princess," Parker hissed. "Hate for Noah to find out about today."

I almost rolled my eyes. If I had to guess, Noah already knew about today. He probably had picture evidence sitting in his text messages as we spoke.

"Stay away from the Valley Boys," Mason ordered, his lips curled into an evil smirk. "You belong to the Southside. Next time, we'll make sure we meet in a dark, quiet place. So, we can show you properly who you belong to." There was no mistaking the threat in his voice.

"Can I go now?" My lip curled into a snarl. "I'm late." Parker jerked his chin, and I stormed off to class. I hated being tied to the Villa Boys. I hated that it felt like they owned me.

"Don't forget my warning, princess," Mason called out behind me. There was no warning. That was a threat. I would pay the consequences if I didn't do what they wanted.

CHAPTER 5

Harper

The clock moved at the speed of a sloth for the following few class periods. I leaned forward on my elbows and watched the clock, my legs bouncing rapidly with each tick. I was anxious to get out of Dodge. I couldn't get caught with Christian and his Valley friends again today.

Ten minutes before dismissal, I excused myself to the restroom with female issues and booked it to the student parking lot.

"Hey," Chloe said, rounding a hallway and stepping up her pace to match mine. We knew they didn't open the school gates until the dismissal bell rang, but we would be ready to take off once they did, long before anyone else made it to the parking lot.

Chloe approached her jacked-up white extended cab 4x4 Ford F-150 and beeped it unlocked. I rounded the front taking one last look over my shoulder; when I slammed so forcefully into something solid, I fell backward, crashing into the pavement. My eyes followed the solid thick legs, up to the crossed tatted arms, over the ripped, muscular chest of Christian Chandler.

Shit!

"How did I know you'd try to bail early," he said, his lips twitching with amusement. Reaching down, he jerked me up by my arm—the same arm still sore from my encounter with Parker and Mason. "Let's go." Dragging me, he opened the back door to one of Lincoln's black SUVs, shoved me inside, and slid in beside me. My gaze flashed to Chloe, frozen in place, gaping at Christian and me.

"9-1-1," she mouthed, and I shook my head no. I had to deal with this on my own.

"Hey, Harper." Maverick grinned from the front passenger seat. I snarled. Laughing, he slid a hand through his dark hair, pushing it off his forehead before he pulled his black ball cap on his head backward. "Funny meeting you here."

"Let me out," I demanded, glaring at Christian. They all laughed. Anger raced through my veins as I grabbed the door handle after the vehicle was already in motion. I would rather take my chances with road rash than spend another minute in this vehicle.

Christian grabbed my arm, effortlessly snatching me back towards him. My elbow met his solid gut, and he briefly released me. Reaching out for the door, I almost had it when he spun me. We tussled, and I felt like I was holding my own before I realized what was happening. I straddled him with my hands pinned behind my back. The corners of his mouth curved into a devilish smirk like he knew he'd won.

"Best not to fight him," Lincoln teased.

"Let me go," I said through clenched teeth. Fighting against Christian's grip, I thrashed hard, trying to free myself. He leaned back, thrusting his hips up, and relaxed like he was enjoying the show. A low guttural growl escaped his lips, and I stilled immediately, realizing what I was doing. His full lips twitched before curving into a smirk. This disgusting pig was turned on by my fight.

"Don't stop, baby," he whispered. His eyes went dark as they trailed over my lips and down to my cleavage, which was on full display with how he restrained me. He sucked in his bottom lip, biting down before releasing it. I had no choice but to sit still and wait until we got to wherever we were going since I wasn't in the mood to get him off with my struggling.

Thankfully, Christian didn't live far from the school. He and most of his boys were from Valley View, an Elite subdivision. It wasn't a typical subdivision that had rows of cookie-cutter houses side by side. Instead, Valley View had enormous mansions tucked away on large acres of land surrounded by lakes, groves, or other landscaping to separate the land.

Christian's home couldn't be seen from the main road; it was tucked behind large oak trees that lined the driveway to the house that was settled on a lake surrounded by groves that were part of his parent's agricultural fortune.

Lincoln snaked his black SUV down the long driveway that led to a 10,000-square-foot mansion. I couldn't imagine living in something so big and beautiful. Last night it had been dark, and the darkness didn't do it justice because seeing it today in the daylight almost took my breath away.

He continued down the driveway to the back of the house, parking behind a black Jeep Wrangler near the two-story pool house that Christian and Aiden lived in. The pool house was larger than the single-wide trailer I lived in.

Christian and I were from two different worlds.

"The house is a mess," he said once he shoved me out of the SUV, and Lincoln pulled off, wishing him luck. He forcefully guided me to the house by placing his hand on the small of my back. "Clean it up." He shoved me through the front door.

"Wait," I scowled, walking into the messy kitchen. "You want me to clean your house?" Cleaning the trailer was something I tried to do regularly, but it wasn't because they forced me to; it was because if I didn't, no one would. Not that cleaning helped. The trailer was disgusting.

Noah only wanted me to do his dirty work if it involved something illegal, so I was relieved that all Christian wanted me to do was clean.

"Yes," he said.

"Why?"

"Because I said so." He wanted me to know he was in

control. He reached back, pulling his shirt over his head before tossing it to the floor.

Swallowing hard, my gaze trailed over every curve of his sculpted torso down to the perfect V leading to... My eyes shot to the ground where his shirt landed. It felt illegal looking at him, even only half-naked. Valley Boys and Villa Girls didn't mix, so being attracted to Christian was unnecessary torture.

The front door flung open, and I was thankful for the distraction until I saw who had stepped through. Alexi Coleman stood in the doorway, still dressed in her school clothes from the day. Alexi was supermodel gorgeous, tall and thin, with long slender legs. Her long blonde hair was always perfectly styled. She flashed an all-white smile when her big blue eyes found Christian half-naked in the stairwell.

"Just in time," she purred, walking up the stairs to him.

"I'm going to get a shower," he said.

Alexi's big blue eyes flicked over her shoulder and widened as she noticed me for the first time; "What's she doing here?"

"Cleaning," he muttered, throwing his arm over her shoulder and guiding her up the stairs. "Oh, and if I even think you've stolen something, I will have my boys hold you down while I strip-search you in front of everyone."

Groaning, I watched the pair disappear up the stairwell. I wasn't a thief! I knew he didn't know that, and I couldn't blame him for thinking I was. I did what I had to do to survive, which was something Christian would never understand.

Noah was cruel. It was his way or no way. Sometimes that meant I had to do things I didn't want to, like break into Christian's house to steal back a bag of weed I wasn't responsible for losing.

The house was eerily quiet until I heard the upstairs shower kick on and then the muffled sounds of Alexi's moans.

Gross!

Aiden's footsteps pounded down the stairs. He jumped over the back of the couch and clicked on the TV. I was thankful for the noise, so I didn't have to hear Christian pounding Alexi upstairs while I cleaned downstairs.

Looking around, I sucked in a deep breath and decided to start in the living room. Even as messy and dirty as their house was, it didn't hold a candle to the dumpy trailer I called home.

Once I found a trash bag, I got started. Christian wasn't kidding when he said it was a mess. It looked like a party house, old red solo cups were lying around, and rotten food, but I gagged when I pulled a used condom from underneath the couch.

"I wondered where that went." Aiden chuckled when he saw what I was holding. "I thought she had stolen it."

Ew!

By the time Christian and Alexi strolled back downstairs, I had everything picked up, a load of laundry started, the living room vacuumed, and I was working on the kitchen.

He led Alexi to the front door, opened it for her, shoved her out, and shut it without a word, no goodbye, no kiss, nothing. It was blatantly obvious Christian didn't do the whole girlfriend thing; in fact, I wasn't even sure he invited a girl back to his bed more than once, except for Alexi. Alexi and Christian had a thing. Not a relationship thing, just a thing. Maybe one day, when he was ready to settle down, it would be more, but right now, it was just a thing.

He grabbed a beer from the fridge, and the front door flew open. Maverick, Lincoln, Sebastian, and Julian sauntered in, taking their places in the living room. Christian's friends were hot and tatted, even if I didn't like to admit it.

Maverick was tall and lean. His dark hair was usually covered with a backward cap, and his lip and eyebrow were pierced. Julian was the shortest of the group, standing only a few inches taller than me, but what he lacked in height, he made up for in muscles. He was thick with dirty blonde hair and dark eyes. Lincoln was tall with full-sleeve tattoos, and his lip was pierced. He usually wore ripped jeans and a white T-shirt. Which was odd considering how much money he had. His dark hair was longer on the top and usually fell over into his blue eyes. Sebastian was the tallest of them all, with the perfect tanned complexion. He had dark hair and eyes. His nose, lip, and eyebrow were pierced. He kept his hair short and usually wore a cap. Sebastian rarely wore a shirt or shoes. From what I'd heard, he was on the basketball team and pretty damn good. Aiden was Christian's younger brother, but the only two similarities the brothers shared were tall, toned, dark hair and eyes. Otherwise, you wouldn't be able to tell they were brothers.

"Damn," Julian said, taking a seat on the black leather recliner. "It looks nice in here. Smells good too."

"What's up, Harper?" Lincoln winked on his way to the couch.

I continued scrubbing the kitchen while they drank and played video games. I was wrapping up when Christian stepped in. He followed me with his dark brown eyes.

"What?" I tied up the garbage bag.

"Who sent you to break into my house?" He was drunk. I had lots of experience with drunken men, which usually didn't end well for me. He stepped into my personal space. "Who?" He knew who. I shook my head. If he expected me to say a name out loud, I knew better than to play this game. He might slap me around, but if I told him anything, Noah would kill me, cut my body into tiny pieces, and feed me to the dogs.

Closing in, he pinned me to the wall, pressing his body into mine, one hand tight on my waist, fingers digging into the sensitive skin, and the other around my throat, forcing my face up to his. His face pressed against mine.

I was used to being manhandled. This wasn't the kind I was used to, though. He wasn't hurting me. Pain wasn't what I felt; it was something else. Something that made my stomach flutter. Something I knew better than to feel.

"You're going to tell me," he whispered against my lips.

"Snitches get stitches," I hissed, not bothering to fight against him.

"You know what bitches get?"

"Fucked!" Maverick cackled from the living room. "We fuck bitches?" My body tensed slightly at the words but immediately relaxed when Christian rolled his eyes and released me with a groan. He wasn't going to force himself on me.

"I really need to go," I said. I didn't need to go, but I didn't want to be there anymore. There was no one waiting at home for me. They didn't care whether I came home unless Noah had dirty work he needed me to do.

"Link, take Harper home."

"No," I snapped, throwing my hand up and pressing my palm flat against his bare chest. His eyes blinked from my hand to my mouth and back to my eyes. Dropping my hand, I braced for impact, unsure whether I would take a hit to the face for touching him. I knew he wasn't mad when the corners of his mouth turned up. He was something else, but I wasn't sure what. "I'll walk." I didn't want them anywhere near my dilapidated single-wide trailer.

"It's eight miles," Christian said. "Link will take you." I opened my mouth to protest but realized it was pointless. He would put me in the truck if I didn't get in it.

So, I sucked it up and followed Lincoln to his truck.

"So, what's the real deal with you and the Villa Boys," Lincoln asked once he swerved into traffic.

"I don't know what you mean," I rolled my eyes.

"You obviously belong to them, but they don't stand up for you when we are harassing you right in front of them. It's weird."

"I do not belong to them." I clenched my teeth. "I don't belong to anyone. I'm not a piece of property."

"Okay." He leaned forward, looking both ways before surging toward forward. "That still doesn't answer my question."

I didn't know how to answer his question. The Villa Boys believed I belonged to them but didn't care what happened to me. They never had. Probably because I didn't fall in line like the other Villa Girls. I didn't willingly participate in anything they were involved in. I didn't want to. I didn't even want to be associated with them, but that wasn't my choice.

"Do you do everything Christian tells you to?" I asked, attempting to change the subject.

"Yeah, when he asks real nice." His tone was filled with sarcasm and humor. "Which house is yours?"

"You can just drop me off here."

"Christian said to take you home." His gaze flicked from the road to me.

"Well, lucky for you, I don't follow Christian's orders." I grabbed the door handle. "So, please stop so I can get out." I didn't want him anywhere near my house not to mention I didn't know what Noah would do if a Valley Boy dropped me off at my house.

He didn't stop.

"Pull over," I ordered. "Or I'll jump."

"You wouldn't," he challenged.

"Try me." I started pulling on the handle, saying a silent prayer that he'd stop and I wouldn't have to jump.

"Okay, okay." He eased the truck to a stop. "You know this is a bad neighborhood to be walking by yourself at night, right?"

I opened the door and slid out. "I live with the devil, so I think I'll be okay." His mouth opened, but I slammed the door shut and bolted into the shadows, where I waited until he was gone.

CHAPTER 6

Harper

Approaching my small single-wide home, the smell of stale weed and body odor assaulted my nose. I shoved my way through the crowd of Noah's thugs scattered around the yard, on the porch, and filling the small living area of the trailer.

Our trailer was a constant revolving door of shady people. If it wasn't the Villa Boys, it was sketchy druggies buying whatever Noah was selling.

This was a typical night in the Villas. Everyone showed up after sunset like creepy vampires to get high and party.

I spotted Parker and Mason in the kitchen, both with a beer in their hand, but I didn't see Noah anywhere, not that I was looking hard. I kept my head down, hoping to make it to my room without being seen. Silently weaving through the guys, I was careful not to make any body contact with them. I wanted to be invisible, and unless Noah wanted something, I usually was.

Stepping into my room, I blew out a breath of relief as I threw the door shut, but it bounced off the size twelve boot wedged between the door and the jam.

"Didn't want to say hi?" Noah asked, his voice low and husky. He used his large-framed body to push inside. I swallowed past the lump forming in my throat. His eyes were dark, filled with evil. Snatching me by my arm, he tossed me across the room, my hip slamming hard into something as I tumbled down, dropping to my hands and knees.

"Noah," I pleaded. I pushed off the ground, knowing I didn't stand a chance on the floor.

"Rumor has it you were cozied up with a Valley Boy today?" He was fast. His long thick fingers wrapped around my arm as he tossed me like an old doll. He whipped me around to face him.

"Noah, I didn't—" I choked on my words when he shoved me so hard that every ounce of air expelled from my lungs. My side slammed into my dresser, hitting it hard before I tumbled to the floor, gasping for air.

"You're a fucking dirty whore," he growled. Reaching down, he pulled me up by my arm and threw me into the door, pinning me hard against it. Pain shot through my body, but I wouldn't give him the satisfaction of seeing the pain in my eyes. "Are you fucking the Valley Boys now, you nasty slut?" I clenched my jaw, fighting back the tears burning in my eyes. "You eat with them, and you fuck them."

"I told him to fuck off," I muttered, twisting my face away from his. "I swear."

Pressing his face hard against the side of mine, his grip tightened on my arms—the tips of his fingers digging in painfully. My jaw tightened and my eyes squeezed shut, the pain so deep I could barely focus on his words.

"You better make sure you did." His tone was threatening. Hot breath, laced with alcohol and weed, burned against my cheek. "You belong to the Southside."

He released me with a hard shove slamming my back hard against the door again. Crossing my arms over my chest, I wrapped my hands around my upper arm, trying to rub the pain out.

Deal or no deal, I couldn't play Christian's game. I would end up dead.

"Come out and socialize with your people," he ordered. I inwardly groaned. I didn't want to socialize with them. I wanted to hide in my room until they were all gone and pretend this wasn't my life, but it was, and if I didn't go out, they'd drag me out.

"Here," Noah said, opening his closed fist in front of me, revealing a tiny white pill. My breath hitched as my gaze blinked up at him. I didn't want to take whatever that was. I didn't do drugs. I was even careful how much I drank around the Villa Boys. I didn't trust them. "Take it." He shook his hand.

"What is it?"

"Just take the fucking pill, Harper!"

Swallowing hard, I picked the tiny white pill up from the palm of his hand and popped it into my mouth, holding it on my tongue, trying not to let it dissolve. Thank god he didn't wait to see if I swallowed it before he disappeared. Spitting the pill out, it hit the floor, and I used the toe of my boot to smash it into the disgusting carpet.

Strolling into the living area, I sank onto the couch, intending to stay there until everyone left or I could disappear into my room without being noticed.

"What's up, Harper?" Mason purred, dropping down beside me. I didn't bother answering because he didn't care. He slid an arm across my shoulders, and I jerked away.

"Don't touch me," I snarled as I scooted down the couch away from him. "Keep your nasty hands to yourself."

"Come on, Harper." He groaned, his glassy gaze lingering on my mouth longer than I was comfortable with. "Don't make this harder than it has to be."

"Mason," I warned, slapping his hand away as he reached out to touch my arm. "If you touch me again, I will throat punch you."

"Hey, Mason," Parker yelled across the trailer. Mason's gaze snapped up.

"Come here," Noah said, leaning over the small wooden kitchen table with a cigarette hanging from his lips. "I need you to make a run."

"I'll be back, princess." Mason pushed off the couch, and I

blew out a breath. It was getting harder and harder to fight them off. Mason joined Parker and Noah in the kitchen, and I quickly slipped out the front door, trying to disappear into the night.

I would wander the streets of the Villas and the lower Southside until the house cleared out or settled down. If I stayed, it was only a matter of time before Mason decided to make good on a promise he'd been making for years.

Since Parker and Mason were second in command underneath Noah, it was only natural that I would marry one of them. That's how it worked here, except I would never marry him willingly. Once I finished school, I was gone. I didn't care if I had to live on the streets while I attended a community college. It had to be better than the life I'd been living.

CHAPTER 7

Christian

The bell rang, and I didn't even bother going to class. Mr. Thompson, my 7th-period teacher, and I had an agreement. I showed up once a week, and he sent me to detention for the rest of the week. Yesterday was a new record for me. I managed to piss him off within the first five minutes of class. It wasn't my fault our personalities clashed. He liked to be the boss, and I *was* the boss.

Pushing through the library doors, I hiked my bag further up on my shoulder.

"Detention again, Mr. Chandler?" Ms. Diaz muttered, but I could hear the flirtatious tone in her words.

Detention wasn't typically in the library. It usually had its own classroom, but Mr. Ward was out for the week.

My gaze flicked over my shoulder to Ms. Diaz standing behind the library desk. She was hot and not much older than me, maybe mid-twenties. Today she had her dark hair pulled up off her neck; she wore a low-cut pale yellow dress that made her tanned skin look even more delicious than usual, and her full lips were wearing my favorite red lipstick. I love smearing that red lipstick with my dick.

"I'll make any excuse to spend my afternoon with you,

Amelia." My lips quirked as I leaned over the counter.

"Christian," she whisper-hissed, her worried dark brown eyes darting over my shoulder to search for anyone who might have heard me. "You can't call me that here."

Amelia started working as our librarian at the end of the year last year, and it took exactly one week to convince her to drop her panties in the copy room.

"No one's here," I said. The corners of my lips twitched, and she cocked a brow. "Fine," I shrugged, "let's go somewhere I can call you Amelia." Her lips pursed as she searched the empty library.

"Meet me in the copy room," she whispered seductively before twisting away from me to busy herself with her library duties.

Eight minutes later, I had Amelia pinned against the wall. We didn't have much time, so I didn't waste any. She always wore a dress and hadn't worn panties since our first time when I ripped them off. This made everything so easy.

"You going to scream for me, Amelia?" I groaned as I grabbed her by the waist and whipped her around, bending her over the copier. I loved it when they screamed, especially if everyone could hear her.

"Just fuck me, Christian." She moaned as I worked my throbbing erection free. I shoved up her dress, positioning myself at her entrance as my hands curled around her hips. I didn't do foreplay. Not that we had time for it anyway, but I didn't fuck these girls to get them off. I fucked them to get *me* off. If, in the process, they got off, too, good for them.

Thrusting my hips forward, I slammed into her filling her. She moaned as she pushed herself up to her toes, and her fingers curled around the sides of the copy machine. I withdrew completely before slamming back into her harder this time.

"Christian," she moaned, and I started fucking her hard and fast, each thrust going deeper than the last. My head fell back as her pussy clenched around me.

"What the fuck?" My gaze flicked over my shoulder to see

Harper standing in the open doorway.

"Omigod, Harper," Amelia cried out as she shoved me off her, quickly correcting her dress, but by the time she was done, Harper was gone. "Move, Christian." Panic spread across her face as I stepped aside, giving her room to freak out. "Omigod, omigod!" She paced the floor staring at the ground, one fist on her hip as she ran the other over her face. "I forgot Harper was here today to complete some of her hours."

"Chill," I muttered dryly, buttoning up my pants. Before Harper broke into my house, I'd never had a run-in with her, not once. We'd never exchanged one word, and now she showed up every time my dick came out.

"Chill?" she hissed. "I could lose my job."

"Don't worry about Harper." I grimaced. "I'll take care of her."

Amelia burst through the doors going left towards the women's restroom, and I went right in search of Harper.

It didn't take long to find her tucked away in the back of the library, hidden in one of the deep rows of bookcases. I let my gaze rake over her soft feminine curves as she reached up to shove a book in the spot it belonged. Her dark straight hair was pulled back neatly in a ponytail. It wasn't down, but it also wasn't knotted up on top of her head, so I'd let it fly.

"What do you want, Christian?" she muttered, dropping to flat feet and flicking a glance my way before turning her back to me to scan through the books on her cart. She snatched a book off the shelf, then twisted around to search for its home, and when she found it, she lifted to her toes, stretching her body to reach the highest shelf. I almost laughed at the fact that she thought she could reach it.

Closing in the space between us, I snatched the book from her hand. "Let me get it." She dropped to her flat feet at the same time I reached up. My body pinned hers against the bookshelf.

"Christian," she hissed, using all her weight to push me off. I shoved the book into a spot and dropped my hands to her hips, keeping her in place.

Leaning in, my lips grazed over her ear, "You didn't see shit today." It didn't cause the same reaction I was used to getting.

"Gross," she growled, snapping her head away from me. "I don't know where your mouth has been. Keep it to yourself."

I took a step back, and she whipped around, narrowing her eyes. "Is there anything you haven't put your dick in at this school?"

"You," I said, my lips twitching with amusement. "Yet."

"I would rather choke on my own arm that I chewed off than ever let you touch me." She sneered.

"I got something you could choke on." I grinned, reaching down and gripping my dick through my denim jeans.

"Eww," she snarled before turning to storm off.

"Hold up," I said, wrapping my long fingers around her tiny wrist and jerking her to a stop. "Keep your mouth shut about what you didn't see in that room today." My tone was low and threatening.

"I mind my own business," she muttered. "It's not my story to tell, but it's only a matter of time before you get caught by someone who it will matter to." I shrugged.

"That day isn't today, baby."

"Can I go?" she asked, her gaze blinking down to my hand, still holding her wrist.

"There's a party at my place tonight. Be there by sunset," I ordered. "And bring some weed."

Her jaw clenched, but she didn't argue with me. I released her wrist, and she stormed off, disappearing around the rows of bookcases.

I didn't typically like a challenge when it came to pussy. I liked my girls easy and wet, but for some reason, Harper was that ultimate conquest I wanted to conquer for the bragging rights to say I fucked her. I thought back, searching my memories for any rumors that ever circulated about Harper being nailed on or off campus, and I couldn't recall any. She probably preferred the older Villa Boys.

CHAPTER 8

Harper

Creeping through the shadows, I searched for Chloe's window. Chloe's parents didn't like me. They didn't know me, but I was from the wrong side of the track, sealing my fate as to the type of person I was. According to them, I was a bad influence on their daughter. I was the reason she was covered in tattoos and piercings and refused to attend formal family functions, which Chloe hated. Chloe was her own person, and I had nothing to do with why she did the things she did, but that didn't matter to them. I would always be the girl from the wrong side of town who corrupted their daughter.

Even though Chloe lived with her parents in the Valley, she was rarely there. She spent most of her time at her cousin Abby's house. I wouldn't dare go to Chloe's parent's house because I'd be sent to the dungeons if I were caught. Not really, but who knew what they'd do because they hated me.

Chloe's aunt and uncle were laid back and not up Chloe's ass about everything, which made it easier to sneak in and out of her window. I didn't know if they liked me, but I assumed not because most people on this side of the tracks, Valley or not, didn't because of Noah and Levi.

I tapped on the window twice. It was my signal. Chloe shoved back the black curtains and quickly opened the window when she saw me.

"What are you doing here?"

"Hiding."

"From who?" She took a step back, shifting her body to move out of the way so I could climb through.

"Christian," I huffed, falling through the window. "Noah. The Villa Boys. The Valley Boys. Everyone, I guess."

"Who knew you were so popular?" She chuckled, closing the window and the curtains. "Why is Christian looking for you?"

"I doubt he's actually looking for me," I said, falling back onto her bed. "But I was supposed to show up to his party with weed, and I didn't."

"He'll be pissed."

I shrugged. "I walked in on him fucking another girl today in the library." I groaned.

"Holy fuck," Chloe exclaimed, sinking into the fluffy dark purple chair beside her bed. "Who knew there was so much fucking happening at school." I laughed. "Who was it?"

"I didn't get a good look," I lied. Ms. Diaz could lose her job if she were caught, and I wasn't going to be the one responsible for that. Even though she was only a few years older than Christian and Christian was of age, she was making bad decisions, and eventually, it would catch up with her if she didn't learn her lesson this time.

"It was probably Alexi," Chloe said, pulling her legs up into the chair. "I heard they fuck a couple of times a week under the bleachers during lunch."

"Eww." I grimaced. "Who has that much sex?"

"Not me," Chloe laughed. "Oh, before I forget." She leaned forward, pulling something off her desk. "Here's a new minutes card for your phone." She tossed it onto the bed beside me.

"You know you don't have to do that. I can live without a phone."

"I like being able to get a hold of you." She shrugged. "And I like you being able to get a hold of me."

Sucking in a deep breath, I picked up the card and sighed as I looked at it. We both knew what she meant. In case I needed her to come to get me to help me clean the blood off my face.

"You crashing here tonight?" Chloe pushed up from her chair. "You can grab a shower, and I'll find you something to sleep in."

"Did I leave any clothes here?" I asked, leaning up on my elbows.

"Yes." She pointed to the white dresser near the closet. "They are clean and folded in the top drawer."

Luckily, Chloe's room had a private bathroom, or I probably would have declined for fear of being caught. I enjoyed the shower until the hot water ran out. Where I came from, a hot shower was a luxury.

Dressing quickly, I stepped out of the steamy bathroom.

"I was starting to think you drowned," Chloe teased.

Crawling into her king-sized bed, I pulled the covers over me. I loved spending the night with Chloe, but I tried hard not to wear out my welcome. So, I only stayed when I had to, or Chloe invited me, and by invited me, I meant ordered me to stay.

"How long do you think this thing with Christian will go on?" Chloe asked, rolling onto her side and snuggling into her pillow.

"He said one month." I groaned, rolling over to my side to face her. "But I'm hoping he gets bored quickly."

"Guys like Christian get bored when they find out you're not easy," Chloe said. "Well, unless they like the challenge, but I don't think Christian's ever been challenged. He usually goes for the easiest girls."

"Let's hope you're right." I yawned. "Hopefully, he got the point after I didn't show tonight."

Chloe twisted and flicked off the last light covering the room in darkness.

"Good night, Harper."

"Good night."

CHAPTER 9

Christian

"I'm skipping lunch today," I muttered, dropping my bag on the floor in front of Bash's locker. Harper didn't show up last night, and I couldn't hide the irritation I was still harboring. "I'm meeting Alexi under the bleachers." I needed to fuck my aggression out.

"Aren't you in, like, a committed relationship?" Bash teased, pulling his locker open. I almost choked hearing the words committed and relationship in the same sentence. I wanted to own Harper, not date her. I wanted every low-life Villa Boy to know their precious princess was mine, and when I did fuck her, they'd be the first to know, but she was making this very hard by refusing to do what I told her.

"Funny." I snorted a sarcastic laugh. "I wanna fuck her, not date her." Harper Brooks belonged to me for the next month regardless of relationship status. She was mine. No one would touch her until I was done with her, or they'd pay the consequences.

Leaning against Bash's locker, I spotted Harper across the hall after third-period dismissal. My eyes roamed over her from bottom to top, tanned legs in a tight denim skirt hugging her soft curves, the low-cut top accenting her full tits, and her long dark hair clipped up.

Seeing her hair tied up annoyed me. It showed her defiance, her stubbornness, and while I thought the whole package was hot, I would make her regret the decision to defy me again.

I followed her and Chloe into Ms. Carter's room, AP English. This was not my class. I didn't have AP anything. Ms. Carter was out on maternity leave, and the substitute couldn't care less if we didn't bother him. Harper's eyes widened as I slid into the seat beside her.

"Meet me at my locker after class," I ordered.

"No," she answered, utterly unfazed by me. She twisted to face Chloe on the opposite side, giving me her back. The only emotion I registered was anger. It surged through me as I pushed my desk closer to hers. Gripping her desk, I yanked with a force that sent silence over the classroom as the steel legs screeched across the old tile floor—putting Harper face to face with me. Her eyes were wide, and her pretty mouth parted in shock.

"Don't be stupid, Harper," I ground out. "Be at my locker." I stood from the desk and walked out of the still, quiet classroom with all eyes on me. I'd make her come to me for her punishment.

The dismissal bell sounded, and I stood perched against my locker, impatiently waiting. Annoyance turned to aggravation when the tardy bell rang, and the halls cleared with no Harper.

"I don't think she's scared of you." Julian chuckled. No, she wasn't but scared wasn't what I was going for anyway. She wanted to play; then we'd play. Today the entire school would think we were fucking, including the Villa Boys.

Like a predator stalking its prey, waiting for that ideal moment to pounce, I stood quietly watching, waiting for that perfect moment when the halls would be full of random students and a group of Villa Boys.

Harper didn't even know what hit her before I pinned her against the locker. Her skirt hiked up, and her legs wrapped around my waist, one hand gripping her ass and the other pinning her arms over her head. She struggled against my hold. Her thighs clenched tightly as I made a show of dry humping her against the locker. The clanking of her ass hitting the metal echoed down the halls.

We had everyone's attention.

"What the fuck?" she growled, struggling against me.

"Play stupid games, get stupid prizes," I breathed against her neck. Everyone hooted and hollered as they passed, heading to class.

"Yeah, get it," a random male student said in passing.

The show must go on. Throwing her over my shoulder, I carried her to the nearest bathroom and closed the door behind me.

"What the actual fuck, Christian?" she said, anger flashing in her eyes when I set her down. She was mad; fury radiated off her as her nostrils flared and jaw clenched.

"You didn't show up at my locker," I scolded, shouldering the wall. I crossed one arm over my chest, and the other hand cupped my jaw.

"I'm not playing your game," Harper spat out. "You broke our agreement." She pressed her finger into my chest.

"What agreement was that?" I asked, rubbing my jaw, slightly amused.

"To keep it between us."

"I never agreed to that." In fact, that would defeat the whole purpose of this. I pushed off the wall, dropping my arms to my sides. "But I'll tell you what. You want out of the agreement?" She didn't say anything, just stood silently, eyes narrowed on me. "Get. On your. Knees." I pointed to the ground in front of me before starting to undo my pants. At this point, a blow job wouldn't be enough. I needed to fuck her. But I wouldn't have offered if I thought she'd actually do it. "And suck my dick."

I was close to pulling my erection free when she finally sighed. "I'm not sucking your dick. Put it away."

"Then take your fucking hair down," I ground out. Harper reached up in haste, pulled the clip out, tossed it to the ground, and stomped on it. "Good girl."

"You're an asshole." Anger colored her tone.

"Be at Tanner's party tonight out on the dirt road back in the groves." I walked out of the bathroom before I finished zipping up to add to the show.

"Did she suck your dick?" Bash mocked just as Harper walked out of the bathroom. She grabbed her books which had gone flying when I grabbed her and were scattered all over the hallway floor.

"Uh uh uh!" Maverick moaned dramatically, dry humping the air. They knew she didn't do anything. By now, we all knew Harper Brooks wouldn't willingly give it to me. She was going to make me work for it. And pussy wasn't something I worked for.

"You're all assholes." She flipped everyone her fuck you finger and stormed off.

"Fuck," Julian said, grabbing his chest. "That cut deep." I rolled my eyes and watched the aggressive sway of Harper's ass as she walked away.

"What was that all about earlier?" Alexi asked, walking alongside me to our next class. I raised my eyebrows at her; I had no idea what she was talking about. "With that Villa girl." I shrugged and kept walking. "Christian!" She raised her voice. I stopped, turning to her. "Are you fucking her?"

I wasn't sure what had gotten into Alexi and why she was acting like a jealous schoolgirl, but that wasn't how we did things. She might be one of the only girls I kept around, but that had nothing to do with liking her. She was easy. I always knew she would drop whatever she was doing to be exactly where I told her to be and do precisely what I told her to do. She would never be more than that.

"What do you want, Alexi?" I growled, annoyed by the questions.

"Do you want to go to Tanner's party with me tonight?" she asked. I almost laughed, thinking she was joking, but when I looked down, I realized she wasn't.

"No." I started walking again. Alexi was me in female form. We didn't date.

"Can I come back to your place after?" she asked.

What had been so great about Alexi, she had just ruined. Not only was Alexi easy, but she was also completely comfortable walking away with no strings attached. We didn't hang out after. We didn't snuggle or make small talk. She left. We weren't friends, and we didn't go to parties together.

"No."

"Are you going with her?" she huffed.

I halted, and she slammed into my back. Spinning around,

I shoved her into the locker with one hand. "Why are you acting like a clingy girlfriend right now, Alexi?" My tone was laced with rage. This was not how we worked; apparently, she needed to be reminded. She shrugged, not making eye contact. I leaned in, putting my face directly in front of hers. "You don't get to ask me questions about who I'm bringing anywhere."

She nodded and, without another word, disappeared around the hall.

CHAPTER 10

Harper

The heat from the fire burned my skin as my gaze locked on Christian through the orange and red flames. My lip curled into a snarl.

"You two gonna eye fuck each other all night?" Ryder asked, pulling me out of my daze of plotting Christian's murder. Christian forced me to come to a Valley party but hadn't said a single word to me the entire night. I'd stood by myself across the bonfire from him, devising ways to unalive him.

My gaze blinked up to meet his curious dark eyes. "Huh?" I asked, my brows pinched together as I stepped back out of the heat of the fire. I wasn't sure what he was talking about.

"You," he said, flicking his pointed finger and gesturing between Christian and me. "And Chandler." I most certainly was not eye fucking him. I was still furious. "You guys a thing now?"

"Not you too," I scowled, snatching the half-empty liquor bottle from him.

"He hasn't taken his eyes off you all night." He shoved a hand into the pocket of his dark denim jeans.

"He's plotting how he can ruin my life." I shrugged, flicking a glance back at Christian before returning my attention to Ryder. Ryder was from the Northside of the tracks but not the Valley. He hated the Valley Boys because he didn't fit into their model of what a man should be, and they tormented him for it. Ryder didn't play sports growing up. He was in the band until high school, when he let them ruin it for him with their constant bullying because they thought he was a band geek. Ryder was tall and unusually thin, with dark hair and eyes. Growing up, he'd had long hair, but recently, after years of bullying, he'd cut it. He had a baby face, and even though he was eighteen, he didn't shave yet. For some reason, all that made him an easy target for the Valley Boys.

As far as I knew, it wasn't necessarily Christian who tormented him, but that didn't matter to Ryder. Christian was guilty by association.

"Anyway, where have you been?"

"Suspended," he answered.

"Again?" He nodded, and I took a drink. Wincing at the harsh burn of the liquor. "What for this time?"

"Ditching." I narrowed my eyes. "What?" He threw his shoulders up. "Mrs. Morgan has a hard-on for me." Ryder was always in trouble. No one had it out for him. He was a natural troublemaker.

Ryder, Chloe, and I were the three amigos. We had all been best friends since grade school. They were the outcasts of the Northside, and I was the outcast of the Southside.

"So, really, rumor is, you and Christian are fucking," he said, taking the bottle back from me. "I didn't think he was your type."

I glanced in Christian's direction. Slouching in an old lawn chair, he was surrounded by girls throwing themselves at him. Two were already topless, bouncing their naked breasts in his face, but he wasn't watching them. His eyes darted back and forth between Ryder and me. I wasn't sure what my type was, but I was sure it wasn't him. I didn't have time to think about relationships and love, I was too busy surviving, but hopefully, that would come someday. But not with Christian.

"It's a long story." I sighed, rolling my eyes, grabbing the bottle again, and taking another long drink. "And no, we are not fucking."

"Your hair is down," he said, reaching up and brushing a strand out of my face. "I haven't seen it down in..." He paused, staring at the strand of hair deep in thought before his gaze returned to meet mine. "Forever."

"Yeah, I lost a bet," I lied, brushing the subject off.

"It's pret—" he started.

"Fuck. Off," Christian growled, storming towards me like a linebacker. Reaching down, he tossed me over his shoulder and stomped towards the grove.

"Put me down," I yelled, but wasting my energy fighting him was pointless. He carried me off the dirt road, past the grove, and down by the small lake before setting me down and pressing me roughly against the wall of the old boathouse.

"I didn't bring you out here to flirt with other guys. You belong to me for the next month. Which means—" He roughly raked his hands down my back and grabbed my ass, thrusting me against his solid chest. "This. Is mine." One hand still on my ass, the other sliding up through my hair and into my scalp, latching onto my hair, he yanked my head back, coming nose to nose with me. "These are mine," he breathed against my mouth before brushing his lips against mine. The sweet smell of liquor lingered on his breath. "Every inch of you. Is mine."

I sucked in a breath, squeezing my thighs together.

I couldn't deny he made me feel things, but I would never give him the satisfaction of letting him know. I was also still furious about his stunt earlier at school.

"You wanna fuck me?" I whispered, sliding my hand under his shirt and slowly running my fingertips along his waistband. Liquid courage coursed through my veins, pushing me to test the limits.

"I want to destroy you." His breathing deepened. His voice was a low, husky whisper. My hand glided up, tracing the curves of his ripped muscles. "Are you ready to beg me to fuck you?"

Sucking in my bottom lip and releasing slowly, a small moan escaped my throat. Spinning me around, Christian pulled my ass tightly against the bulging underneath his jeans, one hand tight on my waist, the other sliding up my stomach through my shirt. His fingertips grazed over the thin lace of my bra before sliding up and gripping my throat. I wiggled beneath his grip, grinding myself against him.

"Go ahead, baby," he breathed against my ear, skimming his other hand down my thigh, pulling my skirt up. "Tell me what you want."

"You want me to tell you what I want?" I whispered, spinning to face him still in his embrace. He nodded. The corners of his mouth turned up in a seductive smile. "I want," I whispered against his lips, skimming my hands up and grabbing both his shoulders, "for you to go fuck yourself." I pulled my knee up hard into his balls. He released me with a grunt. Hunching over, both his hands shot to his groin.

Shoulder back and head held high, I strutted off with a sense of power. That would teach him to fuck with me.

I didn't stick around to find out what Christian did after he recovered. Heading towards the Villas, I realized I couldn't go home tonight. That stunt Christian pulled would infuriate Noah, and giving him a day or two to calm down would help deescalate the situation.

I didn't have anywhere to go. Chloe was on lockdown, Ryder was in a brand-new relationship, and they usually crashed together.

Then it dawned on me. Christian's parents' house was empty. I'd overheard Christian talking to Lincoln about his parents being out of town until closer to graduation, which meant the beautiful 10,000-square-foot home was vacant. Aiden and Christian lived in the pool house and didn't seem to go into the house. The least he could do was let me stay since he was the reason I couldn't go home tonight. Not that I was going to ask permission, though.

Cutting through the groves, I crept to the house through the back of the Chandler property.

Sucking in a deep breath and crossing my fingers, my

heart pounded as I checked the back door, and when it opened, I blew out a heavy sigh. I waited a long moment for an alarm to sound. Nothing. Giving myself a mental high five, I stepped into the darkness of the mansion. Since being bad typically didn't end well for me, I did a little happy dance, even if it was strange that people with so much money and so much to lose just left their doors unlocked.

I stood still as Christian and all his boys pulled up to the pool house. Holding my breath, hoping they didn't come inside, and they didn't.

Turning on lights wasn't an option, so I roamed around the house using only the soft glow of my cell phone. I needed food, a shower, and sleep. I'd missed school lunch, meaning I had nothing but alcohol in my system.

Oddly the fridge was full—so much food. I reached in and then stopped myself. I was hungry, but I wasn't a thief. I shut the fridge and headed up to find a bed. I'd figure out a shower tomorrow in the daylight.

His smell teased my senses before I stepped into the room. I knew this was Christian's room without being able to see anything. My prepaid phone vibrated as I stroked my fingers over his neatly made bed.

It was Christian. I didn't bother trying to figure out how he got my number or how his name and number got programmed into mine. He was slicker than I thought.

Christian - You play dirty, Brooks.

Staring out the second-floor window, careful not to let him see me or the glare of my phone, I watched him reclining in a lawn chair beside the pool, watching his phone.

Harper - It was well deserved.

I expected to see him angry, but he wasn't. He was smiling.
Christian - You know this means war, right?

I wasn't sure what Christian wanted from me, but at that moment, I realized it wasn't to hurt me maliciously.

Harper - Game on ;)

I'd enjoyed teasing him more than I liked to admit, and truthfully, I couldn't wait to see what he came back with.

*Christian - **Be at my house before sunset tomorrow.***

I couldn't help but wonder if he already had a plan or was still working on it. I decided not to respond. To let him wonder whether I'd show or not.

CHAPTER 11

Christian

The following morning, I watched out the kitchen window as Harper carefully shut the back sliding glass door and silently ran down the long driveway disappearing behind the large oak trees that lined the driveway. Switching on my phone, I flipped on the gate camera and watched her load into Chloe's truck.

"Harper leave yet?" Aiden asked, barreling down the stairs wearing only black gym shorts.

"Yeah, Chloe just picked her up at the gate." I set my phone on the countertop and crossed my arms over my chest.

"Are you going to say anything to her?" he asked, opening the fridge, leaning over, and peering in.

"No, and neither are you."

"So, are we taking in strays now?" Aiden laughed.

"She was pretty wasted last night; she probably couldn't go home like that." I had no idea why Harper broke into my house. I didn't know much about her at all. But for some reason, it brought a sense of peace that she wasn't out fucking someone else.

Last night, Aiden and I watched her from my phone on the security cameras from the moment she walked onto the property and followed her until she passed out in my bed.

The entire Chandler property, from the lake out back to the front gate, was covered with cameras, even the bedrooms. The bedrooms were the only rooms in the house with the option to turn them off, but Harper didn't know that.

"You don't think Mom and Dad will see her," Aiden asked, closing the fridge.

"Mom and Dad can't figure out how to turn their phones on and off without help." My parents were brilliant in the business world but weren't very tech-savvy, and I turned off all notifications to the security system a long time ago. So, the likelihood of my parents seeing it was slim.

One knock sounded from the front door before it flew open, and Maverick and Link strolled in.

"What's up tonight?" Maverick asked. "We still having a party?"

"Yes, but I need to take care of something first, and I need your help."

I went over their involvement in my plan; they would direct Harper to my room when she arrived. If she chose not to come willingly, they would carry her, hold the door tight until I knocked, then leave and get what we needed for the party.

As soon as Harper appeared at the front gate, I removed my boxers before pulling on a loose pair of low-hanging jeans and taking off my shirt. Everything was ready for her. I listened as Link told her that I was in my room, and then Aiden explained that he didn't know why I was waiting for her in my room.

"What's going on?" she asked when they shoved her through the door, slamming it behind her. Her gaze scanned over my bare torso. "Why are you half naked?"

Holy fuck, I didn't expect her to look as hot as she did! Her long black-sleeve fitted top hugged tightly against her tits and was short enough to show the bare skin of her tight, toned stomach. Her short tight cheetah print skirt showed off her tanned legs down to her unlaced knock-off Doc Martens.

"Did you dress up just for me?" I asked, the corners of my lips curled into a cocky smirk. She dressed up for me even if she didn't want to admit it.

"What? No," she mumbled, her brows pinched together. "I didn't go home last night, and this was all I had at Chloe's."

"You look fucking hot," I said, my tone low and husky as my gaze lingered on her full lips.

"What's going on, Christian?" she asked again, crossing her arms over her chest, not even realizing she'd pushed her cleavage higher.

"Get on the bed," I demanded, nodding toward the bed.

"What?" Her gaze flicked from me to the bed and then back to me. "No."

"Get on the fucking bed, Harper!" She grabbed the door handle and pulled. "There's no way out." When the door didn't budge, she took a moment assessing the situation before finally deciding to get on the bed. "Good girl, now handcuff your legs and then one of your hands."

"No way! I'm not—" she hissed.

"You do it yourself," I interrupted. "Or all the guys are standing outside waiting to come in and hold you down on the bed." Her jaw flexed as she looked at the door, then down at the cuffs.

Sighing, she put the ankle cuffs on, and after another brief hesitation, she cuffed one of her wrists. After a quick knock on the door to release my boys, I walked to the other side and cuffed her last hand.

"I'm not having sex with you."

"Silly girl." I scowled, a slight edge to my tone. "I don't have sex. I fuck."

I pulled a blindfold from the dresser beside my bed; "Christian!" Sliding it over her eyes, she thrashed against the cuffs, throwing her head back and forth. "What are you doing?"

"Don't worry, I meant what I said," I whispered against her lips, raking my fingers up her inner thigh. "When we fuck it will be because you begged me, down on your knees while sucking my cock."

She sucked in a sharp breath.

"Then why am I cuffed to this bed," she breathed, and I could feel her heart pounding in my fingertips as they trailed over her stomach.

"The way I see it, after last night's little stunt, you owe me. So, tell me where you want it?"

"Want what, Christian?"

"My load."

"Huh, what?" It took a minute to register what I meant. "Christian! No!"

"Calm down," I teased. "I'm going to let you pick. Let's see where to start. The stomach." Running my fingertips over the bare skin of her stomach, I sucked in a breath at the feel of her heated flesh under my touch. Goosebumps spread over her body, and my dick twitched with excitement. "Not my favorite, but if that's what you want."

"No." She yanked hard against the cuffs.

"Okay." Raking my hand up, I shoved her top up to below her bra line. "I can pull up your top and leave it on your perfect tits."

"No! Christian!" Her tone is a mixture of breathy pleas filled with anger and excitement.

"Okay, okay, how about the inside of your thigh," I said, tracing circles on her inner thigh. "Or I can put it deep in that sweet pussy, but you'd have to beg for that." I ran my fingers over the lace of her panties, groaning at the feeling of the soaked material. She was turned on.

Holy fuck! In teasing her, I realized I was torturing myself. My dick throbbed painfully against the rough denim of my jeans.

"Christian, this isn't funny."

"No? Not ready to beg? Okay, well, what do we have left?" I rubbed my thumb roughly over her bottom lip. "Ah, my favorite." I crawled onto the bed, straddling her waist. "I could cum all over that pretty fucking face."

Her breathing hitched. "Christian," she panted, pulling her face from my touch.

"Or you can open your mouth, and I can give you a taste. Would you like a taste?"

"No!" Her words didn't match her tone.

"Well, that leaves one last place," I said, placing two fingers at the entrance of her mouth. Her lips willingly parted for me. Sliding two fingers into her mouth, she closed her lips around them, sucking slightly. My throat flexed on a hard swallow as my gaze stayed fixed on her mouth, and when she willingly sucked on my fingers, I thought I might come in my pants. Fuck! "I can shove it deep in that tight little throat." I pulled my fingers out slowly, feeling the heat from her mouth. I wanted to kiss her. I wanted to taste her. I wanted to fuck her.

"You win, you win! I'll do whatever you want; you win!"

She may have screamed that she didn't want this, but her body said differently. Her nipples pulled tight enough to see their shape through her shirt. I ran my thumb over the hardness, and she arched into my touch.

Lifting and twisting myself, I slid in between her thighs, pressing the weight of my chest into hers. "You're so turned on right now, baby," I whispered before tracing my tongue over her bottom lip. "That pussy is soaking wet for me, and your nipples are begging to have my mouth on them." I pressed my erection against her core to show her what she had done to me. "Are you ready to beg, so I can give that tight little pussy exactly what it's screaming for?"

"You win," she whimpered, thrashing underneath me. "Game over!" With a heavy sigh, I crawled off and adjusted myself. She threw in the white flag, which was all I needed, but I was still painfully hard.

"Christian!" Unbuttoning my pants, my zipper sliding down filled the quiet room. My pants hit the ground. "Christian, what are you doing?" She thrashed beneath the cuffs.

"Do you want to watch?" I whispered. Firmly gripping my cock, I stroked up and down, using the moisture as a lubricant to stroke myself from root to tip. I started slowly, quickly picking up speed and thrusting harder and faster, letting the room fill with the wet sounds of me pumping my dick in and out of my hand.

"Christian!" She fought against the cuffs, tossing around the bed, which caused her skirt to hike up more. My body tensed as my release came closer. Pumping harder, faster, my eyes roamed over her legs spread wide, remembering the feel of her wet panties, her labored breathing through parted lips, her hardened nipples through her shirt. Squeezing my eyes shut, I imagined what she would feel like as I slid my cock inside her soaking wet pussy.

My grip tightened as the only sound in the room was the wet sound of my hand thrusting harder and my labored breathing. My eyes flashed open, and I released myself into my hand with one more hard thrust and a low growl.

Disappearing into the bathroom to clean myself up, I left her cuffed to the bed until I was dressed.

"Game over," I said as I removed the blindfold. "Next time, I'll decide where I put it." I unlocked each of the cuffs. "And I'll choose that tight little pussy."

I'd won. Harper was mine for the next month. She may not be ready to beg today, but she would be soon.

CHAPTER 12

Harper

I was still reeling from what had happened in Christian's bed. My body deceived me, or that's what I was telling myself anyway. Hiding in the downstairs bathroom while Christian waited for me right outside the door, I tried to pull myself together, but chills broke out over my body when flashbacks of his hands, fingers, mouth, and the sounds he made when he released himself pushed forward.

"Ugh, pull yourself together," I whisper-hissed to my vagina, which didn't get the memo that we weren't interested in Christian. "You do not want to fuck him." I was not going to be another conquest conquered by Christian Chandler.

The smell of food and voices pulled me out of my trance, and instead of obsessing about Christian, I was focused on food as I stepped out of the bathroom.

Christian, Aiden, Lincoln, Sebastian, Julian, and Maverick were all piled into the kitchen around the large island in the center, shoving pizza in their mouth and joking around with each other. My senses were in hyperactive overdrive, focusing on the pizza.

"You better hurry up, Harper," Lincoln said, handing me an empty plate. "It will be gone if you wait too long."

Completely lost on what to do, I stood staring between

the pizza and Christian. We rarely had food at the house, but if there was food, it was Noah's, and he would break my fingers if I touched it. I had to work for my food. I didn't want my fingers fractured tonight.

A burst of laughter escaped Christian's mouth, startling me to reality. Still deep in conversation, Christian reached into the box, pulled out two large slices, and slapped them on my plate, and then I remembered Christian was not Noah.

Not long after I finished eating, groups started showing up for the party. The music blared, and people covered the property from the lake to the pool house.

"Hey," I said, tapping Christian on the arm. "Can I go now?"

"No." He laughed, sinking into the couch.

"Why not?" I muttered. "A Valley party isn't my scene." Not that I really had a scene, but this wouldn't be it if I did.

"You're my beer runner tonight."

"Seriously?" He was going to make me fetch him beers all night?

"Yeah, why don't you go get me one now." I wanted to tell him where he could shove his beer, but my body still hadn't recovered from earlier. I was sure I couldn't handle a round two, and who knew what that would entail?

By the time I returned with the beer, Christian was surrounded by girls. The exact girls I wanted to avoid, Valley Girls. Not all Valley Girls were horrible, but very few were friendly to anyone outside the Valley, especially someone from the Villas.

Taking a deep breath, I pushed through the crowd of girls and handed Christian his beer, hoping not to draw attention to myself.

"Ew, who invited the Villa rat?" Ava said, referring to me. I wanted to avoid this—having to defend myself in a house full of Valley brats. Her lip curled into a snarl, and I rolled my eyes. Ava was a typical Valley Girl. She was tall, thin, and tanned, with a perfect body. She had long white blonde hair that I was sure wasn't her natural color and dark brown eyes. She was always dressed in the latest expensive fashion trends with jewelry that cost more than my entire house.

"I did," Christian said matter-of-factly, standing and pressing two fingers against her forehead with a shove. "But I didn't invite you, so why don't you fuck off?"

"I didn't realize you were slumming it with the trash," Ava snarled, her dark brown eyes flicking up to meet mine. She wanted to make sure I knew she was talking about me. I opened my mouth to defend myself, but Julian cut me off.

"You know the Valley's full of rats too," Julian said, bumping my shoulder—a smile twitching at his lips. My brows pinched together. Was he defending me?

"Whatever, Julian. If you guys want to put your dicks in the trash, go for it but don't be surprised if you come out with worms."

Without a word, Christian snatched Ava up by her forearm, dragging her out the front door. His eyes went dark, his face red, and his nostrils flared. Everyone followed, so I did too. It wasn't every day Ava Miller got thrown out of a party.

"You will never talk to her like that again," Christian said through gritted teeth, his face pressed to hers. "Now fuck off and don't come back." With a firm shove, she shuffled away.

In my entire life, no one had ever stood up for me. Ever. Even before my mom disappeared, leaving me with Noah, she never stood up to them when they put their hands on me. But most of the time, she was too far gone on the drugs to care or notice. Even back when alcohol had been her substance of choice before she'd got hooked on the hardcore drugs, she'd never defended me against the men she'd brought home.

Lost in my thoughts, I stared blankly into the blue water of the pool while the party continued around me. Everyone else had gone back inside or scattered throughout the property, but I was still trying to think of a time when someone had stood up for me.

"I thought you bailed," Christian said, pulling me out of my thoughts. My gaze flashed up to him standing beside me, staring into the pool.

"No, I'm still here," I answered. "Thank you for earlier."

"Earlier?" he asked, his brows pinched. He had no idea what he did. Of course, he didn't. He didn't know anything about me. He didn't know that my mom would get drugged out and leave me with men that would hurt me. He didn't know that I had no one.

"With Ava." I forced a smile.

"Ava's a bitch." He shrugged. "Don't go all soft on me, Brooks."

I opened my mouth to change the subject but was thrust into the cold blue water of the pool. Chlorine burned my nose as I came up for air. Christian slicked his wet, dark hair back before wiping the water off his face. His tanned muscles glistened against the blue lights of the pool.

"What the fuck, Christian?" I muttered. Pushing my weight against the water, I moved towards the steps.

Standing in front of the pool, dripping wet, I removed my boots. Everyone was stripping down to their underwear, yelling, laughing, and goading each other on. It wasn't any different from a bathing suit. Unbuttoning my skirt, my eyes locked with Christian's.

"Don't do it, Harper!" His tone was serious, but he stood out of reach. With a smile, my gaze dropped to my soaking clothes. I pushed the skirt down and ripped off my top. I didn't notice Christian charging me like a raging bull.

Using his entire body, he wrapped around me, shielding me from view as he launched us into the water. He was still wrapped around me when we came up for air.

"You're a psycho," I spit out once I caught my breath. I shoved hard against his firm chest, but he didn't budge. The corners of his mouth turned up.

"I don't think you know what you do to me," he whispered against my lips. He pulled my arms around his neck before skimming his hands down, gripping my ass, and pulling my legs around his waist. Everyone disappeared around us. I forgot everything at that moment except how he made me feel.

The heat of his breath tickled my lips as he inched closer. My heart raced with anticipation. His lips brushed against mine with a smile, and I resisted the urge to wet my lips, knowing my tongue would brush his lips too.

"You two gonna fuck or fight?" Sebastian laughed, pulling us out of whatever alternate universe we'd gone to. "Cause you're really confusing all of us." Christian released me and splashed water on Sebastian.

"Grab me two towels," Christian told Sebastian.

Christian refused to let me out of the pool until he had a towel to wrap me in.

"Let's find you something to wear," he said, leading me into the main house and up the stairs. "These are my sister's. She left them when they moved. She told us to donate them, but we haven't gotten around to it. You two are about the same size."

"Are you sure she won't care?" I asked, scanning over all the boxes of clothes. She was throwing away more clothes than I owned.

"No," he said. "I'll meet you back at the pool house."

Digging through a large bag of clothes, I pulled out a pair of ripped-up, faded cutoff shorts. I dug deeper pulling out a tight-fitted black tank. "Perfect." My bra and panties were soaked, so I'd have to go without them.

I dried my long hair using Christian's towel and decided messy hair worked with the outfit.

I gave myself a once-over in the mirror before returning to the party.

"Holy fuck," Maverick purred when I strolled to the beer pong table. His eyes darted over me. "Damn girl, you want to poke the bear, don't you?" I narrowed my eyes. I had no idea what that meant.

"I want to play," I said, pointing to the game of beer pong they were playing. I snatched the shot from Lincoln's hand and shot it back.

"She's on my team," Lincoln laughed. I grew up playing

these games, but I didn't want to win. I wanted to drink unheard-of amounts of alcohol.

Half an hour and countless amounts of liquor later, Lincoln and I were trashed.

"You kind of suck," Lincoln slurred after I missed another shot. I'd lost count of how many drinks we'd had. I nodded, my vision blurring as I watched Maverick shoot. I didn't suck; it took precision to miss the cup that many times.

A song with heavy bass echoed from the house, and my hips swayed.

"I dare you to twerk on the table," Maverick goaded, running his tongue over his lip ring.

"Dare?"

He nodded. I never turned down a dare.

"You're on." Stepping up to the table, Maverick wrapped his long fingers around my waist and lifted me onto it. A couple of sways of my hips, and an audience of boys gathered around. Throwing another shot back, I threw the empty cup at Maverick. Pulling my shorts slightly higher, I placed both hands on my knees.

"What the fuck?" Christian's voice boomed over the music, but I was drunk enough to ignore him. I never backed down from a dare. As the crowd of guys yelled, I popped my ass up and down as everyone crowded closer to the table. One more pop to the beat, and I was jerked off the table and over Christian's shoulder.

He carried me into the main house and straight up the stairs, dropping me on his sister's bed.

"Change," he growled, hovering over me.

"No."

"Change yourself," he hissed against my lips. "Or I'll rip your clothes off and redress you myself."

I could give him a run for his money if I were sober, but I wasn't even close.

"Fine," I muttered, rolling my eyes. This time Christian waited outside the door. I settled for a pair of black leggings and an oversized KISS t-shirt.

"Is this better?" I stumbled out of the room.

"No more table dancing," he barked.

CHAPTER 13

Christian

"What are we going to do with her?" Julian asked, gesturing to Harper, who was passed out drunk in the middle of the kitchen floor. The last partygoers had left, and I was ready for bed, but I couldn't leave her drunk on the ground.

"How much did she have to drink?" I groaned, staring down at her.

"She's really bad at beer pong," Link slurred. All eyes flashed to wobbly Link as he swayed back and forth. He was almost as drunk as her.

"I guess we'll take her home," I answered, shoving my hands into the pockets of my jeans.

"You want to go into the Villas at this time of night?" Bash scowled. Nobody went into the Villas after dark unless they were looking for trouble—the kind of trouble where you ended up dead or in jail.

"She's not staying here," I hissed. Girls didn't sleep here. They fucked, and then they left. We weren't fucking, so she was leaving. "You wanna take her home with you?"

Bash looked down at her, considering the question, and after several minutes of him considering the question, I punched him in the arm. He was fucking with me, he knew Harper Brooks was off-limits, and I would break his face if he touched her.

I couldn't explain why. I'd never been possessive of a girl before, but I'd also never been told no by someone who meant it before, either. At this point, it was about the challenge.

"What?" He shrugged, rubbing his arm.

"I'll get her," I said, nodding toward Harper. "You guys go pull the Escalade around." The front door opened. "And don't let Link drive. He's as drunk as she is." He was twice her size, which was the only reason he wasn't passed out right beside her.

I waited until I saw headlights before scooping her up and carrying her dead weight to the SUV.

Everyone but Aiden, who was driving, piled in the back. I slid into the front passenger side, situating Harper on my lap before shutting the door behind me.

The Hillside Villas Trailer Park was about fifteen minutes by car from the front gate of my house.

"Which one is hers?" Aiden asked, driving through the trailer park, each trailer we passed looking more run-down than the next.

"I don't know." I shrugged. I didn't know anything about Harper other than she was from the Villas. "Link, which one did you drop her off at?"

"I dropped her down the road," he slurred, his eyes closed as his head leaned against the window.

"I told you to take her home."

"Yeah, well, it was that, or she was going to jump from the moving vehicle."

"Bash, call Piper and see if she knows." Piper was a Villa whore that Sebastian shacked up with occasionally and probably the only person we knew who could tell us.

Bash made the call, and a few minutes later, Piper texted directions.

Entering the directions in the GPS, Aiden followed the directions ending at Harper's trailer.

"That's where she lives?" Maverick muttered as we pulled up to the dilapidated single-wide trailer. It wasn't the fact that it was a trailer that was shocking; it was that it was barely standing. Green algae covered the outside and the sagging porch. Trash was scattered around the yard, plywood covered most of the windows, and I was pretty sure the entire trailer was leaning.

"Now what?" Julian asked from the back once Aiden stopped and flicked off the headlights.

"Harper," I said sternly before giving her a firm shake. She moaned, curling her small body into me. "Fuck!"

"Doesn't look like anyone is home," Maverick said, his gaze flashing from the trailer to me.

"I'll just take her in," I said, reaching to open the door.

"No fucking way," Aiden said, gripping my arm. "If they catch you, shit will go down tonight."

"I guess I won't get caught then." I smirked, snatching my arm out of his grip. I was always up for trouble, and it wasn't like I didn't want the Villa Boys to know who dropped off their princess. I wanted them to know exactly who was consuming all her time.

"I'm coming too," Maverick said, climbing over Link, who was now passed out against the window and snoring, to get out of the back and follow me toward the house.

"What's that smell?" Maverick groaned, reaching for the front door. The smell of moldy garbage saturated in cat urine made me wish I was holding my nose, not Harper. He pushed the door open. "Fuck." He gagged at the pungent odor that got worse with the door open.

Maverick stepped inside with his hand covering his mouth and nose.

"Holy fuck!" The inside looked worse than the outside. The walls were covered in black mold and holes, the floors were caving in, and the furniture was ripped to shreds. The small living room was covered in old, moldy food and beer bottles. The even smaller kitchen had broken glass and more beer bottles and cans stacked around the counter. The broken wooden dining table had an ashtray overflowing with cigarette butts and the residue of what looked to be cocaine with hollowed-out pens as make-shift straws covering it.

"I guess they drink their calories," Maverick muttered through his hand, gesturing inside the fridge full of beer and no food.

Focusing on breathing through my mouth, I searched for even the smallest clean spot to set Harper, but it was pointless. The trailer was beyond disgusting. How could she live like this? How could her mother allow this? My jaw clenched as my blood started to simmer. This was why she didn't want Link to drop her off at her house.

"I can't leave her here," I said, unconsciously shaking my head back and forth. I didn't need to see anymore. I didn't know what Harper's room looked like, but it didn't matter. There was no way I could leave her in this filth passed out.

Maverick nodded.

Stepping away from the trailer, Maverick and I simultaneously sucked in a deep breath of fresh air.

"The fuck?" Aiden whisper-yelled, shoving my door open from the driver's side. "I thought you were leaving her here?"

"Change of plans." I slid into the SUV with her still in my arms.

"Man, she's not a puppy," Julian said. "You can't adopt her."

"No, she's not, but I wouldn't leave a puppy there either."

"Yeah, it's pretty bad," Maverick said, climbing back over Link.

"So, what now?" Aiden asked, putting the SUV in reverse and backing out.

"She can stay with us tonight." I groaned. Glancing down at Harper, still deep in sleep, I slid the loose hair from her face back. I knew Harper was from the Villas, but I would never have guessed that was where she lived. "No one says anything about us bringing her home tonight." I didn't want her to feel any different around us.

Harper started to stir once we were back in the Valley.

We pulled up to the pool house, and I slid out, setting her on her feet.

"Stand right there," I said, steadying her before I reached back into the car to grab my phone that had fallen into the seat. Harper was more unstable than I'd realized. My hand slid around her waist as she went down. I couldn't steady myself quick enough, and she took me with her, splashing into the only mud puddle in the yard.

I hated drunk girls. This was exactly why I didn't look after them, along with many other reasons like I didn't care enough and I'd never had a girl pass out in my house before.

I leaned back on my knees, and she threw her head back in a fit of laughter, flinging the mud off her hands. It was the first time I'd seen her smile or heard her laugh. It was contagious. Even covered in mud, she was beautiful.

I climbed off the ground and threw the mud-soaked drunk girl over my shoulder. She didn't fight me, only laughed harder until she hiccupped.

"You smell delicious," she slurred, and I couldn't contain my smile. I liked sober feisty Harper, but drunk Harper was fun too.

"Holy shit, what happened?" Aiden gasped when I stepped into the pool house. I didn't answer as I stomped up the stairs.

I turned the water on before stepping into the shower, fully clothed, still carrying Harper over my shoulder.

Sitting her down on the tile shower seat, I reached back and pulled my mud-soaked shirt over my head, then stripped down to my boxer briefs. I was comfortable being naked, but I wasn't sure how she'd feel about that.

Her lust-filled eyes traveled over the length of my body before settling on my mouth. It wasn't hard to tell what she was thinking.

"See something you like?" I teased, the corners of my mouth turning up.

Harper sucked her bottom lip in before biting down. My breathing deepened as I kneeled to pull off her mud-soaked boots, tossing them to the side.

"You're kind of hot," she slurred, and I smiled at the

confession she'd never make if she was sober. She reached down and pulled her shirt up, fighting to get it over her head. Standing up, I untangled her from it and dropped it on the shower floor. She wasn't wearing anything underneath. My breath hitched at the sight of her. Her bright blue eyes locked on mine, begging me to fuck her. Sober Harper was going to hate herself in the morning.

"Come on." I pulled her up by her waist. "Let's get the mud out of your hair." As much as I wanted to fuck her, I wanted her to be sober when it happened, and I knew sober Harper wasn't ready to submit the way drunk Harper was.

Gripping her around the waist, I held her flush against me under the hot water as it pushed the mud down the drain.

The water cascaded over her skin, trailing over her tits and perky nipples.

Fuck!

Her fingertips traced the curves of my abs, and I released a low growl. She wasn't just hot; she was fuckable and willing. My cock throbbed against the thin fabric of my boxers. I grabbed her hand, stilling her. I wasn't sure how much more I could take before caving to drunk Harper. I honestly didn't realize I had this much self-control.

My fingertips traced the waistband of her leggings, I waited for her to protest, and when she didn't, I slipped my hands in, slowly guiding the wet fabric down her legs, goosebumps following her skin behind my touch. Fuck, she wasn't wearing anything underneath. My eyes trailed over her tanned wet skin.

I said I wouldn't fuck her until she begged me to. Her mouth didn't say the words, but her pleading eyes were begging me to fuck her.

Fuck it!

Scooping her up, I shoved her naked body against the tile wall as she wrapped her legs around my waist. Pressing my body firmly against hers, her fingers slid into my hair. Her full pink lips brushed against mine, her breath tickling every nerve ending before her mouth crashed against mine. I let her start it, but I would finish it.

Running my tongue along her lips, they parted, allowing me access to her mouth. Our tongues collided in a hot wet fight for submission.

I won!

Fisting her hair, I jerked her head back, giving me access to the soft skin of her neck. My lips traced the curve of it as I ground my throbbing erection against her core. A breathy moan escaped her throat, and I almost lost it. There was nothing between us except my boxers, nothing stopping me from pushing deep inside her except a very thin, wet layer of fabric and some newfound conscience that screamed inside my head that Harper was too drunk to remember. I wanted, no, I needed for her to remember.

"Harper," I breathed, pulling away from her and letting her slick naked body slide against mine to the ground. Her face twisted with disappointment as I took a step back. I couldn't believe I was telling her no. I'd never told a girl this hot for it no before, drunk or not. What the fuck was wrong with me?

The mud was gone, so I stepped out of the shower, grabbed two towels, and handed her one.

Helping her into a clean shirt and a pair of boxer briefs, I guided her to my bed and climbed in beside her. I'd never shared a bed with anyone, never snuggled, but I couldn't control the urge to pull her against me. Her small body tucked into mine perfectly, and we were both asleep without another word.

CHAPTER 14

Christian

The following morning, when my alarm sounded and I realized Harper was already gone, a slew of emotions filtered through me. Amusement that she was the one who bailed first, aggravation that she ditched me, and a sense of relief that we didn't have to have the awkward morning-after conversation even without having sex.

I wasn't sure when she'd taken off that morning, but she was gone, along with any evidence she'd been there.

I'd never shared my bed with anyone before, and I never imagined I would, especially with a girl I wasn't fucking.

Strolling into the hallway packed with students, I spotted Harper across the hall; I picked up my pace. My guess was she didn't remember much about last night, and I was going to torture her.

"Why did you take off so early this morning?" I teased, throwing my arm over Harper's shoulder. "Didn't want to stay and cuddle?"

"Get off me," she snarled, shoving my arm from her shoulders and stepping up her pace, but I was right on her heels.

She ignored my questions.

"Hey," I barked teasingly. "So, what? You get what you

want, and now you're going to blow me off?" Both hands dramatically grabbed my chest, feigning hurt. "Are you using me for sex?" I raised my voice so the crowds of students around us could hear. We might as well put on a show for our massive audience.

"Very funny." She fake-laughed, fumbling with the combination to her locker before opening the door. She grabbed a thick textbook and shoved it into her book bag.

"You did kiss me last night," I taunted, leaning against the locker next to hers, my arms crossed over my chest.

"Almost doesn't count," she snorted, slamming her locker. "And that was a moment of weakness." I assumed she was referring to the almost kiss in the pool before she got sloshed. "That I assure you will never happen again." She was even cute when she lied because she *was* lying. She turned to walk away, but I grabbed her wrist, spinning her around to me; my hands gripped her waist, pulling her tight against me.

"I don't think the weakness extended to the shower," I whispered, leaning down eye to eye so only she could hear me. "And yes, we did."

"Shower?" Her pretty blue eyes widened, searching mine for truth before they darted around as she combed through her memories from last night. "We were in the shower?" She paused, swallowing hard. "Like together?" I nodded, cockily smirking. "Na—Naked?"

"Don't worry; I didn't let you take advantage of me in your drunken state."

"So, we didn't—?"

"No." She blew out a heavy sigh, and her shoulders sank as she visibly relaxed.

"Come on." I smiled when the first-period bell rang. Grabbing her book bag out of her hand and tossing it over my shoulder, I threw my arm over her shoulders and guided her down the hall towards her next class, passing all the wide-eyed stares of students as their eyes followed us through the halls. "I'll walk you to class."

I was kicked back in my seat in the back of the classroom, trying my best to drown out the teacher's lecture; I pulled the hood of my black hoodie over my head and closed my eyes. I couldn't stop my thoughts from flashing back to the shower and Harper's naked body.

Last night, I'd made the right decision not to let it go any further. Her not remembering me fucking her was not an option.

Everything about Harper intrigued me, and I needed to know more. Not that my lack of knowledge about her would stop me from fucking sober Harper if she was ready to beg, but I had a feeling we weren't even close to that yet.

My phone buzzed against the desk loud enough to draw attention.

"Put it away," Ms. Morgan demanded. I ignored her.

Maverick - Harper's not in 3rd period.

Leaning forward in my chair, I re-read the text twice, making sure I read it correctly. Harper wasn't the kind of girl who skipped. She was the complete opposite. She was never absent, she was never even tardy except the times I made her late, and she sure as hell didn't skip class.

"Mr. Chandler," Ms. Morgan barked when I stood from my desk, causing the metal legs of the chair to screech across the tile floor. "Sit down!" Ms. Morgan was a small older woman with short silver hair. She barely stood eye-level with my chest, but she wasn't the least bit intimidated by me like the other teachers.

"Gotta piss." I shrugged and strolled out of the classroom and straight to the hall where Harper's class was.

Walking the halls, I scanned each classroom through the long narrow window in the door. Harper wasn't in any of them.

As I passed through the senior hallway, whispers echoed from the girl's bathroom. Leaning up to the open doorway, I immediately recognized the voice. It was Harper, and she was safe.

The deep voice of a male laughing followed whatever she said, echoing out the doorway.

Or maybe she wasn't.

I was going to wait outside, but that wasn't happening now that I knew she was with a guy. My teeth ground together, and my fist clenched as I stormed into the bathroom.

She was locked in the large, handicapped stall with someone other than me who had a dick. Fire blew through my veins. I reared my boot back and shoved it through the weak door. The lock burst off, flying across the stall, and the door slammed open.

"Get the fuck out," I snarled, reaching down and grabbing the wide-eyed punk, spinning, and shoving him out of the stall. He stumbled backward before straightening himself. Bowing my chest out, I bumped mine against his, backing him further away from her. Ryder was the same height as me allowing me to stand face-to-face with him.

"Christian," Harper hissed, jumping up on her feet. "What the fuck?"

The punk stood firmly, shoulders back, head high, his shit brown eyes flicking from me to Harper. Every time his gaze cut to her brought my blood closer to boiling. This fucker was asking for me to pull his eyes out. Ripping him up by the front of his shirt, I drug him out of the bathroom.

"Stop, Christian," Harper yelled, grabbing at my arms. I shoved him hard against the locker. A grunt huffed out as his back made impact with the lockers, my forearm pinning him in place, slowly cutting off his oxygen. My chest heaved up and down as rage consumed me. He struggled against me but was no match for the adrenaline coursing through my body.

"The next time you so much as look at her," I said, my tone low and deadly. "I'll rip your fucking eyes out."

"Let him go!"

I released him, and gasping for air; he scurried off. Spinning around to Harper, I grabbed her by the arm, jerking her back into the bathroom and pinning her against the wall with my body.

"You are mine," I breathed against her lips. "Did he touch you?"

"Ryder is my friend, Christian." She attempted to shove me off her. Pinning her arms over her head with one hand, I filled the other with her ass hiking her up and wrapping her legs around my waist.

"Girls and guys aren't friends," I informed her, releasing her hands. "He only wants to fuck you."

"No, *you* only wanna fuck me," she stated matter-of-factly, a slow smile spreading across her face. "Ryder and I are just friends."

"If he touches you, I'll break every bone in his fucking hand," I ground out. No one was going to touch her but me.

"Christian, you're being ridiculous." She laughed, rolling her eyes.

"It's obvious he wants you."

"Christian, he is not into me." She laughed.

"Is this funny to you?" I asked, not amused, releasing her hands.

"It is because Ryder would be into *you* before *me*. Although, I know for a fact, assholes aren't his type." My brows furrowed. "He's gay, Christian. He has a boyfriend." The tension consuming every ounce of my body disappeared, and my shoulders relaxed.

"Gay, huh?" She nodded, laughing, as I set her feet back on

the ground. The bell rang, and I grabbed her bag for her.

"Bet you feel like an ass," she teased.

An ass, no. Amused, yes, but I did not feel like an ass. I would do it again and again because Harper Brooks was mine, and I would break anyone who touched her.

"Why were you skipping?" I asked, following her out of the bathroom and slinging her bag over my shoulder.

"It's not a big deal." She waved it off. It was obviously a big deal if she went out of her way to skip class and hide in a bathroom stall on a disgusting floor. It definitely was a big deal.

"Harper," I growled, wrapping my fingers around her upper arm and halting her.

"The new sub is a little pervy," she said, shrugging. "That's all."

"Did he touch you?" I asked, keeping my tone level. I didn't want her to think I would freak out, even though we both knew I would.

"No, he just stares." I would deal with that tomorrow. "Creeps me out."

"Are you going home tonight," I asked, stopping in front of her fourth-period class. I hated the thought of her going back to that disgusting trailer, but I wasn't going to invite her to live with me either.

"No," she said. "I'm staying with Chloe tonight." A sense of relief washed over me, and I didn't know why I cared, but I did a lot.

Handing her bag to her, I wanted to kiss her, but I knew right here, right now, wasn't the time. So instead, I watched her disappear behind her classroom door.

CHAPTER 15

Harper

For the first time since I was handcuffed to Christian's bed, I hadn't seen or heard anything from him since yesterday. I assumed he'd had his fill of me and moved on like I'd expected him to do sooner.

Hiking my bookbag higher on my shoulder, I followed Chloe into class.

"What is he doing here?" Chloe whispered over her shoulder as she stepped through the classroom door for third period. I didn't know who *he* was.

Stepping into the classroom, my jaw clenched. Christian was perched on the desk in front of mine, his hands white-knuckling the desk, jaw tight, and eyes focused on the sub.

Oh shit...

"I told him about Mr. Perv," I whispered, sliding into our seats. Her eyes went wide, and her mouth formed an o.

Mr. Pervy's eyes weren't wandering today. In fact, they were glued to his nervously fidgeting fingers in his lap.

I opened my textbook, pretending to work.

"What are you doing?" I whisper-hissed to Christian, who

was still leaning on the desk with his back to me, eyes burning holes into the sub. Every gaze in the classroom was on Christian. The air was thick with anticipation as everyone wondered what was going on. "What did you do?"

"Nothing," he didn't bother to whisper. "I let Mr. Pervert know that if his eyes happened to look at you again, I would remove them from his face." Christian was twice the substitute's size, and the sub was obviously shitting himself.

"Omigod, Christian," I slapped his arm. "You can't threaten a teacher."

"He's not a teacher and won't be back tomorrow. Will you, *Mr. Pervert*?" Not looking up from his hands, he shook his head. "Because if he is, he won't walk out of here." Christian stood from the desk, squaring his shoulders. "I think you owe Harper an apology for making her uncomfortable."

"What? Christian, no," I stammered.

"Go ahead," Christian growled. The sub looked up. Christian's fist slammed into the desk with a force that shook it and made the entire class jump. "I told you not to look at her." His tone was deadly. "The sub's eyes shot back down. "Apologize! To her and every other girl you made uncomfortable, now!"

"I'm sorry," he whimpered, and a roar of applause sounded. The sub ran out of the classroom, and I assumed he wouldn't be back.

Christian spun around to face me. "Let's get out of here."

"What?" I narrowed my eyes. "It's the middle of the day."

"I know," he said, reaching out his hand. "Skip with me today." Every part of me screamed to say no. To shove his hand away and demand he go to his class. "Come on, good girl, be bad with me," he said, his tone laced with seduction.

I knew better. I knew this was a bad idea. But then he said the one thing that ensured I wouldn't say no. "Unless you're scared." I was scared! Scared of how my heart raced and my body reacted to him every time he walked into the room. I was scared that just knowing Christian would scar me for life.

I would also rather die than let anyone think I was scared

of anything.

"I'm not scared," I said, standing up, and grabbing my things. "Let's go!"

"Wait for me," Chloe yelled from behind me. I could almost feel Christian's smile burning into my back.

Shoulders back and head held high, I stormed out the side doors to the student parking lot. I stopped in front of Christian's black Jeep Wrangler, which already had the top off. Lincoln, Sebastian, Maverick, Julian, and Aiden were already waiting for us.

"About time," Lincoln muttered. "We'll take my truck."

"I'll take mine," Chloe announced; the dark green highlights in her short black hair were bolder in the bright sunlight.

"I'll ride with Chloe," I said, spinning towards her truck, but long thick fingers wrapped around the back of my neck before I reached it.

"You'll ride with me," Christian said, his fingers tightening as he spun me back towards his Jeep. I started to protest but then decided against it. I could argue, but he was bigger and stronger, and even if I put up a good fight, I'd lose, and I didn't have the energy to lose today.

Releasing my neck, Christian leaned over and scooped me up before shoving me into his Jeep's passenger side as if I could not load myself into the lifted Jeep.

"I'll ride with Chloe," Aiden said, following Chloe to her truck. Christian shut the door and strolled around to the driver's side. Lincoln's SUV pulled up beside Christian's Jeep with Julian, Maverick, and Sebastian in tow.

"Let's get out of here," Maverick yelled out the passenger side window.

Today was the perfect day to ride topless in a Jeep. The sun was bright, without a cloud in the sky. Trying not to be obvious, I watched Christian out of the corner of my eye. He was dressed casually in a black t-shirt and jeans. The black hoodie he wore earlier was tossed into the back seat before we pulled out.

His dark hair blew wildly in the wind, falling over his forehead when we stopped. One tatted arm perched on the center console, and the other hand gripped the steering wheel. His tongue swiped across his bottom lip as he leaned forward, checking for oncoming traffic. He was hot.

Turning my head towards my window, I stared aimlessly out. I wanted to remember the kiss. Was it everything I'd imagined it'd be, or maybe more?

"Where are we going?" I asked, pulling myself out of my thoughts. The corner of his full lips curved in a devilishly half-smile that screamed trouble, but he didn't answer the question.

Christian drove the topless Jeep over the railroad tracks and then took a sharp right turn into the Southside. I sank into my seat, hiding my face as much as possible with little coverage from the Jeep itself. The last thing I needed was someone from the Villas to see me with Christian and tell Noah.

"What's the deal with you and the Villa Boys?" Christian asked once we were on the other side of town. I pinched my eyebrows. "You don't hang with them. You don't sit with them at lunch. I've never seen you have a conversation with them, but you handle their dirty work." I didn't bother answering, just shook my head, staring out the front window. It was a question I couldn't answer. Discussing Noah and the Villa Boys with Christian was a bad idea that could get me killed. "Why are you so loyal to them?"

"I am not loyal to them." I jerked my head to him. I wasn't loyal; I did what I had to do to survive—no more, no less. I just needed to protect myself.

"So, why do you do their dirty work?" he asked, easing up to a red light.

"Christian," I blurted out, twisting my shoulders to face him. "I'm not going to talk about Noah or the Villa Boys or girls, for that matter, with you." I didn't have a death wish. The light flashed green, and he accelerated.

"Let's play a game," he said after a long moment.

"What kind of game?" I huffed, falling back into my seat.

"If I ask you a question you're uncomfortable answering, you can trade it for a dare," he said.

"Like truth or dare?" I asked. He nodded. "Isn't that like a kid's game?" He shrugged, not taking his eyes off the road. I'd never played truth or dare, but I had a feeling the way Christian played wouldn't be considered a kid's game. I also felt relieved that he was giving me an out to any question I didn't want to answer.

"Okay, I'll play."

"You can go first."

"Where are your parents?"

"London," he answered. "They have a house there." Wow, a house in London too! I couldn't even imagine living in their mansion in the Valley. "My turn."

"Where are your parents?" He turned the question around on me.

I sucked in a deep breath through my nose before slowly releasing it. I hated talking about anything that had to do with my life or family. I hated the looks they gave me after discovering anything about my life and how I grew up, but I also didn't think I was ready for a dare, which I assume was the purpose of this little game.

"My mom disappeared a while ago," I muttered. "And I don't know who my dad is, but he's probably some drunk or druggy."

"Where did your mom go?" he asked, easing up to a stop sign. Looking both ways, he pulled through, picking his speed back up.

"I don't know. She left late one night and never came back."

"Did you report her missing?"

"Yeah, but this wasn't unusual for her. She's a crackhead, but this is the longest she's ever been gone." I paused briefly. "My turn. Are your parents coming back?"

"Yes, they'll be back for graduation," he answered, spinning the wheel left. "What are your plans after graduation."

I shrugged. "What about college?"

"Girls like me don't go to college." I snorted. Those were the exact words my counselor said to me when I asked about scholarships.

"What the fuck is that supposed to mean?" He glared at me.

"It means I'll probably work for one of the Southside clubs. Maybe Show Girls. Or maybe I'll walk the streets at night. Maybe Noah will let me into his little gang, if I'm lucky, so I don't have to fuck for money."

"Harper, that's ridiculous. You're a straight-A student with honors classes. Why wouldn't you get into a college? Did you apply?"

"No, Mr. Cosgrove told me I'd be better off applying to a technical school and getting a trade."

"Mr. Cosgrove?" he questioned, eyebrows shooting up. I nodded.

"How about you? Where are you going to college?"

"I'm not, or not yet, anyway. My parents allowed my brother and me to go to college or learn the family agriculture business and take it over. They plan to permanently move to London after we are ready to take over."

We followed Lincoln's SUV into a parking lot lined with different shapes and sizes of vehicles before finding a spot and parking.

"You ever been here?" Christian asked. I shook my head. I had no idea where here was. I breathed in the smell of salt water, and the sound of crashing waves was close. We were on the coast.

"South Pier Boardwalk," Christian answered my unasked question once we were out of the Jeep. I'd never been to the pier, but I'd heard about it. "Come on." He linked his fingers through mine with a grin and pulled me forward to meet up with everyone else.

CHAPTER 16

Harper

The only friends I'd ever had growing up were Chloe and Ryder. I'd never fit into a normal high school clique; we were all loners that somehow managed to find each other. We all lived very different lives and rarely hung out like other teens. We didn't go to parties together or football games on Friday nights. We spent our friendships hiding from the Villa Boys and trying to escape whatever situation we'd been dealt.

Today was different; I wasn't a Villa girl, Chloe wasn't a Valley girl, and the guys weren't assholes from the Valley. We were a group of teenagers having fun, which was something I'd never done before, ever.

Sitting on a wooden bench on the boardwalk, I watched Chloe and Aiden walk the shoreline and Lincoln and Maverick flirt with a group of older girls. I wasn't sure where Sebastian and Julian disappeared to, but I didn't imagine they'd made it far.

We'd all spent the entire day wasting time like normal teenagers. We'd eaten until we couldn't eat anymore and danced on the beach to music echoing down from the pier. Sadly the sun was close to setting, and the day was almost over. Before long, we'd head back to reality.

"Ice cream," Christian said, holding out a cup of vanilla ice cream with caramel toppings. I wasn't sure I could fit anything else in my stomach, but Christian assured me I couldn't leave the pier without trying the ice cream.

"Thank you." I smiled, taking the cup. He slid onto the bench beside me. It was the first time we'd been alone since we'd gotten here.

"So, what's the deal with you and Alexi?" I asked after several long minutes. It was a question I'd been contemplating asking all day, and now, watching the sunset in what would typically be a romantic setting, I wanted to know.

"Alexi?" he scowled as if the question was absurd. I nodded, taking a bite of my ice cream. "There is no Alexi and me. We had a fling, and she got clingy, so it ended."

"She got clingy?" I repeated, staring at my ice cream as I swirled the spoon around the small cup.

"Yeah, but I was never really into Alexi like that, and I didn't think she was into me like that. We had clear boundaries from the start, and it made things easy."

"Do we have clear boundaries?" I asked, my gaze flicking up to his.

"Are you planning on begging me to fuck you?" he teased.

I didn't answer. I didn't answer because I didn't know what the truth was at this point. Christian was so much more than I'd ever expected. Even though I knew he didn't know how much any of his actions meant to me.

"Then I guess we don't need boundaries." He shrugged, taking a bite of his ice cream. "Why do you get to school so early?" he asked, moving on to the next subject. I've seen you there, but you don't have detention, so why are you there so early?"

This was the first question I wasn't ready to answer. How could I tell him I got to school early to use the washer and dryer? Or I got there early to use the shower because that wasn't an option at my house? We didn't have running water in the trailer.

In the 6th grade, I was bullied and tortured to tears about my clothes and the way I smelled. My P.E. coach tried to help. It was my third time back from foster care, and I would have rather died than return to the system. So, she gave me a key to the girl's locker room and bought me a ton of toiletries and laundry soap.

The bullying didn't improve, but they couldn't say I was dirty or smelled anymore.

"Dare," I mumbled, silently praying we were still playing the game.

"Dare, huh?" Christian asked, cocking his eyebrow, his lips twitching into a smirk. "I dare you to ride that with me." He pointed up to the sky-scraping Ferris wheel to the left of us. "After sunset."

"You're on." Lots of things scared me, but heights weren't one of them.

He tossed our empty ice cream cups into the trash beside him before sliding one arm behind me and pulling me into him. We sat quietly, watching the sun disappear into the horizon in a beautiful display of blended colors.

"You ready?" Christian asked, hopping into the Ferris wheel car, causing it to sway. He extended his hand, and I slid mine into it before he jerked me up into the car. It was big enough to fit four more people inside.

"Anyone else?" the carnie yelled to the line of people waiting.

"Sorry," Christian grumbled. "This car is full." He pulled the door shut and took a seat beside me.

The wheel started to spin, swaying the car back and forth, taking us upward. Christian's hand settled on my bare upper thigh.

"Wow," I gasped, peering out the window at the glowing

city surrounding us. "This is amazing."

The car eased to a stop at the top.

"It's your turn." He smiled. *Hmm.* I had so many things I wanted to know about Christian. What to ask next?

"What did you mean the other night in the pool when you said, 'You don't know what you do to me?'" Those words had been stuck on repeat since he'd said them.

"Dare."

"Really?" I asked, my brows furrowing.

"Dare me to show you," he whispered against my ear, and I ignored the heat that rushed through me.

"Show me what?" I asked, confusion contorting my face.

"Dare me to show you what you do to me."

I knew I shouldn't, but my curiosity overpowered my common sense. "I dare you to show me."

The corners of his mouth curled up, his gaze flickering between my eyes and my lips. He bit down on his bottom lip, slowly releasing it before leaning in and brushing them against mine. Raw desire flashed across his perfect face as his hand gripped the nape of my neck, and his lips crashed into mine in a hot, possessive, demanding kiss that screamed you are mine and only mine. His tongue flicked across my lips, teasing me to open as his fingers gripped tighter around the back of my neck, holding me in place. My fingers curled into the thin material of his T-shirt, pulling him into me. My lips parted, and his tongue pushed through, twisting with mine, teasing and tasting me. Sucking in my bottom lip and catching it between his teeth, he pulled back, slowly releasing it.

Sliding off the seat and onto the floor, finally settling on his knees in front of me, he traced his fingertips down the outside of my thighs. His eyes locked on mine. My heart pounded so hard I thought it might explode, and my breathing was erratic. In the same sense, I was terrified of his touch; I also craved it. Squeezing my thighs tightly, I tried not to give away how much my body wanted him.

Never breaking eye contact, Christian used both hands

and strength to gently pry apart my legs. He pressed his warm, soft lips to my inner thigh, and I sucked in a sharp breath. Closing my eyes, my head fell back as heat flooded my body. Nipping and biting, he slid up my inner thigh, leaving a trail of heated chills.

"Relax," he whispered against my skin. The heat from his words snaked around me, making my head spin. "No one can see us." Sucking in a deep breath, I relaxed, allowing myself to give in to him.

Kissing and licking his way up my inner thigh, teasing every sensitive nerve ending along the way; my legs spread wider, allowing his mouth to slide further up my thighs. My breathing deepened, and a small moan escaped my lips. His mouth hovered over the thin lace of my pink panties, his hot breath caressing the sensitive skin. A rush of heat spread through me, and I couldn't think about anything but his mouth on me and how desperate I was for his touch. He looked up through his long dark lashes, his heated gaze begging for permission. My eyes screamed, *please* don't stop!

But he stopped...

"Did that answer your question," he asked breathlessly.

What?

No!

That answered absolutely nothing...

Now I was even more confused, but I nodded. He'd brought me to the edge and stopped before I could go over. Then it dawned on me. That was how he felt. That's what I did to him. I brought him so close to the edge that he could fall over and then pulled him back.

I opened my mouth to protest as he slid in beside me, but my words lodged in my throat when his hand slid between my thighs. His fingers moved in circles over the lace, adding more pressure to rub the course material against my clit. Squeezing my eyes shut, my head fell back against the window, and my fingers curled into his shoulders.

Christian's lips pressed against my neck as his speed

increased. His mouth moved up my jawline before finding my lips. His mouth closed over mine, swallowing my moans.

"I want to taste this pussy so fucking bad," he purred against my skin. Omigod, I wanted him to taste me. In that moment, I didn't think I'd ever wanted anything more. My chest heaved as my body vibrated against his hand. "You going to come for me, Harper?" He increased the pressure, and my breathing hitched as I exploded in ecstasy.

"Holy fuck," he groaned. "That was so fucking hot."

The ride slid to a stop, and I quickly fixed my clothes as the doors slid open. Christian hopped out and twisted around to me. He didn't offer me his hand like before. Instead, he wrapped his arms around my waist, pulling my body flush against his. He took a few steps out of the way before letting my body slide against his to the ground.

Something had shifted between us. It was intense, electric, and magnetic. It left me craving more. He slid his hand into mine before strolling off, pulling me with him.

Staring down at the hand tangled with mine, I tried to figure out what all this meant. We were born enemies. Valley boys didn't date Villa girls. That's not how it worked.

Maybe I was overthinking this. That was probably it.

Christian didn't do relationships; even if he did, why would he want one with me? I was his for the next few weeks, and then this, too, would pass. We would go back to being the enemies we were born to be.

Chloe and Aiden appeared, and we all headed toward the parking lot.

"Stay with me tonight," he whispered once we'd made it to the parking lot.

"I'm crashing at Chloe's tonight," I lied, knowing what would happen if I went home with him. As much as I wanted him, I wasn't ready to go down the road of being another notch on Christian's bed.

The corners of his mouth curled up into a smirk as he pulled me into him, his mouth covering mine, not in the same erratic desperate kiss as before but in a have-sweet-dreams-about-me-and-all-the-naughty-things-I-could-do-to-you   kind of kiss.

"Text me when you get to Chloe's," he said. I nodded and loaded into Chloe's truck.

Chloe revved the engine, and the boys watched us drive away.

"You crashing with me?" Chloe asked once we were out of the parking lot and on the road.

"I can't. I'm out of clothes. I need to go home."

Chloe hated taking me home as much as I hated going there. She'd never said anything, but I knew she did. There had been many nights she'd helped me clean the blood off my face or body. She also knew foster care would have been my only other option. Unfortunately, with foster care, it was the luck of the draw. You could end up with a decent family who treated you like one of their own, but more often than not, and in my case, you could end up with a family who treated you worse than your own. I'd rather take my chances with Noah. At least I knew what I was getting with him.

None of that mattered now, though, I was eighteen, and foster care wouldn't help me. I was on my own.

She dropped me off and watched me reach my door before pulling out. Too bad the boogie man was inside my house.

I could smell the inside before I opened the door.

"Well, well, look what the cat drug in." Noah sneered when I stepped into the dark, empty house. Noah sat alone in the darkness of the trailer at the kitchen table with a beer in one hand and a lit joint in the other. "I wondered when the little whore would show back up." He tapped his boot on the floor, not bothering to take his cruel eyes off me. "Sit down." He reeked of alcohol.

"I'm tired, Noah," I mumbled.

"I said," he barked as he rose from his seat, slamming his fist into the table. I yelped, flinching. "Sit. The fuck. Down."

Swallowing my fear, I pulled out a chair, reluctantly

sliding in.

"So, you've been hanging out with those Valley Boys?" I started to deny it, but he cut me off. "The neighbors saw them bring you home in that new Escalade the other night. Said you looked to be passed out."

"Wait, what?" I asked. Christian had brought me home. I squeezed my eyes closed. My stomach churned at the thought of him bringing me here.

"You brought those fucking Valley Boys into my home, you fucking bitch?" My eyes flashed open.

"No, Noah! I didn't know, I swear."

"You're going to go back to your little boyfriend's house, and you're going to steal that Escalade he had the nerve to pull into my fucking driveway."

"Noah, please," I begged. I didn't want to steal from Christian or anyone.

He reached around the table, jerking my hand before I could move it. Slamming it on the table, I cried out as pain surged through my arm. He pulled out his pocket knife and pressed the blade against my wrist. My breathing hitched as fear wrapped tightly around my lungs, squeezing every ounce of air out of them.

"You can steal it, or I'll cut your fucking hand off." His smile curled into an evil grin. "You'd be a worthless whore without your hand." I had no doubt Noah would saw my hand off right there at the kitchen table with a smile on his face.

"Okay," I cried out. "Okay." I didn't want to do this, but I also didn't want him to cut off my hand.

"Tonight," he hissed, throwing my hand away from him as he stood from the table. "I want it before morning." He jerked his beer off the table, taking a swig of it before slamming it so hard on the table the glass bottle shattered. "Get the fuck out."

Holding my breath, I stumbled out of the chair and bolted toward the front door. I blew out a heavy breath. I didn't want to do this. I didn't want to steal from anyone, especially Christian and his family. I couldn't explain my feelings for Christian. I was confused. Did I like him, or did I hate him? Regardless, I didn't want to do this, but I also didn't know what other option I had.

CHAPTER 17

Christian

"Christian," Aiden said, shaking me firmly, rousing me from sleep. "Christian!"

"What?" I groaned, rolling over to look at the clock. It was two in the morning. "Aiden, what the fuck?" I shoved him away, falling back onto my bed.

"Christian," he said again. "It's Harper."

"Harper?" I repeated, sitting up. "Is she ok?" I was already climbing out of bed.

"She's here," he whispered. I guess she changed her mind about staying with me. "She's in the main house." Maybe not.

"She's probably just looking for a place to crash." I sat back down on my bed.

"She's looking for something, Christian."

"Like what?" I narrowed my eyes, jumping up and pulling on my pants.

"I don't know, but she was looking through the Escalade in the garage. Then she went into the house. Maybe looking for the keys." I grabbed the keys to the Escalade from my nightstand and bolted into the main house.

I stood silently in the shadows, watching her for several long minutes. Aiden was right; she was searching for something. She scrummaged through each drawer in the kitchen before moving on to the drawers of the old antique china cabinet.

"What are you doing here, Harper?" I asked, my tone low and lethal. A startled gasp flew out of her as she spun around.

"Christian," she breathed, holding her chest as I stepped out of the darkness.

"What are you here to steal this time?" I cut her off.

"Christian, you don't—"

"What, Harper?" I ground out, surging forward.

She stepped back, slamming into the wall. She chewed nervously on her bottom lip but didn't answer.

Anger coiled through me. "What?" I growled so loud she flinched.

"The Escalade." She sighed, dropping her shoulders in the same defeated way she did the first time I'd caught her here trying to find the weed.

"You came here to steal from me?" Anger colored my tone. I couldn't even explain the emotions rolling through me. Rage. Betrayal. Hurt. It was all the same at this point. I thought something had changed between us today: we were no longer enemies, north against south, Villa against Valley. I thought I was Christian, and she was Harper. I was wrong; she was loyal to them and always would be.

"Christian, I'm—" she cried as a tear streamed down her cheek.

Squeezing my eyes shut, my jaw clenched. I couldn't listen to her say my name again. I tossed the keys at her feet as my eyes opened. "Take the car and get out!" My fists clenched at my side.

"Please," she stammered.

"Get. Out!"

She didn't move, eyes flicking between the keys and me as if it was a difficult decision for her. My chest heaved with so much fury that I thought I could physically remove her from the house. When she didn't move, I stepped forward, ready to physically throw her out, but she bolted for the door, leaving the keys.

It took me a few minutes to come to terms with what had happened as I stood frozen, staring down at the keys on the floor. My perception of the Southside had been true. They were all criminals, even Harper. She was the worst of all of them. Befriending me only to steal from me was disgusting. I wanted nothing more to do with Harper Brooks.

"What happened?" Aiden asked, flicking on the lights in the kitchen where I was still standing in the same place since Harper left.

"She wanted the Escalade," I muttered, my gaze flicking up to meet his.

"Harper?" he asked, confusion contorting his face. I nodded. "That doesn't sound like Harper." We didn't know her. I thought I did, but I didn't. She was a Villa whore. What happened between us in the Ferris wheel was probably just another day for her, even if it wasn't for me. How did this happen?

When did this turn into more than a challenge to fuck her? I couldn't answer that, but that mistake would never happen again.

"Actually," I muttered. "It sounds just like Harper." I shrugged. "She's just another piece of Villa trash."

"Yeah, man," he said, his brows pinched as he shoved a hand through his dark hair. "Something seems off to me."

"I'm goin' back to bed." I groaned, shouldering past him. "Harper Brooks is never to step foot on this property again."

"If you say so," he muttered, and I stormed out of the house.

CHAPTER 18

Christian

Slouching back onto the couch, I stared aimlessly at the black television, tipping back the half-empty bottle of tequila. My anger for Harper was still raw, and the liquor helped numb it, but I wanted to forget it. I wanted to forget her.

Heavy footsteps pounded down the stairs.

"Come on, Christian," Aiden groaned. "I'm not going to leave you here sulking in your own misery all night."

"I'm fine," I muttered.

"You haven't left the house in three days." He grabbed his keys from the entertainment center.

"I'm tired." And drunk.

"Christian, get up and let's go, or we'll drag you." The front door opened, and Link, Maverick, and Julian sauntered in. I was too angry to be around people, but I also knew they would drag my drunk ass out the door if I didn't. So, I stood and stumbled out the door.

Julian steered his Dodge Ram down the dirt road and through the woods to the massive bonfire. I slid out the back and went in search of hard liquor. My bottle of tequila was empty, and I still had feelings I didn't want to feel.

Stepping around the front of the truck, I slammed into the only person I didn't want to see, *Harper*. She fell backward, landing on her butt. My immediate reaction was to help her, but I changed my mind. Why was she even here? She never came to parties, especially in the Valley.

"Hey," she said, jumping up to her feet and brushing herself off. When she looked up, the fire illuminated the discoloration on her face: Black, blue, and purple markings and a single gash over her bottom lip.

"What happened to your face?"

"I got into a fight at school," she said, shrugging it off. I didn't care. I didn't want to be friends. I twisted to walk away.

"Christian," she said, her tone laced with sorrow. "I'm sorry. Can I just explain..."

"No." I cut her off. "I said I was done with you. I meant it." I stormed away. I didn't care what her excuse was. I didn't want to hear it.

I spent the rest of the night trying to avoid Harper, but she was right there, no matter where I went or what I did. Going from girl to girl, I tried to focus on anything other than Harper, but she stood directly across from Julian's tailgate on the other side of the fire, talking with Michael Moore. His hand occasionally reached up and touched her, and I tried to remind myself I didn't care. She could fuck whoever she wanted.

Courtney Taylor, captain of the cheerleading squad, climbed up, straddling my lap wearing only the bottom half of her cheer uniform. I forced myself to focus on her, her perfectly round tits bouncing in my face as she ground herself against me.

"Wanna have some fun?" she slurred. She was trashed, and so was I. Continuing to grind herself against me, she ran her tongue over my neck. I closed my eyes, trying to lose myself in the sensation of her hot wet mouth on me, but it was no use. My attention was drawn back to Harper and Michael.

"Hey, Court?"

"Hmmm?" she hummed against my neck.

"Who did Harper get into a fight at school with?" I didn't care, but I was curious to see what the other girl looked like.

"Harper Brooks?" she asked, pulling herself off my neck. I

nodded. "Harper's never been in a fight. Why would you think that?"

"Her face," I answered.

"Seriously?" She snorted. "Harper's been coming to school with bruises since—" She paused, pursing her lips. "We'll since her step-daddy moved in."

My lungs seized with the realization that she didn't get into some catfight; a grown man twice her size put his hands on her. My stomach twisted with nausea.

Courtney reached down, trying to unzip my pants. "Not now, Courtney," I said, swatting her hand. I shifted my weight, putting her to the side of me, and hopped off the truck. I was suddenly sober.

"I need to borrow your truck," I barked at Julian.

"I'll get a ride back to your place with Bash," he said, tossing me the keys. "Just leave the keys in it." I caught the keys and stormed towards Harper.

"Get lost," I growled at Michael, and he didn't say a word as he turned and walked away. "Let's go," I ground out. The anger rolling through me was no longer because Harper tried to steal from me. It was because somebody put their hands on what was mine.

"Go where?" she yelped when I grabbed her wrist and jerked her toward Julian's truck. Lifting her to the driver's side, she slid over into the passenger side.

I didn't say a word on the short ride back to my house. I couldn't. It wouldn't come out as words but instead as fire. I used the silence to steady my breathing and bring the boiling in my blood to a simmer.

Shoving the truck into park, I hopped out and pulled her out behind me. I drug her into the house, into the light, where I could see the full extent of the damage. Her lip was split, and her jawline was bruised along the opposite side of her deep purple cheekbone.

"I can walk by myself," she fumed, jerking her arm out of my grasp, and that was when I noticed that trail of purple markings peeking out from under her shirt.

"Take off your shirt," I demanded, grabbing at it. I needed to see how badly she had been beaten.

"What?" She narrowed her eyes, swatting my hands away. "No."

"Who did this to you?" I hissed, pointing to her face.

"I told yo—"

"The truth, Harper," I demanded. "I know you weren't in a fight at school."

She sighed as her shoulders sank. "Christian," she whispered as her eyes softened.

"Who put their fucking hands on you? Was it Levi?" She shook her head. "Who?" Swallowing hard, she stared at me as her eyes filled with tears. "Harper."

"Noah," she said, dropping her head.

He was dead! "Take off the shirt." She shook her head. "Take it off, or I'll rip it off," I growled. Her eyes swelled with tears, but she turned away from me and lifted her shirt. Her entire back was covered in deep purple and green bruises. He was so fucking dead!

"What happened?" I asked, as my gaze trailed over what he'd done to her. She shrugged it off, pulling her shirt back down. "It's time for the truth Harper."

"You want the truth?" she cried. I nodded. "Are you sure? Because the truth is ugly compared to your perfect life."

"Harper, please," I begged, trying to push the anger aside because I needed to know what had happened.

"Noah was mad that you guys came to the house," she said, her voice trembling. "He told me to steal the Escalade. And if I didn't." She held her hand up to her face before wiping the tears away with the back of her hand.

She took that beating because of me. My head spun, my chest clenched, and my stomach churned.

"Why didn't you tell me?"

"Christian, you can't save me. I was born in the Villas, and I'll die in the Villas. I came to terms a long time ago with my fate.

You should too."

Fuck that! I was going to kill every Villa Boy that ever touched her. "Your month will be over soon, and it will be back to normal."

"Stay here," I demanded, ripping my keys from the counter and storming toward the front door.

"What? Christian, no," she begged, chasing after me. "You'll only make this worse for me. Please!"

I stopped. Even though she was never going back to that house, she was right. I couldn't do anything until I could make sure she was safe.

"Christian!" I turned to face her. My gaze met her pleading eyes. "Please promise me you won't do anything. That you'll leave this alone."

There was no way I was leaving this alone, but she didn't need to know that, and I wouldn't do anything until I knew they couldn't get to her.

"Fine," I groaned, dropping my keys back onto the counter.

"You promise?"

"I promise," I muttered, my tone laced with anger and irritation. I reached out for Harper, pulling her into me. Wrapping my arms around her, she buried her face in my chest. "How many times has this happened because of me or the guys?"

"Christian," she whispered, pushing against my chest. "Don't do this to yourself."

"How many, Harper?"

"A few."

Guilt wrapped painfully tight around my chest, squeezing hard.

"Go get a shower." I released her. "You're staying here tonight. You can find something to sleep in, in my dresser."

She disappeared up the stairs, and I pulled out my phone, shooting the guys a message.

Christian - 9-1-1 - Meet me at the pool house ASAP.

Pacing the floor, I tried to calm myself, to remind myself that I had to control my temper for now. I needed to focus my attention on finding a safe place for Harper.

The sound of the shower turning on echoed through the quiet house until a diesel engine pulling up drowned it out.

"Hey, what's going on?" Aiden scowled, rushing through the front door, followed by Julian, Maverick, Bash, and Link.

"Who's here?" Maverick asked, his gaze staring up at the ceiling at the sound of running water upstairs.

"Harper is upstairs showering."

"Oh, thank god you two kissed and made up," Aiden muttered, running a hand down his face. "Even she was acting stupid.

"Yeah, she got into a fight at school," Julian said. "She never gets into fights."

"Did you see the fight?" I asked. They all looked at each other, eventually shaking their heads. "She didn't get into a fight at school."

"Where did she get those bruises from?" Aiden's brow knitted together.

"Noah."

"Wait," Julian said, stepping forward cocking his head to the side. "Are you saying Noah put those bruises on her face?"

I nodded.

"Her back and body are even worse," I muttered as guilt wrapped tightly around me.

"We can all fit in my car," Link said, throwing his thumb over his shoulder.

"I promised I wouldn't go after Noah." I groaned, shoving my hands into the pockets of my jeans.

"I didn't promise anything," Aiden shrugged, his gaze flashing from me to Link. "Did you, Link?"

"Nope," Link answered.

"Yeah, me either." Maverick shrugged.

"Noah will get what's coming to him," I warned. "But first, I need to make sure that Harper is safe and that they can't get to her." They all nodded in understanding. "I need to find a safe place for her to live first."

"And after that?" Julian asked.

"You guys can have him and every Villa Boy that ever put his hands on her."

CHAPTER 19

Harper

Pounding down the stairs, the whispers went silent. I hadn't heard the guys show up, but it didn't surprise me that they were here now. They were always here. Stepping off the last step and onto the hardwood floor, my eyes flashed between Christian and his friends.

He'd told them. I knew that look in their eyes. Pity. I hated that look.

Chewing on my bottom lip, I shifted on my feet and tried desperately to hide my discomfort. The awkward silence filled the room for what felt like an eternity.

"Hey, Harper," Maverick said, breaking the silent stares. "We were trying to decide what we wanted to eat." I knew they weren't discussing food but I appreciated the subject change anyway.

"Little late for food, isn't it?" I asked, moving up to the massive guys towering over me.

"What?" Lincoln scowled, rubbing his rock-hard stomach. "It's never too late for tacos."

"Are you hungry?" Christian asked, stepping behind me, his hands settling on my hips. My stomach rumbled before I had the chance to answer. I *was* hungry. "Let's go get tacos."

"We're glad you're back, Harper," Lincoln said. "I don't

think we could have taken another day of Christian sulking around in misery all day."

"Funny." Christian rolled his eyes, and my cheeks heated. I knew it wasn't true, but thinking of Christian Chandler pining over a girl was funny. "Go pull the truck around. I'll take Harper to get some clothes."

Ten minutes later, I bounced down the main house's stairs, changed out of Christian's tee and boxers, and into a sundress from Christian's sister's old clothes.

"I'm ready," I said, passing by him towards the back door. Christian's long fingers wrapped around my wrist, stopping me before pulling me into him. One hand curled around my hip and the other cupped my face.

"I'm sorry, Harper," he whispered, running his thumb over the bruise on my cheekbone. "I know I can't change what happened, but I want to make it better."

"Christian, this is not your fault," I said, closing my eyes and leaning into his touch. "And you don't owe me anything. You're not obligated to help me out of guilt."

"I like you." He smiled. "I want to help you because I like you, and I would rather die than let that happen to you again because of me or not." His hands cupped my face, and our eyes locked together. I swallowed hard; my heart pounded against my chest. "By the way, you look amazing," he whispered. Biting down on my bottom lip, I leaned on my tiptoes, inching closer to his mouth, and tangled my hands into his black shirt to help steady myself against him. He dropped his face, brushing his lips against mine, his hands holding my face. He was going to kiss me, but a horn blew from outside, startling both of us.

"Let's go." Christian sighed, leaning his forehead against mine. "Before they die of starvation."

Sliding into the back of Lincoln's SUV, I situated myself between Maverick and Christian. Sebastian and Julian were behind us in the third-row seating, and Aiden was in the passenger seat next to Lincoln.

"Everyone ready for tacos?" Lincoln laughed, pulling

his SUV out of the driveway. Everyone separated into their conversations, none of which I could pay attention to because Christian's fingers curled around my upper thigh just under the hem of my dress. The small gesture was oddly intimate. His fingers slowly caressed the bare skin as he stared out the window.

"We're here," Aiden announced as we pulled into The Taco Shack. "You ever eaten here before?" I nodded. Chloe brought me tacos from here a while back.

Everyone piled out of the SUV and headed for the entrance. Christian slid his fingers into mine and led me to the door. My heart raced as we stepped closer to the door. I didn't have any money to buy food, and the anxiety of telling everyone that I wasn't that hungry, so they didn't know I couldn't afford food was overwhelming.

"Go grab a table," Christian said. "I'll order. What do you want?"

"I'm okay." I turned to grab a table, but Christian was on my heels.

"Harper, what do you want?"

This was hard for me. It wasn't just hard for me to ask for help; it was hard for me to accept help. I didn't want to assume he was going to pay for it, and I didn't have the money to pay him if he asked for it, which was embarrassing for both of us. As if sensing why I was apprehensive, he said, "It's on me, Harper."

"Get me the same thing you get," I said, and he headed toward the front to order.

Pulling out a chair, I slid into the seat and waited. The restaurant was mostly filled with late-night drunks because this was the only place that stayed open late.

"Hey baby," a young dark-haired man moaned. "Why don't you drop the zero and get with a hero." He was a sloppy drunk, and I could smell the booze seeping from him and his friends.

"Ew." I scowled. "Does that line actually work?"

"What the fuck did you say, bitch?" the same dark-haired man growled, shoving out of his chair.

"I asked if that bullshit you spewed actually worked on women." His mouth opened but snapped shut as his eyes lifted over my head. I didn't have to turn to see what he was looking at.

"You should pick your next words very carefully," Christian snarled. "Or you'll end up choking on your teeth." My guess was not only was Christian behind me but also the rest of the guys.

"I don't want any trouble, Ms." He grunted. "My apologies." He and his friends collected their food and practically ran out the door.

"You okay?" Christian asked, setting the food on the table and sliding into the chair next to me. Holy shit, that was a lot of food. The guys piled in around the table, and I felt normal for the second time in forever. I wasn't the white trash girl from the Villas. I was another teen laughing and hanging out with her friends.

"We ready?" Lincoln said, pushing out of his chair and rubbing his stomach.

We all gathered our things and cleared the table before strolling out to the SUV.

"Uh," Julian whined. "I don't think I can climb in the back seat. I'm too full."

"Harper and I can take the back," Christian offered, jerking open the door. I climbed in and over the back row, careful not to show off my panties as I did, and Christian followed me. He lifted the second-row seats so Julian and Sebastian could climb in before settling back in.

Lincoln cranked up the music before pulling the vehicle into drive and taking off.

Christian slid one arm across the back of the seat behind me, and his other hand slid up my thigh as he leaned over, pressing his lips to my ear. The scruff of his five o'clock shadow tickled my skin in a way that sent a jolt of electricity straight to my core. "How quiet can you be," he whispered, and my brows pinched. I had no idea what he was talking about until his hand slid under my dress.

My gaze shot up, eyes wide with panic.

"Trust me," he whispered.

"No," I whisper-hissed. Christian pressed his lips to the skin behind my ear, and I almost melted into him.

"Trust me," he breathed against my skin. "They won't even notice." I relaxed as his hand slid up further. "Don't make a sound." His hand slid under the thin cotton of my panties before he ran his fingertips through my slick flesh. "Holy fuck, you're wet." He groaned against my ear, and the raw sounds and vibration nearly made me fall apart before he started.

My legs spread wider as his fingers circled my swollen clit. I swallowed my moan fighting hard to act as normal as possible. My hand found his thigh. Digging my fingernails into the denim helped alleviate the need to cry out. His fingers dipped to my entrance, circling it before sinking a finger deep inside. My lips parted as my chest heaved, but I managed not to make a sound.

"I'm going to fuck your pussy with my fingers until you come all over them," he breathed against my ear. "Okay?" My words lodged in my throat; all I could do was nod. We weren't too far from Christian's place, so we only had a few minutes.

I slid forward in the seat, giving him better access to me as he pumped a finger in and out of me, slowly giving me time to adjust to the delicious invasion. "Fuck, you're so tight."

He slid another finger in, stretching me as his thumb flicked at my throbbing clit. His speed picked up, doing exactly what he threatened. His fingers fucked me fast and hard as his thumb stroked my clit, finding the perfect rhythm that pulled me closer and closer to the edge.

My eyes squeezed closed, and my body shook as my core tightened. I was so close. "I want this tight little pussy to come all over my hand, baby," he purred, and I clenched around his fingers. "Let go, baby, and come for me." And that was all it took to send me soaring so hard over the edge I gasped for air as my fingers dug deeper into the denim covering his thigh before quickly remembering where we were and who was with us.

He pulled his hand out, and my entire body shuddered as

it slowly came down from its high. He brought his fingers to his lips, sucking each clean as I watched.

"Next time," he grunted, "I want to taste you when you come all over my face."

Holy fuck... Next time...

CHAPTER 20

Harper

It felt good to pretend to be a typical teenager, and it was always fun with Chloe.

"How about this one," I pulled a glittery royal blue dress off the rack and held it up. Chloe turned up her nose. I shoved the dress back on the rack and flipped through the dresses.

"Oh, wow," Chloe gushed, holding up a shimmering silver mermaid-fitted dress. "You should try this one."

"I'm not going to prom," I reminded her. "You should try it on."

"Come on." She shoved the dress against my chest. "Live a little. You try that one and..." She paused, twisting and grabbing a fluorescent pink dress off the rack that we both knew she'd never wear. "I'll try this one."

My lip curled as my gaze raked over the sparkly gown. "Fine."

We both entered the dressing room. By the time I stepped back out, Chloe was waiting for me in front of the mirrors.

"Wow," Chloe gasped. "That dress was made for you."

"And that one was definitely made for you." We laughed as I stepped onto the raised platform. My gaze followed my hands as they slid over the dress that perfectly hugged every curve of my body. "It really is beautiful, isn't it."

"It's perfect! You think it would look that good on me?"

"Yes." It would look amazing on Chloe.

"Sold. Let's change and find shoes to go with it."

We'd spent the rest of the day trying on clothes, shoes, and jewelry. Even if I couldn't buy anything, pretending was still fun.

By the time we left, we were both exhausted, and I was ready to eat and relax.

"Are we headed back to your Aunt's?" I asked Chloe when I noticed we were going in the wrong direction for her house.

"No, I was under strict orders to bring you back to Christian." I rolled my eyes dramatically, sinking back into the seat. "Sorry, but he's bigger and scarier than you."

Overprotective wouldn't be a strong enough word to describe Christian the last few days. If he wasn't with me, one or all the guys were. My only private moments were in the bathroom. When Chloe asked me to go, I was surprised he didn't push me to come, but he hadn't even asked.

Chloe whipped her truck inside the gate.

"Drop me here. I want to walk up."

"Are you sure?" she asked. I nodded.

Christian's property was beautiful, and the weather was perfect today. A walk in the quiet alone was exactly what I needed. I hadn't had much time to think about what I would do next. I'd spent the last few nights with Christian but knew I couldn't stay much longer. I was getting low on clothes and didn't want him to tire of me. He was fueled with hate and guilt, but that would wear off eventually, and I'd have to go home.

Rounding the main house, I spotted both Christian and Aiden waiting outside the pool house.

"What's going on?" I asked, stepping up to Christian. "Is everything ok?" He pulled his hand out of his pocket and held up a keychain with four keys. My eyes narrowed as they followed his hand. He grabbed my hand, forced it open, and placed the keys in it. "What is this? What's going on?"

"It's the keys to the pool house," Christian answered. My eyes went wide. Was he asking me to move in with him? Panic rose in my throat. "Aiden and I moved out this morning." I blew out a heavy sigh. It wasn't that I didn't want to live with Christian; well, actually, that was precisely what I didn't want. I wasn't even sure what Christian and I were, and there was no way we were ready to live together.

"Wait," I said, my eyes flying to Aiden. "This is your man cave."

"And now it's yours," Aiden said, smiling softly.

"No." I shoved the keys into Christian's chest. "I'm not pushing you out of your home."

"You're one of us now," Aiden said, bumping my shoulder with his. "We take care of our own, plus, I've already moved my stuff, and it was a lot of work, so..." I laughed.

"You'll be safe here," Christian said.

"What about your parents?""

"It was Mom's idea," Aiden said. Christian grabbed the keys, unlocked the front door, and gestured for me to go in.

It was no longer a dark, stinky man cave. It was bright, clean, and smelled like fresh linen.

"You did this today?" I gasped. He nodded. My chest swelled. I didn't even know what to say in a good way.

"This will be your home," Christian said, and I smiled. "You can stay as long as you want to."

"I'll have to go and get my things," I said, smiling.

"No," Christian said, his tone and posture tense as his long fingers curled into my arms, squeezing hard enough to get my attention. Leaning down, he pulled me closer, nose to nose. His tone was no longer gentle. "You will never go back to that house!" He squeezed my arms tighter to my sides. "Harper, do you understand me? You will never go over the tracks to the Southside again."

Never going over the tracks to the Southside again was unreasonable.

"Christian, I have no clothes," I said.

"Well, lucky for you," Chloe sang, appearing at the front door that was still open. ""We have that taken care of." She dropped the shopping bags from today on the table and floor. Christian released his grip on my arms, but I knew this conversation wasn't over.

"And I have everything else," Ryder said, stepping in behind her.

"How—"My eyes widen in shock. They did all of this for me.

"Christian called us yesterday," Chloe cut me off, handing Christian a black rectangular piece of plastic. "We weren't actually shopping for me today, and Ryder picked up toiletries and..."

"New sheets," he interrupted. "Who knows how many bare asses have been on that bed."

"Just mine." Christian laughed. Ryder passed Christian and gave a sincere nod, insinuating peace between the two or mutual respect for one another. Maybe both.

"What would you have done if I said no?" I asked Christian.

"Tied you to the bed until you changed your mind." He chuckled. "Too bad it didn't come to that. Could have been fun."

"Gross," Ryder scowled.

"We should get you unpacked," Chloe suggested, grabbing a handful of bags. "Everyone ready to help?"

"Let's do this," Ryder said, carrying a few bags up the stairs.

"Thank you," I said. Christian threw his arm across my shoulder.

"Promise me you won't go back to the Villas," he said. I knew I'd eventually have to go back. When whatever this was with Christian was over, I'd have to return, but this promise wouldn't matter at that point.

"Promise."

We spent the entire afternoon setting up the apartment. Chloe took charge of delegating jobs, making sure everyone was busy working.

"Oh," Chloe said as we finished unpacking. "I almost forgot this." She held up the silver shimmering prom dress I'd tried on at the dress shop earlier that day.

"What am I supposed to do with that?" I chuckled. Chloe nodded, indicating to look behind me. When I turned, Christian was smiling behind me.

"Prom," Christian said, answering my question. My eyes flashed between the two. "Will you go to prom with me?"

"You want me to go to prom? With you?" He nodded. "Are you asking me, or do I have to go?"

"I'm asking." His lips curved into a smirk.

Going to prom had never been in the plans for me. It had never even been on my radar, but how could I say no when he'd gone to this much trouble for me to go with him?

"Yes. I'll go with you."

A knock sounded from the first floor, distracting everyone.

"That's the food," Christian stated, and we all barreled down the stairs.

I was surprised when I saw Maverick waiting outside to be let in. Christian's boys didn't knock or wait to come inside the pool house. He'd already told them.

Everyone stood in the kitchen, all eyes on me. "What?"

"Are you going to let them in?" Christian laughed, jerking his head toward the door. "Or tell them to fuck off?"

"They have food," I said. "Of course, they can come in." I opened the door.

"All right, Harper," Lincoln said, holding up a new Xbox game when he stepped through the front door. "You in?"

"Of course," I said, following him into the living room.

"After you eat," Christian said, grabbing my waist and guiding me back to the kitchen. He handed me a plate and started filling it with more food than I'd eaten last week. It was nice for once in my life having someone who cared if I ate or starved, but I didn't want to get used to it either. Tomorrow it could be gone.

After Chloe and Ryder left, I realized I hadn't seen Christian in a little while.

"Where are you going?" Maverick asked when I pushed off the couch.

"Lincoln can play for me." I tossed the controller to him.

"No, Link sucks," Maverick whined, throwing his arms in the air.

The guys went back to yelling at the game and throwing back shots before I stepped out of the house.

Christian sat on the pool's edge, legs hanging over the side in the water, lost in thought.

"Want some company?" I asked before sitting beside him. He nodded without looking up from the water. "Everything ok?"

"I don't get it," he said. "Why would you have said no?"

It took me a minute to realize what he was talking about. He didn't understand why I would say no to living here when my life was so horrible at home.

"I learned a long time ago; I can't count on anyone but myself. I can't trust anyone but myself."

"You can trust me," he said sincerely. "You can trust us." He gestured towards the pool house, and I assumed he meant all the guys. Deep down, I knew I could, but I also knew that this good thing happening right now was temporary, and I knew that someday when Christian moved on or tired of me, I would be fending for myself again.

"You're 18, why haven't you left?"

"And go where, Christian?" I sighed. "I have no money, no education, no car, and I can't get a job because no one in this small town will hire me because of who I'm associated with." I absentmindedly kick the water. "I don't have any options."

"You should have told me."

"Told you what, Christian? Should I have told you that I never miss a day of school because it's my only opportunity for a meal and that I'm starving by Monday? Or should I have told you that my first kiss was with one of my mom's drunk boyfriends who couldn't tell the difference between my mom and me? Should I have told you I go to school early because it's the only place I can shower? Do you really want to know everything you have no control over in my life?"

"Yes." A sound of irritation escaped him. "I do, but I most definitely want to know if my or my friend's actions are causing you to take a beating."

"If it wasn't you, it would be something else. Noah is an angry person. Plus, I hate telling people anything because I hate that look."

"What look?"

"The 'I feel sorry for her' look. The one you're giving me now." He shook his head as if to shake the look off his face. "I've had to take care of myself since I was five. I've learned to live with the cards I was dealt." He nodded, like he understood. "But I didn't want anyone's pity." That was one of the reasons I loved Ryder and Chloe so much. They never made me feel like I was less than them. They never made me feel like I owed them because of their help.

Lincoln and Maverick stumbled out of the house, tripping over each other, drunk.

"I should take them home," Christian said. "You should get some sleep. I'll see you in the morning."

I guessed that answered my question about whether he would stay with me tonight.

CHAPTER 21

Harper

Jerking the front door open, my smile faded at the sight of Aiden dressed casually in jeans and a t-shirt filling my doorway. It was six in the morning, and I was expecting Christian because we rode to school together in the mornings.

"You ready?" Aiden handed me a to-go cup of coffee and reached for my bag. Aiden was a morning person—the annoying kind. No matter how late he stayed up the night before, he was ready to go bright and early the following day with a smile. I, on the other hand, was only a morning person if I got a full ten hours of uninterrupted sleep.

"Where's Christian?" I mumbled, taking the coffee and relinquishing my bag to him. He tossed the bag over his shoulder.

"Not sure," he said, flashing an all-white smile. Aiden was hot. On top of being hot, he was also charming. He could make your panties melt off with a wink of his deep brown eyes. He was taller and leaner than Christian, but they shared similar facial features. His torso and arms were covered in colorful ink, his lip, tongue, and eyebrow were pierced, and I was sure there was more I hadn't seen. "He left early this morning and told me to make sure I got you to school." Christian didn't need to clear his schedule with me, but I wondered where he was. "Are you ready?" I nodded and followed him out to his truck.

Fifteen minutes later, we were parked and walking through the school doors, where Christian was leaning, his arms crossed over his chest against my locker. My breath caught in my throat when his dark brown eyes locked with mine, and his lips curved into a seductive smile. He made my heart flip, and my stomach fluttered with the curl of his lips.

"Where were you this morning?"

"I needed to take care of something." He pushed off the locker. "Ms. Cruz is waiting to talk to you in her office."

"Ms. Cruz," I repeated. "The guidance counselor?" He nodded. "She's not my counselor."

"She is now, and she would like to talk to you about what options you still have for scholarships and applying for college." My chest swelled, tears burned the back of my eyes, and my mouth dropped speechlessly. Christian never ceased to amaze me, and I couldn't understand why? He'd done more for me in the last few days than my mother had in my entire life. For once, I didn't live in fear; I wasn't worried about going home and what kind of mood Noah would be in. Or in what condition I'd find my mom.

I'd spent my entire life worried that I'd come home and find my mom dead, either a drug overdose or some man finally killed her, but instead, she'd done me a favor and left.

I'm almost too shocked to speak. "You did this," I stuttered.

"Is that okay?" he questioned, unsure if my reaction was good or bad.

"Yeah," I nodded, jumping up and wrapping my arms around his neck. College was my only chance to get out of this town and away from the Villas.

"Go." Christian ushered me off. "She's waiting for you."

I walked the short distance from Christian to the office.

"Good morning, Harper," Ms. Smith, the front office assistant, said. "How can I help you?"

"She's here to see me," Ms. Cruz said, rounding the corner into the front office. "Good morning, Ms. Brooks. You can follow me." I followed her down the short hallway and into the small office. "Come in and have a seat. I already let your first-period teacher know you'd be late."

"Thank you," I said, sliding into a chair in front of her desk.

"Well, I've gone over your grades and GPA; you have the highest GPA in the school," she smiled. "Did you know that?" I shook my head. "That's amazing, but I must be honest that most college application and scholarship deadlines have passed." My shoulders sank in disappointment. "But we still have a few options for the upcoming year." I sat up a little straighter. I would take whatever I could get. "We have a couple of scholarships offered to students at this school from personal donors. The only problem is that your application must be submitted by the end of the week."

"I can do that," I exclaimed.

"I knew you'd say that," she said, pushing a stack of papers forward. "Here's the paperwork and directions on how to apply." I reached out to take the paperwork from her. "Now, college applications, there's always the option of community college, and if you're hoping to get out of town to go to college, we could apply in a different county. A few private colleges have not yet cut off their applications, but again you would need to complete those applications by Friday."

"I can do that."

"I'm going to take you out of art because you don't need it and put you in study hall," she said. "You'll be able to use that time to complete the applications."

"Thank you." I skimmed through the paperwork.

"If you need more time during the day, please let me know. I can try to talk to your teachers."

"I won't need more time," I said. "It will be done by Friday."

"Do you have any other questions?" Did I have any other questions? I didn't know I was doing this today, so I didn't know if I had any questions. I shook my head. "Well, if you think of anything or if you have any problems, you can email me or stop by and see me."

"Thank you, Ms. Cruz."

"No problem, Harper. You can head to study hall and get started. Mr. Hall is expecting you and will provide you with a computer to use."

Collecting all the paperwork, I stood and headed for study hall in the senior hallway. The halls were empty, and second period had already started. Following the brightly lit corridors decorated in the school's colors, black and gold, I looked over the paperwork in my hand. I couldn't wait to get into study hall to get started.

Rounding the corner, I saw Christian waiting outside the large double doors that led into study hall.

"Are you waiting on me?" I stopped directly in front of him.

"How did it go?"

"Great." I held up the paperwork. "I need to get inside and get started on these. They are due Friday."

"I saved you a seat."

"Wait, you're in study hall this period?" He nodded, grabbing the left side of the double doors and jerking it open. Of course, he was. Second period was my only class without Christian or one of his friends.

For the rest of the week, I spent every free moment working on all the applications. Christian came over to the pool house during meals to make sure I took a break to eat and then gave me my space to get what I needed to done. And I appreciated him for that time.

Friday at 10:12 p.m. I submitted my last application before

PLAYING WITH FIRE | 119

the deadline. Throwing myself back on my bed, I smiled at the ceiling. Now I played the waiting game, praying I'd be one of the lucky ones that get a scholarship and be accepted to any University or Community College away from the Villas and far from Noah and his gang of thugs.

Pulling out my phone, I sent Christian a text.

Harper – WYD?

I watched the screen waiting for a reply.

Christian – About to shower. Want to join me?

It was a nice offer, but I'd already showered.

Harper – Thanks, but no. Come over when you're done?

Christian – What are you wearing?

My lips curled at his attempt to flirt.

Harper – Clothes.

Christian – See you in ten.

CHAPTER 22

Christian

Ten minutes after Harper's text, I pushed through the front door of the pool house, spotting Harper curled up on the sofa watching TV wearing only a thin pink tank top and a tight pair of black gym shorts.

"Did you finish your applications?" I sank onto the sofa beside her.

"Yes." She smiled. "Now we wait and see what happens." She seemed hopeful, and that made me match her energy.

"So, what's up?"

She shrugged as her gaze flicked to mine. I recognized that look. It was the same look she'd given me in the shower that night, but she wasn't drunk tonight.

"Harper," I said, the corners of my lips curling into a smirk.

"I didn't want to be alone." She shifted on the couch to face me. "Can you stay with me tonight?" I matched her movements and nodded.

"Is something wrong?" I reached out and brushed a strand of her dark hair out of her face. Her eyes closed as she leaned into my touch.

"No," she whispered. When she opened her eyes, there was no hiding the burning desire blazing in them. Her tongue swept across her lips as her gaze dropped to my mouth, lingering longer than usual before biting down on her bottom lip as her gaze flicked up, meeting mine. I was sure she was seeing the same burning in my eyes that I saw in hers.

Hooking an arm around her waist, I jerked her onto my lap. She didn't fight me as she sank down, straddling me. My fingertips curled into the thin material of her gym shorts. She shifted, situating herself on top of me, and I groaned as my dick strained against my shorts, desperate to come out and feel her heat.

My hand cupped the back of her neck, and I yanked her mouth close. "I'm going to kiss you, Harper," I breathed before I claimed her mouth with mine. She pushed her tits forward as the kiss deepened, and when her lips parted, I thrust my tongue through, exploring every inch of her mouth.

My heart pounded as I fought for air. I craved this. I desired everything about her: her touch, taste, sounds, and feel.

Her hands cupped the back of my neck as my hand slid down, gripping her ass and guiding her hips over the thickness under my shorts. Her head fell back, and she gasped, feeling me between her thighs as my lips trailed down her throat. I shoved up her shirt as she continued to grind herself against me. She wasn't wearing a bra. My mouth raked down her throat, nipping and biting. God, she was so fucking hot. I sucked her nipple into my mouth, and she pulled my face harder against her as her fingers curled into my neck.

"Christian," she moaned, grinding herself harder against me.

"That's it, baby," I breathed against the skin between her tits, my tone low and raspy. "Fuck me." My teeth sank into my bottom lip as my gaze flicked up to watch her. Her eyes were closed, and her lips parted on a breathy moan. "Do you feel me" baby?" She hummed a yes. "Ride me like my dick is inside you, and come all over my lap."

The heat of her body radiated against mine as I lifted my hips, and she rolled hard against my thick length. My body clenched, and my dick twitched as her fingernails dug into the skin of my neck. I welcomed the pain.

She was close.

I wanted to flip her over, strip her naked and fuck her hard and fast, but even if she was willing, I didn't think she was ready.

Her body vibrated against me as she cried out, her speed picking up with each thrust hitting her clit through the very thin layer of clothes she wore.

When her body tensed as she exploded, coming apart on top of me, I wrapped my arms around her pulling her hard against me, feeling her chest heaving as she came down from her high. Her head dropped to my shoulder as her breathing steadied.

"You are so fucking hot when you come," I purred against her throat, and she smiled against my shoulder. "You still want me to stay the night?"

"Yes."

I lifted from the couch with her still wrapped around me and carried her to bed. I crawled onto the bed, releasing her. My mouth captured hers in a slow, deliberate kiss that heated my insides. I broke from the kiss and rolled to the side of her knowing I wouldn't be able to stop myself if I kept going. I pulled her into me, which was exactly how we fell asleep.

CHAPTER 23

Christian

Glancing out the window, I noticed Chloe's truck parked in front of the pool house. She was here earlier than I expected. Today was prom, and Chloe and Harper were going to spend the day getting ready. I pulled my shirt over my head and headed down the stairs to the first floor.

"Christian," Aiden yelled. I rounded the corner into the kitchen, where Harper stood fist on hips, her dark brows furrowed, and lips thinned into a line.

"What are you doing here?" I let my gaze travel over the length of her. I wanted to pull her into me and kiss her, but she didn't look like she was in the mood. Her hand flattened on the counter with a smack, and my credit card was sitting on the counter when she lifted it. I wasn't exactly sure where this was going. I'd given the credit card to Chloe to take care of anything Harper needed today, but for some reason, Harper was slamming it on the counter.

"Christian," she hissed. "I can do my own hair and make-up for prom." I narrowed my eyes. I wasn't sure what she was getting at. "I appreciate everything you've done for me. Everything. But I can't be your girlfriend and your charity case." Raising my brows, my head tilted, and the corner of my mouth curved up.

"Did you just refer to yourself as my girlfriend?" I teased. Her face fell, and her cheeks flushed. I reached out, running my thumb over the pink in her cheeks. We'd never laid a label on what we were. It never occurred to me that I would need to. She was mine. I knew it, she knew it, the guys knew it, the entire school knew it, and if the Villa Boys didn't know it yet, they would soon.

"I don't know what this is or what to call it," she started.

"Then we should clear it up right now," I interrupted. "I like you, and I don't want anyone to touch you ever again." I cupped her face forcing her to look up at me. "Not for pain, not for pleasure. So, I guess that makes you mine. My girlfriend."

She smiled, and I leaned in, pressing my lips to hers. Her eyes closed as her body melted into mine.

"Now," I said, pulling myself out of the kiss, "that we've established you aren't my charity case." I reached over, sliding the black credit card off the counter. "And I am just a boyfriend doing something nice for my girlfriend. Take the card and have fun with your friend. Please!"

Grabbing her hand, I put the card into her hand and closed her fingers around it. Her gaze flicked from me to the card, then back to me before she finally nodded. As I watched her disappear out of the house, a smile spread across my face knowing she had just let me win one of the hardest battles I'd ever have with her, and that was not only getting her to realize she could depend on me but also her accepting help from me.

Standing in front of the mirror, I readjusted the vest of my black tuxedo before sliding my arms into my jacket. I hated formal events, but I wanted Harper to have the opportunity to have a normal high school experience, and I couldn't wait to see her all dressed up tonight.

"Christian," Aiden called out from downstairs. I was ready. I turned and strolled down the stairs.

"What's up?" I met Aiden at the bottom of the stairs. Aiden was wearing a similar black tux without the jacket, his dark hair a disheveled mess, and black flip-flops in place of his dress shoes.

"Rumor has it," he said. "Noah is looking for Harper." My posture stiffened at his name in the same sentence as hers. "Some are saying the Villa Boys will start trouble tonight at the dance."

"Is everyone going tonight?" I knew Aiden was going with Chloe, but I didn't know if Bash, Link, Maverick, or Julian planned to go too.

"Yes." He nodded. "They will be here shortly, and we'll all ride together. We have reservations at Nineteen31 for all of us in..." He trailed off, glancing at his watch. "Thirty minutes."

"Okay," I said, inhaling a deep breath. "Are you ready?" My eyes scanned down to his flip-flop.

"Yes." He winked, his lips curling into a grin.

"Let's go get our dates." I chuckled. Chloe was going to punch him in the throat when she saw his flip-flops.

We walked a short distance from the main house to the pool house. The door was unlocked.

"Harper," I called out before stepping inside. "Chloe. We are here."

"Come in," Chloe yelled from the second floor. "We'll be down in a minute."

The rumble of a diesel engine roared from outside as Julian's truck pulled up to the pool house.

"You boys ready for this?" Chloe called out.

I was ready.

"Hell yeah," Aiden shouted.

"Go," Chloe whisper-yelled. I laughed, picturing Chloe pushing Harper. When I looked up, Harper appeared at the bottom of the steps. My gaze locked on her as my jaw dropped. I was speechless. Harper's silver sparkling dress hugged every one of her perfect curves. The dress hung low in the front with a slit up her thigh. Her long dark hair was pulled up from her neck, and I couldn't wait to put my mouth on the bare skin.

"Wow," I managed to choke out. "You look beautiful."

"Thank you," she smiled.

"Holy shit," Aiden exclaimed. We all looked to see a blonde standing at the bottom of the stairway. Holy shit was right. Chloe's black hair with deep green highlights was gone, and her natural dirty blonde was back. Her tattoos were still visible, but she replaced all the piercings on her face with a simple small diamond stud in her nose. "You look amazing," Aiden finally said when he found his words.

"Are we ready? Everyone is outside waiting."

"Wait," Chloe stopped us. "Where are your shoes?" She didn't look amused by Aiden's flip-flops. I couldn't help but laugh as Aiden stuttered his way out of this one. Ultimately Chloe won, and Aiden put his dress shoes on.

Twenty minutes later, we pulled into Nineteen31. Aiden pulled the Escalade up to the door, and we all piled out.

"Where are your dates?" Harper gaze narrowed on the guys. Maverick, Bash, Link, and Julian were all dressed in similar tuxedos to Aiden and me. I was pretty sure we all got them at the same time for some stupid formal event at the country club. Our moms probably went shopping for them together.

"You're looking at 'em." Link laughed, gesturing to Bash, Maverick, and Julian. "We don't really do dates." My guess was they wouldn't even be going if it wasn't for the Villa Boys threatening to cause trouble for Harper tonight.

"We made it," Ryder said, pushing through the door with his date in tow. A tall blonde guy I'd never met before, but apparently Harper had because she ran to greet them both with a hug.

"Your table is ready," the hostess said. "Follow me."

"Wow," Harper whispered, her gaze flicking around the

room. "This is fancy." It wasn't the fanciest restaurant I'd ever been to, but it was one of my favorites. The restaurant's ceiling was lit with white lights like stars flickering above us. Each round table was dressed in a white tablecloth and a floral candle centerpiece.

We spent two hours eating and socializing. Harper seemed to be enjoying herself, and I thought it was even better that Chloe and Ryder were here with her. Even though she was coming around to all of us, she still seemed more comfortable with Chloe and Ryder.

"I forgot my phone in the car," Chloe said. "Harper, will you come with me." Both girls pushed away from the table.

"Hold on," I said. I threw the white napkin on my empty plate and pushed it away from the table. "I'll come with you."

"Christian." Harper threw a hand out to stop me. "That's girl code for I need to talk. Alone."

"Okay." I hesitated. I didn't want her outside without me, but I also didn't want to ruin the night by bringing up Noah and the Villa Boys. I hadn't told her about the rumors yet; they were only rumors at that point, so I didn't want to say anything. "I'll be here if you need me." I could see the Escalade from the window by our table.' I'd watch her from here.

CHAPTER 24

Harper

The cool night air sent a chill across my skin. The sun had set over an hour ago, and the night air was still cold even though it was late spring. Crossing my arms, I ran my hands over my arms to warm them. This dress didn't offer much coverage from the cold.

"What's going on?" I asked Chloe once we got to the Escalade, but she didn't have the chance to answer.

"Hey, Harper." My heart lurched at the sound of the familiar voice. Noah appeared from the shadows in front of the Escalade. "Look at you all fancy." He reached out for one of the loose strands of hair, but I jerked my head away. "Where you been?"

Grabbing Chloe's arm, I pulled her behind me. I didn't want her caught in the crossfire. It didn't matter; Noah's boys stepped out of the shadows surrounding us. Panic surged through me.

"What do you want?" I hissed. My heart slammed against my chest, dread twisting in my gut. Noah had never come looking for me before. I'd disappeared for weeks at a time, and never once had he cared. Why was he here now?

"We came to get you"," Noah said. The threatening tone of his voice sent chills surging over my body. His eyes were dark and soulless. "To bring you back home. To the Southside. Where you belong." Noah reached out, wrapping his long fingers around the bare skin of my upper arm. Trying to escape his grasp, I realized there was nowhere to go. We were surrounded. There were only three of them, but they were all twice the size of Chloe and me.

"Why don't you and your friends fuck off?" Chloe suggested.

"Take. Your. Fucking hands. Off her," Christian's voice boomed from behind me. His tone was laced with venom. "Or I'll break every bone in your fucking hand." Noah and Christian were the same height, but Noah was leaner, and Christian was pure muscle.

"Harper belongs to the Southside," Noah taunted but released my arm.

"Harper belongs to no one," Christian seethed.

Noah's taunting demeanor disappeared and was replaced with fury. His fist clenched at his sides. Noah already didn't like the Valley Boys, and for them to take something Noah thought was his would declare war. Christian knew it. His defensive posture said he was ready for battle. I wasn't, though. I didn't want Christian or his friends hurt because of me. Noah was outnumbered today, with only Mason and Parker with him. The war wouldn't happen today.

Mason and Parker crowded behind Noah, and Christian's boys stood behind him. Chloe and I stood in the center of them.

"This has nothing to do with you," Noah said.

"Yeah," Christian said. "It does. Don't you get tired of beating on girls? Maybe it's time to pick on someone your own size."

"Fine," Noah scoffed, throwing up his hands. "Go ahead and let him pop that cherry. We'll finish breaking you in when you come crawling back because he's done with you." Noah's eyes locked on mine. He never saw it coming. Christian's fist slammed into the side of Noah's face sending him tumbling to the ground as chaos broke out around us.

"Don't you ever talk to her like that again," Christian snarled. His tone low and lethal. Noah was back on his feet and charging for Christian.

Lunging forward, I was jerked back against my will by Sebastian. Aiden had Chloe, and Sebastian had me, hauling us to the opposite side of the Escalade and away from the fight.

"Stay here," Sebastian ordered, setting me down to open the door, but I took off. No way was I letting anyone get hurt because of me. Aiden reached for me but caught one of the thin straps to the top of my dress, snapping it.

Sirens echoed from a distance. Someone had called the cops. Sliding around the back of the Escalade, I didn't waste time assessing the situation. I went straight for Noah.

"What are you doing, Wonder Woman?" Lincoln hissed, grabbing me around the waist before I could get to Noah and jerking me back. It wasn't like Christian needed my help. Christian stood over Noah with Noah's shirt balled in his fist, using the other to pound into Noah's face.

Maverick, Sebastian, and Julian stood ready to pounce if Noah's boys stepped in, making the fight unfair.

"We need to go," Lincoln shouted. "Cops."

Christian dropped Noah and backed away. His chest was heaving with anger.

Noah fumbled to his feet, wiping the blood from his lip and mouth. His eyes locked with mine. His mouth curved into a purely evil smile as blood dripped from his lips.

"See you soon, Harper," Noah muttered, backing into the shadows with his boys. Christian surged forward, reaching out for Noah, but Maverick grabbed him, shoving him into the Escalade.

We all piled inside, and Lincoln spun out of the parking lot. Five minutes down the road, he pulled over, and we all got out.

"Doesn't look like we will make it to prom," Chloe said, grabbing the broken strap of my dress. My dress wasn't even half as damaged as Christian's tux, not to mention the shiner on his cheekbone.

"You guys should still go." They shouldn't miss out on tonight because of me. "You don't have to miss it."

"Fuck that," Chloe said. "We were only going for you." Chloe's gaze flicked around to everyone. "Does anyone still want to go?"

Everyone shook their heads.

"So, now what?"

The guys all passed glances before simultaneously chanting, "Lake house."

"What is the lake house?"

"Lincoln has a house on Lake Cannon," Maverick said. "We'll, spend a few hours out there instead of going to prom."

Lake Cannon was deep in the Valley behind all the massive mansions tucked deep in the woods.

Twenty minutes later, Aiden pulled the Escalade down the long-isolated driveway ending at a two-story house built on Lake Cannon.

The house was as beautiful as the location. It looked more like a luxury cabin with large windows, a wrap-around porch, and a large pool and hot tub in the backyard that overlooked the lake—something I'd only ever seen on TV.

"Let's go Netflix and chill," Aiden said to Chloe, reaching for her hand and heading into the house.

"We are hitting up the hot tub," Lincoln said, and Maverick, Sebastian, and Julian followed.

"What are we doing?" I turned to Christian.

"Come on." He smiled, taking my hand and leading me

past the house and down to the dock over the lake. The trail down the dock's path was lit with white lights, the only light other than the full moon that danced across the black water.

"Wow, this is so beautiful."

"Yes," he said, grabbing my hand and spinning me. "You are." My cheek burned, and my stomach fluttered with butterflies. I didn't know how he did it, but he made me feel things with the simplest gesture.

Releasing me, he sat down on the edge of the dock, hanging his legs over into the water. "Sit." He patted the wood beside him. Hiking my dress up, I sat down, removing my shoes before putting my feet into the water.

"Sorry about tonight."

"That was not your fault," he said. "You have nothing to apologize for."

"You know it's never going to stop, right?" I treaded my feet through the water. "You declared war with Noah; if I don't go back, there will be a war between the Villa and the Valley."

"Yes," he said, turning his gaze to mine. "You aren't going back if that's what you're getting at. Noah fucked up the minute he put his hands on you, and tonight when he threatened you, he declared war with us regardless of where you are." He ran his hand through his thick dark hair pushing it out of his face. "I want to kill him for hurting you."

"I don't want anyone to get hurt because of me."

"Harper," he said, staring off into the water. "Was what he said tonight true?"

Sucking in a deep breath, I closed my eyes. I wondered if he'd ask me what Noah said earlier about popping my cherry. My virginity was the one thing I managed to keep through all of this. Through all my mom's perverted boyfriends' Noah's friends, and even Noah.

"Yes," I sighed. "Does that bother you?"

"No." He shook his head. He jumped up to his feet and started unbuttoning his pants.

"What are you doing," I was thankful for the subject

change even though I wasn't sure exactly what he was doing.

"Skinny dipping." He laughed. "You coming?"

Turning away from me, he slid out of his pants and shirt, and then his boxer briefs were lying in the pile of clothes on the dock. My breath hitched at the sight of him. His body was made by special order from the gods. Every inch of his tanned chiseled form was perfection, his torso and arm covered in black artistic ink. He dove into the water with a splash.

Standing up, I peered over into the darkness of the water. Ever since I was a little girl, I had an unrealistic fear of deep water that wasn't clear and lit up like a swimming pool. It terrified me, not knowing what was under me. Christian emerged from the depths of the darkness, and I blew out a breath.

Looking back at the house, I wiped my damp hands on my dress. Beads of sweat formed on my forehead, and my heart raced.

"Harper," Christian said, running his hand over his face. His words were muffled by my heart pounding in my ears. My words caught in my throat. "Harper, are you okay?"

"Uh," I muttered. "Uh yes, I uh need to go to the bathroom." I bolted for the house.

"Harper," Christian called out, but I didn't stop. I kept going until I found the first bathroom, shut the door, and slid down onto the floor, drawing in long, slow breaths.

I'm not sure how long I sat on the bathroom floor before Christian knocked once and then walked in.

"Harper," he whispered. "Are you okay?" He'd changed out of his tux into shorts and a white T-shirt. He slid down to the floor when he saw me there. "'Harper, what's wrong?"

"It's stupid," I admitted.

"Was it because I was naked?"

"No." I snorted a laugh. "Trust me; it's stupid."

"Then tell me, please".

"I'm scared of the dark water."

"The water?" He laughed. "Thank god; I thought my naked

body terrified you." I laughed. "Here." He handed me some clothes that appeared to be his. "Get dressed, and we'll go Netflix and chill with Chloe and Aiden."

CHAPTER 25

Christian

The sound of feet pounding pulled my eyes up to see Harper standing sleepy-eyed at the bottom of the steps.

"Good morning." I set a coffee cup on the counter. She stopped, taking in the bedding on the couch. The evidence that I'd slept there.

"Did you sleep here last night?" She grabbed the coffee cup. "On the couch." Her eyes narrowed on me.

"I did," I answered, pouring coffee into her cup as she slid onto a stool at the bar. "I didn't want to wake you, and I felt like I should be close if you needed me." I didn't know how far Noah and his thugs would take this, but I wanted to ensure she was safe if they brought it here.

"Did you make breakfast?" She changed the subject.

I nodded, making her a plate. "I wanted to make sure you ate before we left today."

"Left?" she asked as I set the plate in front of her.

"It's spring break," I answered as if that meant anything to her. "Everyone from the Valley heads over to the coast, and we rent a bunch of beach houses for the week." Plus, I seriously doubted Noah or any of his wannabe thugs would come to the coast to stir up trouble.

"Sounds fun," she said as I ran up the stairs taking them two at a time. "What is that?" she asked when I reappeared with a suitcase.

"Your luggage." I opened the front door and set the suitcase outside. Harper narrowed her eyes. "Chloe packed it for you the day you moved in," I answered her unasked question.

"Uh, yeah, I'm going to need to go through that." She chuckled.

"No time; eat, shower, dress, and let's go."

The ride to the coast was long, and Harper wasn't a very patient passenger. By the time we made it, everyone was already settled in. Chloe and Aiden met us in the driveway.

"Please, someone shut her up." I groaned, jumping out of the Jeep.

Chloe snickered. "Let me guess." Chloe met me at the back of the Jeep. "She's a terrible passenger." I rolled my eyes and grabbed our luggage.

"I get claustrophobic." Harper shrugged. "I can't help it."

Harper reached for hers; "Don't insult me," I muttered, jerking the bags out of her reach. She threw her hands up and backed out of my way.

"Have a Snickers, man." Aiden chuckled. "You're hangry."

"Harper is the worst car rider I've ever met," Chloe said matter-of-factly. "The furthest I've ridden with her is an hour. So, I can only imagine how four hours went." She laughed, and I stormed into the house.

After a quick trip to the bathroom and some deep breathing, I was back to normal when Harper met me upstairs.

"This is your room." I set her luggage down on the bed. "My room is next door." I opened the French doors in her room, leading out onto a balcony overlooking the ocean, and then the second set of doors that led to my room.

Harper stood speechlessly on the terrace overlooking the white sandy beach and clear bluish-green water. She leaned over the rail, sucking in a deep breath. Her long dark hair caught a gust of wind flying around her face.

"This is amazing," she finally said, running a hand through her hair to tame it. "Who all is staying here?"

"In this house, there's me, you, Chloe, and Aiden. There's also Maverick, Link, and Sebastian. Julian is staying over there," I pointed to a large white beach house two houses down, "with some girl he met."

"I didn't realize the house was that big." She stepped back into her room.

"It has seven bedrooms."

"Seven?" she questioned, and I knew what she was asking.

"Chloe and Aiden are sharing a room." Her eyes went wide, but I wasn't going to elaborate on Chloe and Aiden. She'd have to talk to Chloe.

"We should figure out dinner," I changed the subject.

Harper rolled her eyes. "Christian, we just got here," she whined, tugging at my arm. "I'm still digesting breakfast and lunch. Let's go down to the beach."

"Yeah." I smiled, wrapping my arms around her waist and pulling her into me. How could I say no to those piercing blue eyes pleading with me? "You want to go for a walk and check out the sights? Sunset will be soon."

Sliding my hand into hers and tangling our fingers together, we walked barefoot in the sand down the beach towards the pier. A few other beachgoers were out walking, digging for shells, or waiting for the sunset. Even with the other people, it was still peaceful, with very little noise other than the sound of the crashing waves that came up, occasionally wetting our feet.

"I've never been to the beach before," Harper admitted. "I've only seen the ocean on TV."

"Is it what you expected?"

"There's no way a TV could do this justice."

Harper and I stopped turning towards the crashing waves to watch that last minute when the day turned to night. The sinking sun disappeared behind the horizon, leaving a symphony of colors in what could only be described as breathtaking. I'd visited this beach for years and never once watched a sunset.

"Harper," I said after several minutes of silence. "Do you ever think about looking for your mom?" I didn't mean to start such a heavy conversation, but it was something I'd wondered about.

"Yeah, I used to think about it a lot, but really it hurts less to think she's dead than she abandoned me, leaving me with Levi and Noah."

"Do you think she's dead?"

"I don't know." She sighed. "I just can't believe she didn't come back for me. She'd always come back."

"Did she know they hurt you?" I asked, already knowing

the answer.

"I don't know," she shrugged. "She was too far gone most of the time to know anything."

Looping an arm around Harper's waist, I pulled her back to my front and wrapped my arms around her holding her tightly against me. We stood silently, watching the sun disappearing into the ocean and breathing in the fresh air and salt water.

When I got home, I planned to dig into the disappearance of Harper's mom. It sounded like she was mixed up in a lot of bad things that could have ended her life, and I wasn't sure what I'd find when I started digging. Harper deserved to know the truth about her mom's disappearance, even though I wasn't sure the answer would bring the peace I hoped it would.

CHAPTER 26

Christian

The following day, I stood impatiently waiting outside Harper's bedroom door.

"Are you ready yet?" I shouted through the door. "How long does it take to put on a bathing suit?" The lock clicked, and I flung the door open. I sucked in a breath at the sight of her. Her tan legs looked tanner in the tiny black bikini that showed her entire ass. She moved to the door. "You're not wearing that." Grabbing her waist, I spun her back around, guiding her to her suitcase.

"Find something else." I flung the suitcase open.

"You should have let me go through the suitcase." She giggled. She grabbed a sheer wrap and started to wrap it around her waist.

"Yeah, no," I said, pulling it off her. "If you wear that, I will get into a fight."

"All the bathing suits are like this." She sifted through them.

"Put on a pair of sweatpants."

"You think Chloe packed my sweatpants?" She laughed. She snatched the sheer wrap and rewrapped it around her waist. "This will have to work." She disappeared around the corner, and I groaned.

We spent the entire day together, going from beach and sand to pool and tanning, only going in for lunch. Before we knew it, the sun was gone, and it was bonfire time.

The heat of the fire felt good against my chilled skin. A large group of us were gathered around the fire pit, joking and telling stories. Limited on seats, Harper sat on the arm of my wooden Adirondack chair.

"Omigod," Brianna laughed, pointing towards the walkway from the beach to the house. All eyes turned to see Julian's pale white skin saunter up the path, completely naked. He used his hands to cover his manhood.

"What happened to you?" Maverick teased.

"She kicked me out." Laughter roared through the group. "Can I crash here?

"All the rooms are full," I answered. "But the couch is yours, buddy."

"Wait," Harper whispered, turning to me. "The couch?" I pulled her onto my lap and was slightly surprised when she didn't put up a fight.

"Yes, the couch." I slid my hand over her bare thighs. "Where else would he sleep?"

"Wasn't he originally supposed to stay here?"

I rolled my eyes. Now Harper thought she was taking his room. I shrugged, not willing to answer.

"He can have my room. I'll take the couch."

"You're not sleeping on the couch."

"Christian, that couch is better than what I was sleeping on in the trailer. I'll be fine."

"It has nothing to do with that. Look around." I gestured to all the drunk guys running around stupidly. "I'm not taking the chance of some drunk fool getting stupid and you getting hurt in the process." I paused for a moment as a thought popped into my head. "But you can share a bed with me, and he can have your room."

Her lips pressed into a thin line as her gaze locked on mine before finally agreeing. "You can have my room, Julian," Harper said, standing from my lap.

"Hey, we are all headed down to the pier," Link called from the beach. "Y'all coming?"

"Nope," I said, standing and swooping Harper over my shoulder. "We are going to bed." She burst into a fit of laughter.

CHAPTER 27

Christian

I sat on the second-floor balcony watching the activities on the beach while I waited for Harper to move her things into my room. While my eyes focused solely on the beach, my mind dwelled on Harper in my bed with me tonight. We'd only shared a bed once, and she'd been too drunk to even know which bed she was in.

"All done," she said, falling into the chair next to mine. "You didn't want to hang out with your friends tonight?"

"I've spent every spring break with them since I was a kid. I'm where I want to be." She shivered, wrapping her arms around herself, and I stood, grabbing a blanket and wrapping it around her. She pulled her feet into the chair, covering most of herself. "I thought we could talk."

"What do you want to talk about?" she asked, avoiding eye contact and nervously chewing on her bottom lip. She busied herself with adjusting the blanket tighter around her. She was uneasy about sharing a bed with me. On the beach, it didn't seem to faze her, but now alone, she was anxious.

"I want to make sure you are comfortable sharing a bed with me," I said. "We don't have to do anything you don't want to."

"I'm not nervous about sharing a bed with you." She

sighed. "I trust you."

"Then what is it?" I narrowed my eyes.

"I feel like this is all going to blow up in my face," she said. "I'm terrified of what Noah will do if I have to go back there."

"Harper, listen to me; you will never go back to the south side. I meant that. I don't know what will happen with us yet, but you will never go back to Noah, and I will kill Noah if he comes after you again."

"I don't want to ruin this," she whispered. "I've never had anyone who cared whether I had a clean place to sleep or food to eat." She shrugged. "And I just don't want to do something that's going to screw this up, but I also don't want to cause trouble for any of you either."

"Harper." I scooted forward in my chair. "I promise that if you need me, I'll be there no matter what." Grabbing her chin, I forced her to look at me. "Even ten years from now, if some asshole isn't treating you right and you need me to come to get you, I will." She smiled. "You will never be hungry again. You will never not have a safe place to sleep again."

She leaned forward, dropped the blanket, closed her eyes, and softly kissed me. Every part of my being wanted to grab her and pull her onto me, deepen the kiss, tear off her clothes, and make her mine, but this was her moment, and I'd let her have it.

Pulling away, she stood, placing her hands on my shoulders; she slid onto my lap, straddling me and curling her legs underneath her.

"Harper," I whispered, but she shushed me, pressing her mouth to mine, stealing my words. Running her tongue along my lips, they parted slightly with a heavy breath, and she dove her tongue into my mouth. Our tongues dancing together, I filled my hands with her ass pulling her harder against me.

The kiss turned frantic and messy, and all I could think about was her skin against mine. Pulling her top off, I flung it across the deck. She wasn't wearing a bra. My hands trailed up her sides, and she shivered against me. The heat from her bare skin burned into mine, setting a fire deep down. She ground herself against the throbbing in my pants, pushing me over the edge. I needed her.

Gripping her ass, keeping her tight against me, I didn't break from the kiss as I rose, carrying her to the bed. Lowering her onto it, I stood back, taking in every inch of her perfect, almost naked body, every curve. I flicked the fly of my pants open, dropping them to the ground before my boxers were gone too.

Biting hard on her lip, her eyes raked over me, her eyes widening when they dropped below the belt line. Her gaze lingered for a long moment before roaming back up and locking on mine.

She was breathtaking.

Hooking my fingers into the sides of her pink lace panties, I slid them down her legs. Dropping to my knees, I dropped them on the floor beside me. The room was dark, with only the light from the moon illuminating the room and the cool ocean breeze blowing through the open terrace doors. Watching her through my lashes, I pried her thighs apart, trailing my lips and facial stubble across her, teasing her sensitive skin. I pressed scattered kisses over her thighs and bare pussy, and when she rocked her hips into my face, my lips curled into a smirk. She wanted me as much as I wanted her.

My arm wrapped around her thighs, spreading her wide as I slid my tongue through her heat-wet flesh before drawing her flesh into my mouth, sucking and biting. She whimpered as her fingers tangled in my hair. My mouth continued the slow torture of her clit as I slid a finger inside her, slowly pumping. She gasped when I added another finger, spreading her open, giving her time to adjust to me, stretching her so she could take all of me.

"Christian," she pleaded, arching her back as her pussy tightened around my fingers.

"Fuck," I groaned against her heat flesh. "Come for me, baby. Come all over my face. I need to taste you before I fuck you." My tongue flicked her clit as my fingers thrust deeper. Her eyes closed, and her back arched as her body vibrated against me. I added more pressure, pumping in and out in a rhythm that made her legs tremble. Her body tensed, and her pussy walls squeezed. I pulled my fingers out, swiping my tongue over her entrance as she exploded. I spread her wider as I lapped up every drop of her orgasm.

I needed to be inside her.

I trailed my lips over her hips, stomach, and chest, kissing and nipping every inch of her as I slid up her body. She arched into my mouth, a moan escaping her lips. My hand slid over her breast, my thumb grazing her taut bud as her hand slid into my hair.

My mouth covered her breast, sucking in her nipple, teasing it with my tongue. Her body shook underneath me as goosebumps covered her skin.

"Are you sure?" I breathed, releasing her breast and hovering my mouth over hers. I wanted her, but I wanted her to want me just as much.

"Yes," she whispered; she pushed her hips into mine, rocking slowly against me. "I want you, now, please." Her big blue eyes were pleading and desperate. That was all I needed. Sliding her hands over her head and tangling our fingers together, pinning them in place, I took her mouth with mine in a hot, possessive, demanding kiss that told her she was mine.

She moaned into my mouth as I stroked myself against her, working my way to her entrance. As much as I wanted to dive deep into her, she was a virgin, and I had to take it slow. Hovering over her entrance, I slowly worked myself inside, allowing her time to adjust with each movement. She sucked in a sharp breath as I eased deeper. Holding myself deep, I paused but when she rocked her hips forward, begging for more of me. I almost lost control.

My mouth released hers, trailing down her jawline. I groaned against her skin as I rocked into her, each thrust harder, deeper. Her hips met mine, moving in sync together. Releasing her hands, I grabbed her thigh, pulling her legs higher.

Closing my eyes, I lost myself in the feeling of her. My thrust grew quicker, harder, deeper. My body tensed as she pulsated around me.

"Harper," I groaned against her lips as her body vibrated underneath me. She was close; I was close. With a hard deep thrust, my body shook.

"Christian," she moaned into my mouth as her entire body tensed. Another thrust, and I exploded with a low growl. Her body went limp, and my head fell into the crook of her neck as our rapid breaths were in sync.

With a sigh, I rolled to the side in exhausted satisfaction.

"Are you okay," I asked, leaning up on my elbows once I caught my breath. Harper smiled, nodding, her chest rising and falling rapidly. She hadn't caught her breath yet.

"Are you on birth control?" The realization hit me. We'd had sex without a condom or any protection. Of course, she wasn't on birth control. She was a virgin. That was a stupid question. Panic set in, and my head spun. I'd wanted her so badly that a condom never crossed my mind. This had never happened before.

"Yes," she said. My head twisted to hers, and my brows furrowed. "I've been on birth control since the first time one of my mom's boyfriends snuck into my room thinking I was her. Plus, I never knew if or when Noah or his friends..." She trailed off. She didn't need to finish. I didn't want her to. Swallowing hard, I forced the anger down.

No one would ever have the opportunity to hurt her again. EVER!

CHAPTER 28

Harper

"Holy shit." Maverick snorted a laugh. "I was wondering when you'd come up for air!" I rolled my eyes, but the truth was I wasn't sure we'd ever leave the room again, and if I hadn't been starving, I probably wouldn't have. Everything about the last 36 hours had been perfect, and I was scared it would end once I left the room.

"Good morning," I mumbled, grabbing a cup and filling it with coffee.

"Breakfast?" Maverick grinned, holding up an empty plate with a ridiculous smirk plastered across his face. Maverick was undeniably hot. A backward baseball cap covered his dark hair. His full lips had a piercing at the corner of his mouth that hid his all-white smile. He stood shirtless, with a perfectly sculpted torso covered in black ink, and his black gym shorts hung low on his lean hips.

"Why are you up so early?" I asked, taking a seat on a wooden stool at the breakfast bar.

"It's my morning to cook breakfast," he said, stepping out of the way and showing the feast behind him.

"You take turns cooking?" I took a sip of my scalding hot coffee, wincing when it hit my tongue.

"Just breakfast." He handed me a plate full of more food

than I could ever eat. "So, will you two love birds be joining us for our annual scavenger hunt tonight after dark?" Maverick set a stack of plates out.

"Scavenger hunt?"

"No," Christian barked behind me. "She will not be participating in your stupid scavenger hunt tonight."

"She?" Maverick laughed. "What about you?"

Christian leaned in, kissing my forehead before saying, "We will not be participating in your stupid game."

"Wait, why not?" It sounded like fun.

"Just trust me." Christian grabbed a coffee cup. "Eat." He shoved my plate closer to me.

Rolling my eyes, I took a bite.

"What about the after-party," Maverick laughed.

"No!" Christian took a seat beside me. His eyes narrowed on Maverick's and his lips pursed, challenging Maverick to keep going. "We will not be participating in any of your games tonight."

"Someone want to fill me in?" I threw my hands up.

"Christian?" Maverick questioned, adding more pancake batter to the hot pan. Christian didn't answer.

"Unless you're scared, you won't win."

"We'll play," I said, standing my ground. I wasn't scared of a stupid game.

"No, you won't," Christian growled. "The scavenger hunt is nothing but a big perverted checklist of random sexual acts that have to be performed by random strangers on the boardwalk for your group to win." He put his face level with mine. "You're mine, and if anyone touches you, I'll kill them."

I swallowed hard. He was right. We shouldn't play the game. I didn't want Christian to go to jail, and performing sexual acts on strangers didn't sound like a good time.

"So, you have to walk up to a stranger and ask to fuck them?" My mouth twisted with curiosity.

"Not exactly," Maverick answered. "Your checklist could say go down on a random stranger or make out with a stranger.

Everyone in the group must do something on the checklist."

Considering I'd had sex for the first time yesterday, this probably wasn't a game I'd be good at anyway.

"The after-party is a big orgy where everyone ends up fucking everyone," Christian said. "The only person you'll be fucking tonight is me."

I couldn't argue with that.

"Looks like we're out." I shrugged.

"Party poopers," Maverick teased.

Standing on the second-floor terrace, I watched each movement of the glittering ocean sparkle against the moonlight. The beach was packed, with everyone getting ready for the scavenger hunt.

"Why would anyone want to play a game like that," I asked when Christian stepped out of the bedroom and onto the terrace dressed in a tee and shorts.

"It was fun once upon a time ago," he chuckled, leaning on the railing beside me. "Before you." We watched Chloe, Aiden, and Maverick reviewing their list below us.

"Have you played before?"

"A few times," he nodded.

"Do you wish you were playing tonight?"

"No," he laughed, stepping behind me and placing a hand on each side of the rail, trapping me in.

"I want to be right here with you." I smiled, relaxing into him as he pressed his lips to my bare shoulder.

"Come on, let's go for a walk on the beach and watch these fools play their games."

Christian grabbed his shirt off the back of the chair and pulled it over his head before we strolled down the stairs, out of the house, and down to the beach where everyone was gathering.

"Did you guys decide to play?" Lincoln asked when he noticed us on the beach.

"No," Christian said. "Just taking a walk."

"Come on, Link," a tall thin brunette yelled across the beach.

"Gotta go." He took off towards the girl.

We walked in silence, watching the chaos around us. Everyone was running everywhere, yelling and laughing. Talking about what crazy things they'd done, some of the stuff so wild it made me blush to hear it.

"I've never done anything like that before," I whispered. "I've never done anything crazy."

Christian smiled, wrapping his fingers around my wrist. He stepped into the shadows underneath the peer and drug me with him.

"Shhhh..." he whispered. Spinning me, he pulled my back to his front. Wrapping his arms around my waist, holding me in place. "Look." He pointed out of the shadows to the edge of the boardwalk where Maverick stood shirtless, his hand tangled in a blonde's hair on her knees in front of him. It took me a minute to take in exactly what was happening.

"Omi..." Christian's hand slid up, clamping over my mouth, silencing me, his other arm holding me in place and my arms at my sides. I squeezed my eyes shut.

"You've never done anything crazy," he whispered against my ear. "Have you ever watched?" I hummed no against his hand, frantically shaking my head. "Open your eyes."

This felt so wrong. So dirty, but I did what he told me and opened my eyes.

Maverick's toned and sculpted body flexed with each bob of the blonde's head. His head tilted back, and his lips parted as he fisted the girl's hair tighter, guiding her head exactly where he wanted it. He released a low moan, and I squeezed my thighs together. This was wrong, yet I couldn't pull my eyes away. The blonde was topless, and Maverick was bottomless, but we could only imagine what was happening in their position.

"What are we doing?" I whispered when Christian's hand dropped to my shoulders, releasing my mouth. My heart raced, hoping they didn't see us.

"We're watching," he purred against my neck. My eyes closed, and my head fell back against his firm chest as the heat from his breath feathered across my skin. Leaning down and pressing his soft lips to the nape of my neck, he slowly slid the straps to my dress down, all the way down, freeing my breasts. I panicked, my eyes flashed open, and my pulse pounded in my ears. We were in public where anyone could see us.

"What are you..." I scrambled to find my straps, but he stopped me.

"No one can see us," he whispered, wrapping his arm over my chest and holding my body tightly against his. "Don't take your eyes off them." Sucking in a deep breath, I did as he said as his hand moved under my dress, sliding up between my thigh as his fingertip dipped into my panties.

I tensed, and even though I wanted to search the area for anyone who could see us, I didn't take my eyes off Maverick and the blonde. His fingers slid through my folds. "Holy fuck, you're so wet. Does this turn you on, Harper?" Throwing my head back into him, I moaned at the sensation of his fingers and the cold breeze brushing across my nipples, hardening them.

It did turn me on. The thrill of being caught, plus Christian's hands on me, was almost too much.

My breaths came hard and fast as I watched Maverick look down at the blonde. His body tensed as he fisted her hair, snapping his hips harder and faster into her mouth. Her hands gripped his thighs, resisting his hard brutal thrusts.

Christian's finger slid inside me while his thumb circled my clit. I winced, still sore from the last few nights. His mouth sucked and tasted the hollow of my neck. My heart pounded against my chest as I gasped for air. Waves crashed around our feet as the tide came in. His grip around my chest tightened, holding me hard against him. Christian's finger pumped in and out, finding the perfect rhythm before he added another one.

His pace picked up, and my breath hitched as I inched closer and closer to the edge. His other hand cupped my breast as his fingers continued to pump, his thumb stroking my clit. It was almost too much.

Maverick was close to his climax. His eyes were closed, his moans deeper. I was close too.

"Christian," I whispered. My body vibrated against his, and my pussy clenched around his fingers as everything inside me exploded in euphoric ecstasy.

I spun in Christian's grip facing him; my body went limp in his arms in satisfied exhaustion.

"Holy fuck, that was hot," he breathed against my lips before taking them with his as white-hot electricity exploded between us.

Breaking from the kiss, he slid the straps to my dress up my arms and back to my shoulders.

"We should head back before I fuck you right here."

My gaze flicked to the edge of the boardwalk, but Maverick and the blonde were already gone. Christian tangled his fingers into mine, and we returned to the beach house.

CHAPTER 29

Christian

Every year our house held the annual last-day pool party. Everyone from the Valley celebrated the last official day of spring break, even though we still had Saturday and Sunday before returning to school. It was our last day at the beach. Everyone was close to trashed from partying all day already before the nighttime bash even started.

Sitting on the pool's edge, I watched Harper and Chloe gossiping at the other end. They had no doubt discussed every dirty detail about the week's event, and I couldn't help but smile when the thought of last night crept into my mind.

My phone vibrated in my hand.

Alexi - *I need to talk to you.*

I didn't answer, instead hitting the side button and declining. My phone vibrated again.

Alexi - *It's important. It's about Harper and Noah.*

She had my attention.

Christian - *Meet me at my house on the third-floor terrace.*

I didn't want to go, but Alexi hung out with the Villa Boy sometimes, and if she knew or heard something, I needed to know so that I could protect Harper.

Christian - On my way.

Harper was consumed with Chloe, so I didn't bother her. I'd be back before she knew I was gone.

"What is it, Alexi?" I asked, annoyance in my tone when I made it to the terrace. Alexi stayed in the house next to mine. I had a clear view of the party from her terrace.

"I could suck your dick first," she purred, tracing her fingertips down my torso to the waistband of my bathing suit.

"Alexi," I warned, wrapping my fingers around her wrist and stopping her.

"Okay, fine," she groaned, snatching her wrist out of my grip.

"You said this was about Harper," I growled. "Is it or not?" I leaned over the railing on my forearms.

"Can't blame a girl for trying." She shrugged.

"Alexi," I hissed.

"Fine. So, you know, sometimes I run around with Mason?" I nodded. "Well, I met him at a party and overheard them talking about Harper." I nodded, urging her to continue. "They said she was already spoken for."

"What does that mean?" I narrowed my eyes.

"I don't know exactly," she shook her head. "But I got the feeling it would be something against her will."

"Do they know where she is?"

"No, they don't know she's here at the beach, and they don't know she's staying with you. They know she hangs out with you, but they think she's staying with Chloe or maybe even Ryder."

I leaned further over the third-floor terrace from Alexi's beach house and down to the pool behind my beach house.

Chloe, Harper, and Aiden sat on the pool's edge, laughing about something.

This put them in danger.

Reaching for my phone, I sent a group text.

*Christian - URGENT! Meet me at the
beach house now. 3rd-floor terrace.
Don't say anything to anyone.*

"I appreciate you letting me know," I said dismissively, twisting to face her.

"You know we could still be friends," Alexi purred, placing the palm of her hand on my chest.

"I don't think you would ever be satisfied with just friends, Alexi."

"I meant with benefits," she whispered against my lips, sliding her arms around my waist. I'd never in my life turned down easy pussy, but Alexi wasn't who I wanted. For the first time in my life, I only wanted one girl, Harper, and I didn't want to do anything that would screw it up.

I shoved her out of my personal space before saying, "No."

"What's up?" Maverick asked, pushing through the double doors to the terrace.

"I'll let you boys chat," Alexi said, disappearing into the house.

I filled them in on all the details I had.

"Wait," Aiden said.

"That means Chloe's place will be the first place they hit."

"If they do anything at all," Link interjected. "They could be all talk."

"Well, I'm not willing to bet Chloe's life on that," Aiden stated.

"I agree," I said. "They are pissed right now. Not only because we have Harper but because of what happened the night of prom."

"What do we do?" Sebastian asked.

"We let everyone enjoy their last night out here. Then, tomorrow after we're loaded, we come up with a plan together." They all nodded in agreement.

CHAPTER 30

Harper

I kicked the cool blue water with my feet and laughed at Chloe's corny jokes. The sun had set hours ago, and the entire Valley was partying around the pool, celebrating their last night of Spring Break.

"How often do you come here for Spring Break?" I asked Chloe.

"I used to come with my parents when I was a kid, but when they stopped, so did I."

"So, you've never come out here with the rest of the Valley kids?"

She shook her head. "No, I've never really fit in with any of them, but I have to admit this has been fun."

She was right. It had been more fun than I'd had in a long time. I'd been worried that the Valley wouldn't accept me, and I still wasn't completely convinced they had, but no one was treating me any differently than anyone else. Of course, that could be out of fear. No one wanted to stand toe-to-toe with

Christian.

Aiden sank onto the concrete pool deck on the opposite side of Chloe. "What are you two chatting about?"

"Do you really want to know?" Chloe laughed. "You might be embarrassed."

"Well, now you have to tell me."

Chloe and Aiden fell into their own conversation, and my gaze flicked around the pool deck. "Where's Christian?" I muttered mostly to myself because no one else was listening. Sebastian and Lincoln were still in the same spot where Christian had been. Pushing off the deck and hopping to my feet.

I strolled around the pool deck, through the house, and then down to the beach. It wasn't like him to go far without letting me know, not that he had to check in with me, but he usually did.

Twisting back to the house, I froze when my gaze landed on the third-floor balcony of the house next to the pool party.

It was Christian, and he was with Alexi. Alexi leaned into him as her hands touched his bare chest.

I stood there paralyzed as my heart shattered into a million pieces.

"Hey, Harper," a voice said from somewhere behind me, but I didn't bother looking to see who it was. I needed space.

I stormed down the beach, rage mixed with pain coursed through my chest, sucking the air from my lungs.

"Hey," a deep voice called out. "Are you okay?"

I stopped twisting to see Mike. I knew him from school. "I'm okay."

"You don't look okay." His brows pinched with concern. "Where are you headed?"

"Um." I didn't know where I was heading. "For a walk."

"Okay, how about I walk with you? It's kind of dangerous to walk the shoreline alone at night."

"Yeah, sure," I murmured. I didn't really want the company, but I also didn't want to be alone.

"I need to change. My house is right there." He pointed to an ocean-blue house just down from the boardwalk. "We can do that and then head over to the boardwalk."

I nodded and followed him to his house.

CHAPTER 31

Christian

    Looking over the terrace, I scanned the pool for Harper, but she wasn't there. After checking our house, the pool, and the beach, I found Chloe.

"Where's Harper?"

"She went looking for you." She pointed toward the beach.

"How long ago?"

"Right after Aiden disappeared. Maybe she went to bed." I shook my head no.

"Hey," I stopped a random person passing by. "Have you seen Harper Brooks?" She shook her head.

"What's going on?" Julian asked.

"Have you seen Harper?"

"No." He shook his head.

"Hey, man," someone yelled from behind me. I spun to see Ben Davis walking up to me. "I saw Harper." He threw his thumb over his shoulder towards the boardwalk as he pulled his blunt to his lips and inhaled. "She took off after she saw you up there." He pointed Alexi's third-floor balcony. "Making out with Alexi. She was pretty upset."

Fuck! "She took off alone?" I shoved my hand through my hair.

"Uh, no, man," his friend Josh said, grabbing the blunt

from Ben. "She bumped into Little Mikey, and he invited her to the boardwalk."

"Little Mikey is here?" Little Mikey graduated last year. He had a reputation for being too handsy with girls, but that probably wasn't something Harper knew because she didn't hang with the Valley kids.

"Who invited him?" Julian asked. Ben and his friend shrugged.

"Split up," I ordered. "Find her."

Searching the path of the boardwalk, I took off, stopping everyone who passed and asking if they'd seen her.

Stopping, I spun, shoving my hands through my hair, searching the beach and boardwalk. Where was she?

"Harper," I yelled.

"I'll go down to the boardwalk and search," Maverick yelled, catching up to me.

"Hey," Sebastian called from behind me. I turned. "Missy saw her going into that house. She said that's where Mikey is staying." He pointed, and we both took off.

"Let's split up," I said, not bothering to knock on the door.

Searching the first floor, Sebastian ran up to the second. Flinging doors open, I rushed through each room.

"Christian," Sebastian yelled, and I took the stairs two at a time. Flinging myself around the doorway, Harper sat on the floor, knees to her chest, and Sebastian checked the pulse of Mikey, who was lying beside the bed with a shattered lamp next to his head.

"Is he dead?" I asked, moving to Harper.

"No, but he's going to wish he was tomorrow morning," Sebastian said.

"Harper," I leaned down, pulling her up.

"No." she shoved me away and stormed towards the door. Gripping her wrist, I spun her around. Her right hook caught me in the chest. We'd attracted an audience. Chloe, Ryder, and all my boys had trickled into the room.

"Fuck off, Christian." She swung, aiming for my face but

missed when I ducked out of the way. Gripping her wrist, I jerked her to me and threw her over my shoulder before carrying her to a separate room and slamming the door behind me.

"Christian," she hissed.

"Put me the fuck down." She was pissed, and I couldn't blame her.

"Harper," I said, setting her down, holding her tight against me, and trapping her arms at her side. She turned her face away from me. Releasing her and grabbing her face with both hands, I forced her to look at me. She struggled against my grip, but I only held tighter, pressing my face firmly against hers. "Harper, I'm sorry."

"You could have just told me you got back together with her," she cried.

"I didn't," I whispered. "I'm not sorry that I kissed her because I didn't. I'm sorry that I put myself in a situation that would make you think I did."

"Why were you with her?" she asked, grabbing my wrist that still held her face.

"She said she had something she needed to tell me about you," I said.

"And?"

"Can we just go back to the house?" I asked, releasing her face. "It concerns everyone."

"So, you didn't fuck Alexi?"

"No."

We stepped out of the room, where everyone stood silently, waiting for us to return.

"Chloe and Maverick, will you take Harper back to the house?"

"Wait, you're not coming?" Harper asked.

"Yes, but there's something I need to take care of first."

"I already whooped his drunk ass," Harper hissed. "Just let him be."

"Not a fucking chance in hell."

"I'm staying," she said, crossing her arms over her chest.

"Maverick," I shouted, my gaze meeting his. I didn't need to say anything else. He knew what that meant: take her out of here, willingly or not. I didn't want her to witness what was about to happen.

"Don't you do it," she snarled at Maverick as he moved to her. She leaned forward, ready to attack.

"Please don't hurt me," Maverick whined.

"Go help him." I shrugged to Julian.

"Come on, Harper," Chloe said. "Let the boys clean up this mess, and you can tell me how you laid that jerk out." Her eyes flipped back and forth between Chloe and me before hesitantly agreeing.

CHAPTER 31

Harper

When we made it back to the beach house, Christian sat Chloe and me down and explained why he was talking to Alexi and the information she'd had given him.

"So, let me get this straight," Chloe huffed, crossing her arms over her chest. "You want me to go into hiding because a group of loser thugs thinks Harper is staying with me?" Aiden nodded. "No, that's crazy. Tell them to bring it!" She leaned into Aiden dramatically. Chloe was taller than most girls, and Aiden still towered over her, but she wasn't the least bit intimidated by him or his size. "I got something special just for them."

"Chloe," Aiden grumbled in exasperation, shoving his hand through his dark hair. Chloe and Aiden stood toe to toe in the center of the

living room while the rest of us stood in a circle around them, ready to intervene if Chloe knocked Aiden out, and I think we were getting closer and closer to that happening.

"It would only be temporary," Christian intervened.

"Temporary is still too long to hide from a bunch of juvenile bullies."

"I could make you," Aiden threatened, leaning down eye to eye with her. His nostrils flared on a long-inhaled breath.

"And I could beat the shit out of you," Chloe snarled, pressing her nose to his. They stood eye to eye for several long seconds before Aiden blew out a guttural growl, bawling his fists and spinning away from her.

"I think we all need to chill for a minute," Ryder exclaimed, releasing a sigh and moving closer to Chloe so he was now between her and Aiden. "This isn't getting us anywhere."

"He's right," Christian agreed, running a hand over his face.

Aiden threw his hands in the air, spinning on his heels, and stormed out of the house, and Chloe mimicked him, going in the opposite direction towards their bedrooms.

"Well, that went well," Maverick said, slumping into a chair.

"I'll go talk to Chloe," I said, blowing out a breath.

"Actually," Christian said, stopping me. "Let me talk to her. Why don't you see if you can get Aiden to calm down." I nodded.

Stepping into the cool night air, I spotted Aiden at the edge of the patio, staring out into the darkness of the night, his hands shoved in his pockets, his expression pained.

"Why does she have to be so impossibly difficult?" Aiden growled through gritted teeth when I stepped up beside him.

"Because if she weren't, she wouldn't be Chloe." I smiled. He cut his eyes to me before his gaze moved back to the darkness. "You want to take a walk?"

"Yeah," he said, nodding.

Kicking my sandals off, I sank my toes into the soft white sand. I stepped in beside Aiden as he stormed towards the pier. I wasn't sure if he was actually walking fast or if my legs, which were half his size, had trouble keeping up with his long strides.

"Hey," I squealed. "Did you want to walk or run?"

"Sorry," he said, stopping and giving me a chance to catch up. "It's just." He paused and started walking again at a much slower pace. "I just got her back, and I don't want something to happen to her." *I just got her back.* We would circle back to that later.

"I would rather go back than let something happen to anyone because of me," I said, staring down at the sand around my toes.

"Harper," he snapped, grabbing my upper arm and pulling me to a stop again. "You can never go back." His grip tightened on my arm. "Not just because they will kill you but because Christian will die to protect you." My gaze locked with his. "Going back would put everyone in more danger because they will have leverage over us."

"Leverage?" I asked, pinching my face. How would going back give anyone leverage? It would only make the Villa Boys back off.

"Whether you go back or not," Aiden said, releasing my arm, "this war is happening."

"What does that have to do with leverage?"

"You," he said. "All of us, Christian, Chloe, Me, the guys, they'll use you against us. You can't go back, Harper."

I nodded in understanding. There was no going back to the Southside. If I left the Valley, I'd have to leave town, which was a terrifying thought.

Aiden turned away from me and moved towards the pier, and I stepped in line with him.

"So, what did you mean you just got her back?"

"We broke up in freshman year," he said.

"Broke up?" My head jerked up to him. "You dated?" I didn't remember Chloe ever mentioning anything about Aiden's freshman year, or any other year, for that matter.

"You didn't know?" His brows knitted together. I shook my head. "Yeah, for almost all of freshman year."

Chloe and I were friend's freshman year, but we all attended different schools until sophomore year when Valley View Prep closed its doors. Chloe had always told me everything, so I didn't know why she never mentioned Aiden.

"What happened?" I stepped under the pier and letting the water swirl around my feet.

"I fucked up," he muttered, leaning up against one of the

massive pillars holding the pier. "And I don't want to do that again." He didn't want to tell me what he did, and I wasn't going to push either. It was obvious that whatever he did, he seriously regretted it.

"We'll figure this out," I reassured him. "We should head back and see if Christian had any luck with Chloe." I spun in the sand. "Looks like they found us."

Christian and Chloe were walking toward us. "You want to trade?" Chloe said when they made it to the pier.

"Yes," I said, sliding an arm around Christian's waist. "Is everything okay?"

"Everything is good?" Her gaze flicking to Aiden. "I need to talk to Aiden, though." I nodded, and the two strolled away, hand in hand, back towards the beach house.

"How did it go?"

"She's going to stay in the second bedroom of the pool house for a few days while her parents are away," he said. "Hopefully, we can figure this out before she has to go home."

"Will you and Aiden be staying on the couch?" I laughed, remembering the bedding on the couch before we left to come here.

"I can't speak for Aiden, but I think I'm going to stay with you." He curled his fingers around my hips and pulled me against his firm, hard-naked chest. His lips pressed to mine. "We should go back to the room."

I nodded, but as we turned to head towards the house, my eyes flashed to the spot just below the boardwalk where we'd watched Maverick and the blonde. I wanted to be that spontaneous, even if it was only once. My mind filled with the memories of Maverick and the feeling of Christian's hands on me, making my stomach flutter like it did that night.

Sliding my hand into Christian's, I yanked him towards the same spot. The light from the boardwalk shined over us, but darkness from the wall that held the boardwalk over the beach covered this spot. If anyone walked to the edge, they would see us, and something about that sent adrenaline coursing through my veins.

Placing my hands against his chest, I shoved his back against the concrete wall into the shadows. Christian didn't say anything; a cocky smirk tugged at the corners of his mouth like he knew what I was doing.

A wave of nerves washed over me as I reached out, flicked the button on his jeans, and slowly slid the zipper down. Dropping down in the sand to my knees, I tugged his jeans and boxers down, setting his cock free. I sucked in a breath. It was the first time I'd really seen it. It was huge and hard. Hard for me.

My hand wrapped around his thick girth, slowly stroking him up and down. He sucked in a sharp breath as I stroked tip to root, slowly rolling my wrist as I moved. I glanced up through my lashes, continuing my movements. He tilted his head back, and his lips parted as his chest rose and fell with ragged breaths. The look of pleasure on his face with his movements sent my confidence skyrocketing.

I wanted to bring Christian the same pleasure he'd brought me.

Gripping him at the base, I leaned forward, brushing my lips against the tip before licking my lips and tasting the evidence of his arousal. I flicked my tongue out, tasting more of him.

Fisting his hand into my hair, I opened my mouth, sliding the tip of his cock between my lips and rolling my tongue around his swollen head. His abs flexed as his body tensed.

"Fuck," he groaned, his grip tightening in my hair. He bucked his hips forward, thrusting himself deeper before pulling my head back so my eyes locked on his as he slowly pulled himself out.

My grip tightened around his base as I moved my mouth and hand towards each other, finding a rhythm as I sucked and pumped his length.

"Fuck," he grunted as I continued, harder, faster, deeper. "Harper." His head fell back as his body shuddered, and I knew he was losing control. He thrust his hips forward, hitting the back of my throat, eliciting a low groan.

Squeezing my thighs together, I continued sucking him with quick, deep pulls. He gasped, and the overwhelming sensation almost sent me over the edge. The thrill of being caught, the noises he made as I pleased him, the ache in my jaw, his hand in my hair, all of it.

His hand fisted tighter in my hair, and I dropped my hand as he thrust his hips forward; simultaneously, he pushed my head down, shoving his cock deep down my throat.

"Fuck." His body tensed as he held me in place. "I'm gonna —" I gagged, placing both hands on his thighs to brace myself as I felt the warm salty liquid shoot down the back of my throat.

He pulled himself out, and I gasped for a breath, dropping my hands to my thighs to hold myself up.

"Are you okay?" he breathed.

I gave a slight nod, still trying to catch my breath. Everything about that was hot, and I wanted more of him. "We should go back to the beach house," I said breathlessly. "Before I fuck you right here," I repeated the exact words he said to me the night we watched Maverick.

CHAPTER 32

Harper

Spring break was over, and it was back to reality. I rode the long ride back to the Valley with Chloe. I wanted to ask her about Aiden and freshman year, but I didn't want to pry. If she didn't tell me, she must have had a reason. So, I left it alone, for now anyway.

We quickly packed a few things for her and then headed to Christian's.

"You sure you don't mind me crashing with you?" Chloe asked, focusing on the road in front of her. "It's not too late for me to go home."

"What?" I asked. "Of course not." She pulled her truck down Christian's driveway, around the house to the back, and up to the pool house. Hopping out of Chloe's truck, exhaustion overwhelmed me. I wanted to spend the next two days in bed before returning to school.

Grabbing a bag from the backseat, I headed inside, rounding the front of the truck. Christian stepped out the sliding glass door from the main house. Aiden stepped out behind him, and then a tall thin, dark-haired woman followed Aiden out. The woman was an older, more mature mixture of Christian and Aiden, and I knew immediately it was their mother.

"Mrs. Chandler," Chloe said with a tiny squeal of surprise. 'Her wide eyes flashed from Christian to Aiden. I assumed she had the same question running through her mind: *Did you know she would be home?*

A flood of panic surged through me.

"Chloe," Mrs. Chandler smiled, leaning in to hug Chloe. "So good to see you again."

"When did you get back from London?" Chloe pulled out of the hug.

"Last night," she said, her gaze flicking to me. "You must be Harper."

Panic coursed through me, my pulse drumming in my ears. Moms hated me. All of them. Chloe's mom. Ryder's mom. My mom. They all hated me. I was from the Southside, and even worse than that, I was the stepdaughter of Levi, a well-known drug dealer. I wasn't ready for this.

Rubbing my damp hands down my jeans, I struggled to push past the panic. To say something, anything, but I couldn't.

"Mom," Christian said, sensing my panic. "Why don't we let Harper and Chloe get settled, and we can all catch up tomorrow?"

"Of course," Mrs. Chandler said. I somehow managed to return her smile though I wasn't sure how genuine it looked. "You girls get settled tonight; perhaps we can chat tomorrow."

I swallowed the lump forming in my throat. Tomorrow. Tomorrow I would have to sit down and have a conversation with his mom, and she would hate me, and then what? Would she kick me out?

"I'm going to help them unload," Christian said. "I'll be in, in a few minutes."

"Come on, Mom," Aiden said, placing a hand on her back. He led her back towards the house.

"Did you know she was back from France?" Chloe whispered, following Christian back to her truck.

"No," Christian muttered, grabbing the suitcases from the

back seat. "She was here when we pulled in." I unlocked the door, and they followed me inside.

Chloe dragged her suitcase up the stairs.

"Don't panic," Christian said, spinning to face me. "My mom is going to love you."

"You don't understand," I groaned. "Moms don't like me. Like none of them. I'm from the wrong side of the tracks."

"Harper." He stopped me, brushing a loose piece of hair out of my face. "I promise you my mom will love you." I gave an unconvinced nod. "Aiden and I are taking her to dinner tonight to give you and Chloe time to settle in." He leaned in, pressing his soft full lips to my forehead. "Maverick and Link are coming to hang out with you two while we are gone."

"I don't think we need a babysitter," I muttered.

"They are not here to babysit you or Chloe," he said. "They are here if Noah or his thugs decide to show up while we are gone." He grabbed the door handle and opened the door. "I trust them to keep you and Chloe safe." He leaned in, pressing his lips to mine. "Aiden and I will stay out here tonight. I should be home by nine, and we can watch a movie."

"No." I scowled, shaking my head. "Your mom is home; you can't stay out here." He laughed, walking out and shutting the door behind him. I wasn't laughing. I didn't want to add to her reasons to hate me.

Sinking into the couch, I closed my eyes, blowing out an exaggerated sigh. Maybe this wouldn't be as bad as I thought it would be. Who am I kidding? This was worse. If Christian's mom didn't like me, she could throw me right back to the Southside, and I was positive that's what would happen.

"Christian's mom is pretty cool," Chloe said, pounding down the stairs. "She will love you. I'm sure of it."

"Like your mother loved me, or Ryder's mother loved me." I groaned, not bothering to open my eyes. "Hell, my mother didn't want me."

"My mom is crazy, and she hates everyone," Chloe said, sinking into the couch beside me, pulling the throw pillow to her chest and hugging it. "And your mom. Well, your mom is an addict, which has nothing to do with you."

Two taps sounded at the door before Maverick pushed it open.

"Everyone decent?" He laughed. Link followed him through the door with pizza in his hands.

I wasn't in the mood to entertain tonight. I wanted to shower and sleep, so I woke up refreshed and ready to impress tomorrow.

"I'm going to shower and sleep," I mumbled, pushing passed them to head upstairs. "I'll see you guys later."

"After dinner," Maverick said, hooking an arm through mine and guiding me back to the kitchen.

"Not hungry," I whined as he led me into a chair.

"Christian said to make you." Link laughed, shrugging. He pulled out a plate, slapping a piece of pizza on it. "Please don't make me force-feed you. That doesn't sound fun." He dropped the paper plate on the table in front of me.

I rolled my eyes. "How am I supposed to eat? Tomorrow, I have to talk to Christian's mom."

"Christian's mom is cool," Link said, handing Chloe a plate.

"I tried to tell her that." Chloe laughed, adding a slice of pizza to her plate. "But she's freaking out."

"That's easy for you to say." I groaned, dropping my head into my hands. "You don't come from the Southside, and you're not associated with criminals."

"Harper," Maverick said, his blue eyes zeroing in on me. His tone made it clear he was serious and no longer joking around. "You are not your family. You are not the Southside. You are not where you are from, and you are not your mother." After a long pause, he continued. "No one here defines you by where you came from, and Mrs. Chandler won't either. Give her a chance. She might surprise you."

He was right. I couldn't expect her to give me a chance if I'm unwilling to do the same.

CHAPTER 33

Harper

I tossed and turned in bed until I heard the bedroom door creak open. My eyes flicked open, and I leaned up to look at the clock on the nightstand. It was just after nine p.m.

The room was dark, with only the moonlight shining through the small window above the bed.

"You're awake," Christian whispered, reaching back and pulling his shirt off before dropping it to the floor. As he removed his pants, I dropped my gaze, sweeping up and down his perfectly sculpted torso. It didn't go unnoticed. Kneeling on the bed, he leaned in, his lips brushing mine. "Like what you see?" A cocky grin tugged at the corners of his lips.

"Maybe," I teased, tugging him closer. I needed to feel him, to alleviate this overwhelming anxiety in a way only he could. I needed him to make me forget all the craziness running through my head, to help me release my stress.

His mouth crashed hard against mine with a force that stole the air from my lungs. He shifted over me and situated himself between my thighs as I wrapped my legs around the back of his thighs, desperately attempting to pull him harder against me. I moaned into his mouth as his hips rocked into mine, and I could feel every inch of his rock-hard erection press into me.

This is exactly what I needed.

Desperate for more, I slid my hands down his torso to the top of his boxers, desperately trying to shove them down.

"I want to taste you," he breathed, breaking from the kiss. "All of you." He pushed to his knees, twisting to reach into the nightstand's top drawer, and pulled out a pair of cuffs. "Do you trust me?"

"Yes," I said without an ounce of hesitation, throwing my arms over my head. I did trust him—more than anyone in this world. The corners of his mouth turned up in what could only be described as a devilish smirk. He handcuffed each hand before situating himself back between my thighs.

He lowered his body over mine, our lips fusing together with a desperate hunger for each other. His mouth trailed down, brushing his lips along my jawbone before sucking and nipping down my neck to my collarbone.

I whimpered when the heat of his mouth left my skin to slither further down my body. I wanted to grab his head and force his mouth back to my skin, but he was teasing me.

His lips grazed the sensitive skin above my panty line as his hand slowly slid my shirt up until my breasts were bared to him. My nipples hardened as the cool air hit them.

I gasped, arching my body into his mouth as the heat from his trail of kisses along my panty line had every part of my body aching for him. I can feel his smile spread across my skin.

His mouth moved lower over the thin lace of my panties as his thumb brushed over my nipple. A breathy whimper escaped my parted lips as a desperate plea for more. The heat from his breath caressed the sensitive skin underneath my panties as he ran his lips up and down my length. I bucked my hips forward, desperate to have his mouth on me.

"Please," I begged, struggling against the cuffs. Christian looked up at me through thick dark eyelashes continuing his slow sweet torture.

He moved up my stomach dusting my flesh with his lips and tongue until he found my breast. He trailed a line of kisses around my nipple before he drew it into his mouth while his fingers slid under the thin lace of my panties. His tongue flicked the hard bud sending a jolt of electricity through every nerve ending in my body. His fingers slid up and down the length of me, teasing me. I rocked my hips into his fingers as he continued his slow torture of my nipple.

"Fuck, you're so wet, baby." He groaned against my heated flesh, removing his fingers. He slid to the end of the bed, hooking his fingers into the side of my thong and peeling them down my legs, trailing his knuckles along my skin as he moved down. Goosebumps rippled over my body.

"Christian," I pleaded, pulling hard against the cuffs.

"Not yet, baby," he whispered against my inner thigh. "I need to taste all of you." A moan pushed past my lips when his head dipped between my legs, and he mapped kisses along my inner thigh and pussy. I arched into him, but he continued his slow, deliberate torture—only making my need for him more desperate.

When his tongue darted out, striking my clit my entire body vibrated, my head fell back, my body arched, and my hands gripped the cuffs. His tongue circled my swollen bud, flicking it faster each time.

"Christian," I cried out as my orgasm got closer.

His tongue continued to taunt and tease my most sensitive spot as he slid a finger inside me, pumping in and out before adding another. His mouth formed a suction over my clit as he continued to pump his fingers in and out.

It was too much.

A choked sound ripped from my throat as my entire body shook uncontrollably, and my orgasm exploded around him. I pulled against the cuffs, frantic to delve my fingers into his hair. His suction released as he removed his fingers and lapped up every bit of the hot liquid, tasting every bit of me.

"I need you to fuck me." I moaned. He leaned on his knees, licking his lips as his heated stare raked over every inch of my naked body. I wanted to cover myself but couldn't, and he knew it. He shoved his boxers down, freeing his huge, thick erection.

"You taste so fucking good." He groaned, positioning himself over me. My body still trembled with euphoric spasms.

A rush of heat spread over me as he positioned the head of his cock at my entrance. His lips claimed mine as our tongues tangled, and he devoured my mouth. His fingers skimmed my breast as he buried himself deep inside me. I cried out in pleasure, rocking my hips against his.

He released a raged breath as he withdrew and pushed in deeper. "Fuck." His head fell into the crook of my neck, his hot deep breaths adding to the intensity. His thrust grew harder, going deeper each time—each one bringing me closer to the release my body was begging for. I clenched around him, my core tightening with each thrust as he drove deeper, harder, and faster inside me. I rocked my hips forward, meeting his thrusts. He groaned into my neck.

His mouth claimed mine again, demanding my surrender. My lips parted as his tongue delved past them so he could taste every inch of my mouth. I hummed against his lips as the intensity between my thighs increased.

"Harper," he groaned into my mouth, thrusting deep before grinding himself. "Fuck!" I bucked my hips up rocking harder against him. Pleasure built up, and my body shook as it overtook my body; I let go, bursting into an orgasmic high, and he followed right behind.

Our skin slick with sweat, he kissed me softly before collapsing. We both lay silent for several minutes, allowing our breathing to slow.

"Shower?" he reached up and releasing my cuff.

Hoping for round two, I agreed.

CHAPTER 34

Harper

This was what having a mom was like. Sadness twisted in my gut as I watched Mrs. Chandler flip through a clothing rack, pulling random items off and holding them out. Blinking back the tears, I forced a smile, nodding approval of everything she held up.

As far back as I could remember, I'd never had this with my mother. As a baby, she left me with my grandmother, who passed away when I was six. She didn't have much money but always ensured I had what I needed. After she passed, I went with my mother.

I was seven the first time my mom disappeared for a week. Her boyfriend, Rick, and my mother were high on their newest drug of choice when they left the house and didn't return. They left me with no food, running water, or electricity. It was the first time I was put into the foster care system. I wished that had been a better experience, but it wasn't, and I would have rather starved to death than be put back into the system. Unfortunately, I was in and out of foster care thirteen more times before I turned eighteen. Each home was worse than the last. Even harder to swallow was that no one cared what happened to you anymore after you turned eighteen.

I knew that not all moms took you shopping and spent

way too much money, but I didn't know what it was like to have a mom at all. My mom never packed my school lunches or attended a school function or teacher/parent conference. She never made my breakfast, lunch, or dinner. She never even showed up to pick me up when she was supposed to.

Christian had that. Mrs. Chandler was great, but I wasn't sold that I wasn't going to get the 'you're-not-good-enough-for-my-son talk.'

"What else do you need?" Mrs. Chandler said, pulling me from my thoughts. "Do you need any personal items? Or shoes?" She glanced down at my worn knock-off Doc Martens. "We should get you new shoes."

I'd given up arguing with her three stores ago. She was even more stubborn than Christian. So, I forced a smile and nodded.

My phone vibrated underneath the pile of clothes I was carrying. Shifting them to one side, I checked my messages. A smile spread across my face when Christian's name appeared on the screen.

Christian: Is she smothering you with clothes yet?

I snapped a quick selfie of myself covered with piles of clothes with a caption that said, 'send help' and hit send.
Harper: Yes, how do I make her stop?

Christian: Fake your death.

I snorted a laugh before remembering I was in public. My gaze darted around the shoe department. While it was busy, it didn't seem anyone noticed.

Christian: If you need me to, I'll fake mine.

Harper: Thanks, but I'll be okay.

It was nearing sunset when Mrs. Chandler finally decided we were done shopping. Her entire Range Rover was filled to the brim with shopping bags. Some were for her, but most were for me, even though I tried to tell her I didn't need anything.

Sitting in the restaurant booth waiting for our food, a sense of panic rushed over me. It was just her and me in front of each other with nothing to do but talk while we waited for our food.

"Christian tells me you are planning to go to college after graduation," Mrs. Chandler said, her dark blue eyes piercing mine. "Where are you planning to go?"

"I'm not sure yet." I shrugged. "I had some issues applying, and because it was so late when I did apply, I'm not sure if I'll be accepted anywhere but the community college."

"I have a few friends that work at a few different universities." She swirled the straw in her soda around the cup. "I could give them a call."

"Thank you, but I have to have a scholarship. I've applied for a few but haven't heard back yet."

She twisted in her seat, reached into her purse, and pulled out her keys, phone, and wallet, setting them on the table in front of her.

"You don't need to worry about that," she said, pushing the items she pulled out of her purse across the table toward me. "My husband and I would like to sponsor you."

"I'm sorry?" I narrowed my eyes, unsure of what she was saying. "I don't understand." Was this when she would offer to pay for everything if I broke up with Christian? Chloe's mom had done the same thing. She'd bribed me with money to stay away from Chloe. I'd declined then, and I would now too.

"We would like to pay for your tuition, books, and anything else you need to go to school," she said. "You'll need a car." She pointed to the keys in front of me. "You'll need a more reliable phone." Her finger moved to the cell phone in front of me. "And you'll need a credit card for essentials." Her finger moved to the wallet. "You just let us know what you need for school or anything else, and we will take care of it."

My jaw dropped because this was not what I expected. There was a catch. There had to be a catch. There was always a catch. Unable to form words, I sat silently, waiting for the other shoe to drop, for the you're-not good-enough-for-our-son speech. But it never came.

"Did Christian tell you I was from the Villas?" I shook my head. He'd never told me anything about his family. "I was born in the Villas. I was raised by a single mother who chose men over me." My chest clenched tightly as a swell of agony ripped through me. She understood. She'd walked a mile in my shoes. "I was removed from her custody when I was ten, but the damage was already done by then."

I didn't know what she meant by damage, but I could only imagine. I had my own. I didn't dare ask her because scars like that were deep, and asking someone to dig them up would only bring back an emotional rollercoaster of all the suffering and trauma shoved down deep so that you could be a functioning human being in society. If she wanted me to know, then she'd tell me.

"I was put into a wonderful foster home with a couple who ended up adopting me. I don't know where I would be today if that couple hadn't stepped up and helped me. I want to do the same for you."

"It's hard to accept that someone wants to help me." I shrugged. My throat tightened as I shoved back the tears stinging the backs of my eyes. I avoided eye contact for fear of a tear breaking free. So many emotions swelled through me, and I didn't know how to control them. "I've been on my own for a long time."

"Sometimes, the hardest thing in life is realizing we need help." She smiled, placing a hand over mine. "And even harder to admit and accept it, but I promise my husband and I truly just want to help. No strings attached."

We spent the next hour talking about everything. We talked about my life, my mother, Noah, and Levi; she shared a little of hers. We had more in common than I could have ever expected. I never once felt like she was judging me, my life, or my decisions.

I released a sigh of relief. They had all been right. Mrs. Chandler did surprise me.

CHAPTER 35

Christian

"Did you see the tits on her?" Bash laughed, holding his hands out in front of him, demonstrating the exaggerated size of her chest. "And that ass." He sucked in his bottom lip, biting down. "Damn."

"I'd titty fuck her," Lincoln said, biting his lip as he dry-humped the air. A new transfer student had all the guys worked up.

"You'd fuck anything," Maverick laughed, slamming his locker door closed. I rolled my eyes, leaning against my locker while I waited for Harper to come out of the classroom.

The first week back to school, surprisingly, had been relatively quiet. I expected more commotion from the Villa Boys, but they'd stayed on their side of the school without a word.

Shoving off my locker with my shoulder, I glanced across the hall at the classroom door that Harper should have come out of already. Her class was right across from my locker. I'd made it to my locker before the dismissal bell sounded, and when the rest of her class left and Harper didn't, I wasn't suspicious because it wasn't unusual for Harper to hang back for various reasons, but she seemed to be taking longer than normal.

Pulling my phone out, I texted her to ask if she was still in class.

Even though the week had gone smoothly, we didn't let Chloe or Harper move around the school without one of us with them. No one knew what Noah's next move would be, and I was being cautious. Aiden had gone to meet Chloe at dismissal, and I was waiting for Harper. It was the same plan we'd used all week and would continue to use until Noah was dealt with.

After a few more minutes of waiting, I flipped my phone over to check for a response from Harper. Nothing. It hadn't sent. I had no service.

Chloe appeared in my peripheral vision.

"What's up, Chloe?" She clenched her books tight against her chest. Swallowing hard, her head dropped as she peered behind her from the corner of her eyes. Something was wrong. My eyes followed hers over her shoulder as a group of Villa Boys passed, laughing.

Harper!

"Chloe, where's Harper?" She was in shock. Scanning her over, I noticed blood soaked through the knees of her ripped jeans.

"Chloe, where's Harper?" My tone is both desperate and demanding. Harper was supposed to be in 6th period, the classroom directly across from my locker.

"Mason," she croaked through hysterical sobs.

Grabbing hold of her shoulders, I gave her a slight shake. "Where?" I ground out.

"The field." She shifted, pointing toward the back of the school. I knew exactly where she was—the only part of the school deserted at the end of the day.

I bolted into a sprint across campus, anger swimming through me, causing my chest to tighten and pushing my legs harder and faster. When I heard her screams from down the hall, red-hot rage surged through my veins. My boot impacted the door, bursting it open. My vision blurred with rage. My jaw clenched and my nostrils flared. I was ready to commit murder.

Mason's large body pinned Harper to the floor as he pawed at her body. Harper screamed, fighting hard to get him off her.

Reaching down and grabbing the back of his shirt, I launched him across the bathroom, slamming him into the wall. Twisting my fist into his shirt, I scrapped him off the floor. A loud crack followed by a low grunt; the sound of bone meeting bone filled the room as my fist pounded into his face. Mason's fist flew up, cracking against my jaw. I didn't feel it. Rage made my body numb.

"You're dead," I growled, throwing another punch and smashing his nose. Mason gurgled as blood filled his mouth, running down the back of his throat. Another, and the blood splattered across me and the walls. The rage pounding in my ears muffled the screaming in the background. I couldn't stop myself. The anger consumed me, egging me on.

Straddling him, using my body weight to pin him to the ground, I wrapped my fingers around his throat, using the palm of my hand to cut off his airway. Mason's eyes went wide as he struggled underneath me. He gasped as his fingernails clawed at my hands, begging for air.

Mason's body fell limp at the same time Link jerked me off him. I pushed Link away. Mason wasn't walking out of here alive.

"Holy fuck," Maverick said, sliding into the bathroom, taking in the bloody scene and Mason's bloody body lying lifeless on the floor. My gaze traveled from person to person before snapping down to Harper, who sat curled in the corner, her clothes torn, her body bruised and bloody.

"Are you okay?" I sank to the floor with her and pulling her into me. Her head fell against my chest, her body still trembling. I had no idea why Chloe and Harper were on this side of the school, but that would have to wait.

Chloe's frantic cries sounded from the opposite side of the door. They wouldn't let her in. No one knew what mess they'd find once they got inside the bathroom.

"Aiden is pulling the truck around," Maverick said. "He'll meet us at the back of the school. Christian, get Harper out of here. The rest of us will clean this mess up."

"Is he dead?" I asked, anger vibrating through my body.

"I don't know." Maverick shrugged, glancing down, eyes narrowed on Mason.

"I'm not leaving until he's dead. Bash, take Harper and Chloe back to my place. I'm staying."

"Christian." Maverick scowled, shoving a hand over his head.

"Guys, we don't have time to argue about this," Bash said, cutting Maverick off. "We need to get Harper out of here and this mess cleaned up now before someone comes to this side of the campus.

"Aiden and I will take Harper and Chloe," Julian said. "You guys do what you need to."

"Take care of her," I said, scooping Harper off the floor and handing her to Julian, who carried her out of the bathroom, leaving Maverick, Link, Bash, and me to take care of Mason.

Link leaned down, placing two fingers at the pulse point on Mason's wrist. "It's weak, but he still has a pulse."

"What are we going to do with him?" Maverick asked, nodding toward Mason's body.

"We are going to deliver him to Noah." I hovered over Mason's body. "With a message." I reared my boot before bringing it forward and smashing it against Mason's bloody face.

CHAPTER 36

Christian

"Come out, you fucking pussy," I yelled, slamming my car door shut and storming toward the beat-down trailer. My chest heaved with anger; my fist balled at my side. I was ready for a fight. "Pick on someone your own fucking size."

Maverick and Link dragged Mason's limp body across the gravel, dropping it on the broken steps that led up to the trailer.

"He's not there," a female said, strolling up behind us. "What happened to him?" My gaze flicked to Piper, who stopped beside Bash.

"He fucked with the wrong person."

"Is he dead?" She leaned forward to get a better look at him. My eyes hardened, warning her not to ask questions she didn't want to know the answer to.

"Where is he?" My fists clenched at my sides.

"I don't know." She shrugged, smacking her gum and flipping her long blond hair over her shoulder. "I saw them load up about ten minutes before you showed up."

My gaze flicked back to the trailer before they darted around the park, looking for something I could destroy what remained of this shit hole trailer park. My eyes settled on a red and yellow gas can.

"Let's light this bitch up," Link yelled, running to the gas can. He knew exactly what I thought when my eyes landed on that can of gas.

"Woah." Piper scowled, grabbing my arm. "If you do this, they will kill you."

"Tell them where to find me," I said, my eyes locked on hers. I jerked my arm out of her grasp before taking the can from Link and heading toward the trailer.

"You should go home," Bash warned. "You don't want to be tied to this."

Piper sprinted back to her trailer. She stood for several long minutes before finally going inside.

Bash dragged Mason's body off the steps, dumping him on the ground before we started. I wanted Noah to find Mason's lifeless body and see what his fate was. I wanted him to know he fucked with the wrong person, and I was coming for him next.

We all found gas cans scattered throughout the park and covered not just the outside but also the inside. I wasn't just dousing Noah's home; I was smothering every bad memory Harper ever experienced in this home and setting fire to it. I couldn't erase her past, but I could eliminate it from becoming her future.

The guys ran back to start the truck as I flicked the match, tossing it to the porch. An ombre of yellow, orange, and red roared to life, lighting up the dark trailer park.

Heat blasted my face as I watched the fire engulf more of the trailer, growing taller and wider. I stood mesmerized, watching the fire claim the trailer and every horrible thing that Harper ever endured with it. She would never come back to this trailer again, and knowing it was gone now sent a wave of relief flooding over me that I didn't realize I was harboring.

"Let's go," Maverick yelled from the truck's passenger side, pulling me from my thoughts.

I jumped in the truck, and Link sped off before my door closed.

"Harper's not safe at your place anymore," Link said what we were all thinking as he swerved the truck out of the trailer park. "Chloe, either."

"School either," Bash said. "We have three weeks until the senior's last day. Maybe your mom can help organize a way for her to finish from home."

I nodded. Harper was no longer safe in this town. She would never be safe if Noah and Levi were alive, making the calls in the Southside. Even hidden behind the thick iron bars surrounding the Valley, she wouldn't be safe anymore. They would come for her to get to me.

"Noah's going to send his goons after her," Maverick added. "He's too big of a pussy to come himself."

"I want him dead," I said, my tone laced with venom. "Levi too."

"That's inevitable, man," Bash said. "But we need to be smart about this."

Link took a sharp left, and my gaze flicked out the window to the sky-high thick black smoke as the sound of piercing sirens zoomed by us. They were undoubtedly heading to put out the fire I'd started. A smirk tugged at the corner of my lips, knowing they'd be too late. Noah's trailer was long gone, but maybe they'd make it in time to save the rest of the trailer park. Not that it'd hurt my feelings to see the entire park burned to the ground. How many of them knew what was happening to Harper? How many turned a cheek and let Noah beat her? How many participated? Nope, I'd be fine with the Villa Boys taking their dirty business elsewhere.

Before Link came to a complete stop in front of the pool house, I had the door open and jumped out.

"Where's Harper?" I stood in the living room.

"She's showering," my mom answered, pointing up toward the bathroom upstairs.

"What happened," Aiden gaze flashed between me, Bash, Maverick, and Link.

"We heard there was a fire in the Villas," Julian added.

"Yeah," I said dryly. "Noah's trailer is gone." He nodded in understanding. "Chloe, what happened today? Why were you guys on that side of the school alone?" I needed to know who had sent Harper and Chloe out to that side of the school so I could eliminate that problem too.

"Harper said someone from the office buzzed into her class and told her to report to the field immediately."

"Who, why?"

"I don't know," Chloe shrugged, her voice a shaky whisper. "I just happened to be coming out of the bathroom when she was headed towards the field." Chloe looked down at her fidgeting hands. "She said she didn't recognize the male voice. I thought it was weird, so I tried to text you but had no service. Mason came out of nowhere."

"So, someone in the office is working with Noah," Bash shoved his hands in his pockets.

"Possibly," I said. "But it's also possible that someone got into the office and accessed to the intercom." He nodded. "Mom, can you do some digging and see if anyone has ties to Noah or the Villa Boys working in the office?"

She nodded. My mom had a private investigator, Ricky Gonzalez, on retainer; he was the best. "I'll call the school tomorrow and see if Harper can finish out her senior year from a safe location," my mom said.

"No." Everyone's gaze flicked around to see Harper standing at the bottom of the stairwell. My heart clenched at the black and blue discoloration covering her face. "No," she repeated, this time a demand. "I'm not going to let them take anything else from me. I'm finishing my senior year and walking at graduation."

"Harper," I said. "We can discuss this once you are safe. Go upstairs and pack a bag."

"Christian," she said. "I'm not running and hiding anymore. I'm going to do what I should have done a long time ago and stand up for myself."

"Harper," I hissed. Now was not the time for her to be brave. They were going to kill her. "I'm not giving them another opportunity to hurt you. So, go pack a bag, or I'll do it for you."

"No." Stepping into her, my heart sank when she flinched. She had just been assaulted, and here I was, trying to intimidate her. I didn't want to scare her; I wanted to protect her. But paralyzing fear consumed me. The fear that the next time they came for her, I wouldn't be there to protect her, and they'd kill her.

"Christian." My mom hopped to her feet. "Take a walk." I backed away from Harper.

"I'm sorry, Harper," I said before walking out of the house and down to the lake.

An hour later, I was lost in my thoughts when my mom sat beside me on the old wooden boat dock.

"I just want to protect her," I said after long minutes of silence.

"I know," my mom reassured me. "And so does Harper, but she is tired of being the victim, and I understand. I know you disagree with her, but you should respect her decision and try to devise a solution you can both live with."

I couldn't live with any solution if there was a possibility of something happening to her. Even though I wanted to pick her up, shove her in a vehicle, and hide her somewhere until this was all over, I wouldn't do it against her will, even if I wanted to.

"Ricky just dropped this off," my mom said, holding up a large manilla envelope.

"What is it?" I took the file.

"It's all the information he found on her mom," she answered, pushing up to her feet.

"I'll deal with that once we deal with Noah," I said,

climbing to my feet and heading toward the house. I could only deal with one issue at a time, and right now, I had to negotiate with Harper about her safety.

"Christian," she said, stopping me. "You should look at the file now." Her eyes were wide, and a warning infused her tone, which piqued my interest. I flipped open the envelope and pulled out the thick stack of papers and pictures, scanning them.

"What the fuck?" I hissed, my eyes flashing up to meet my mom's. The warmth of anger traveled up my neck as I clenched the papers in my hands.

"I know where she is," my mom said.

CHAPTER 37

Christian

Sitting behind the tinted windows of the Escalade, Aiden and I watched for any signs of life in the large house on the opposite side of the road.

We'd staked out the place for the last week and noticed little movement. Only the staff appeared to be working within the house and on the grounds, not the actual residents.

I wanted to confirm with my own eyes that this was, in fact, Harper's mom before I said anything to Harper. I didn't see any reason to hurt her if it wasn't necessary.

"Maybe they have Harper's mom tied up in the basement," Aiden suggested.

That was the only situation that would make sense right now. The million-dollar home sat on close to twelve acres just outside the Valley on the opposite side of the county line. The last place I would expect to see a tricked-out druggie living. So, what would Harper's mom be doing here? It didn't make sense at all.

"We don't even know that it's Harper's mom," I reminded him.

"Well, we've been sitting here for days, Christian." Aiden groaned, slouching back into his seat. "Where are the people who live here? Where is this woman they think is her mom? Because honestly, the place looks vacant."

He was right. We had seen nothing but groundskeepers coming and going for a week.

"We should head back," Aiden said, holding his phone in front of his face. "Link said Harper is starting to wonder where you are."

"Yeah," I mumbled, not taking my eyes off the house. "You're right." With a sigh, I hit the button, and the engine roared to life. "I'll get with Mom's PI and see if he can find any other info on the woman." I reached for my cell phone, checking it before we pulled out. "We'll come back tomorrow."

My phone buzzed as I moved to set it down. Harper.

Harper: Are you okay?

Sucking in a deep breath and exhaling slowly, I reread the text before responding.

Christian: Yes, I'll be home soon.

"Christian," Aiden said, drawing out my name. His tone was different. My head snapped up as my gaze flicked to his wide eyes. I followed his line of sight to a white Lincoln Navigator that had just killed the ignition in the driveway. This vehicle was new, not one of the random vehicles we'd seen coming and going from the property.

All the door doors of the vehicle flung open as three small children unloaded from the back one by one. A tall thin man from the driver's side stepped out, slamming his door, and a petite woman from the passenger side stepped out stretching. I sucked in a breath, holding on to it as I silently prayed that "it wouldn't be Harper's mom when the woman turned around.

The kids played in the driveway as the man began unloading luggage from the trunk as the room reached back into the vehicle.

They had just returned from a family vacation. My

stomach rolled at the thought of this being Harper's mom. It couldn't be, right? Because what kind of person, no, what kind of mother, would leave her daughter in a home with someone who hurt her? Alone and hungry, with no way to take care of herself so that she could start a whole new life.

"Come on," I muttered, leaning forward like it would give me a better view. I wasn't sure what I wanted to happen. If it wasn't Harper's mom, it was back to the drawing board to figure out where she was and pray that I don't eventually have to tell Harper her mom was dead. If it was her mom, I'd have to tell her that her mom left her behind and started a new life without her. I didn't know what pain would be worse for Harper. Regardless of the outcome, Harper was going to be hurt.

The woman spun, a smile spreading across her face as she looked at the three children playing in front of her.

"Is it her?" Aiden gaze flicked from the woman to me.

"Yep." I sighed. I had no doubt it was Harper's mom. I didn't need to look at the picture because Harper was a clone of her mother. The photo I had was an old mugshot from six years ago when Harper's mom was arrested for drugs and solicitation. She didn't look like that now. She looked healthy, happy even.

Harper's mom, Dana Brooks, was a few inches taller than Harper, her hair dark like Harper's, her eyes the same bright blue, but what really gave it away was the same smile, high cheekbones, and dimples.

Gripping the steering wheel and rolling my fingers around it with a force so tight my knuckles turned white, I clenched my jaw. Every part of me wanted to get out of the car. I wasn't sure what I would do, but it wouldn't be good. When I first started searching for Harper's mom, I never thought this might be the outcome. I hoped to give Harper closure, and I was truly hoping to tell her that her mom had a genuine reason that she never returned, like she was incarcerated or hospitalized.

"She definitely doesn't look like she's being held against her will," Aiden said.

My gaze flicked back to the happy family as the man

leaned into the woman holding the youngest of the three children, a little girl, pressing a kiss to her lips before throwing an arm across her shoulder and strolling happily together towards the house. My chest heaved with anger as I sucked in long, slow, deep breaths. The more I watched, the angrier I got. I'd hoped she was being held against her will. I'd hoped she hadn't abandoned her daughter, leaving her with someone who hurt her to start a new life.

"So, what now?"

"We leave," I muttered after a long moment, "and I tell Harper." I would tell her that her mother was a disgusting piece of shit who cared more about herself than her flesh and blood.

Aiden's eyes softened as the realization washed over him.

CHAPTER 38

Harper

I winced as the initial impact of the chilly water hit my skin before going from warm to hot. Holding my breath, I let the hot water scold my face before running down my body. I never knew a hot shower held this much power. The power to heal aches and pains. The power to wash away the feeling of disgust. The power to make me feel better. A hot shower was a luxury where I came from. I was lucky to have running water. I didn't most of the time, and it was always cold when I did.

I closed my eyes and listened to the bathroom door open and then click close. I knew it was Christian. He'd been gone all night. He hadn't said where he'd been, but I knew it had something to do with Noah and protecting me. I hated that this was the relationship we had to have. I hated that he was in danger and that I was the cause.

"Harper." He sighed. "I need to talk to you." Spinning to him, I reached out, filling my hand with his black tee, and jerked him into the shower.

"It can wait," I whispered, grabbing the hem of his shirt and shoving it up his chest. He reached back, pulled the shirt off, and dropped it on the floor. His pants followed. I didn't want to hear any more about Noah or the Southside for tonight. I wanted to be an ordinary eighteen-year girl who didn't come with the load of baggage being dumped onto Christian's shoulders.

Right now, I just needed him.

Tracing my finger over the curves of his perfectly sculpted torso, I let my gaze follow my finger, memorizing every curve, every tattoo, every scar of his perfect body. I walked my fingers down his torso, stopping at the massive erection. I wrapped my hand around his hardness and caressed him. I slowly stroked him as my gaze locked on him. He sucked in a ragged breath as my grip tightened at his base, stroking up and rolling my wrist around his swollen head.

He leaned into me, pinning me against the cold tile wall as his mouth collided with mine. He wrapped an arm around my waist and lifted me up to him before deepening the kiss. His tongue pushed past my lips, tangling with mine.

Pulling my legs up, I wrapped them around his waist as he pressed his body flush against mine. Our mouths tangled together in a frantic need for more. He needed this as much as I did.

His hands gripped my ass as he positioned me where he wanted me. Sliding his thick erection through my slick flesh, rubbing the tip over my swollen clit. My head fell back against the wall, and a moan escaped my parted lips as he slid his lips down the side of my throat, sucking and licking my tender flesh as he trailed down to the hollow point of my throat. My pulse thrummed in my ears as my heart pounded against my chest.

My nails dug into his shoulders as his cock nudged my entrance. I bucked my hips forward, begging for more. Grasping at his shoulders, I desperately pulled him closer, needing to feel more of him.

His mouth claimed mine as he pushed inside me. His tongue slipped through my parted lips, swallowing my moan. He grabbed my wrists, pinning them with one hand as he used the other to grip my ass tighter, driving himself deeper inside me. My chest rose and fell with deep, ragged breaths. Our eyes locked as he filled me. At this moment, he and I were one. Our bodies fit perfectly together, and I knew nothing would ever feel as good as him.

The water turned cold, but it didn't break his rhythm as he drove in and out of me, each thrust harder, deeper, faster. My body tensed as the pleasure built inside me. I bucked my hips forward on a hard snap of his hips. He groaned against my lips as he ground his hips against mine, pushing deeper. He released my wrist, and I clung to him as his mouth claimed mine. My core tightened as we continued our rhythm.

My breathing hitched as he pushed inside me, my body vibrating against his as his muscles tightened, and I cried out as the pleasure grew. His breathing accelerated with each pump of his hips. His head fell into the curve of my neck; his warm breath sent chills racing over my skin, and the overwhelming sensation of all this threw me over the edge. I cried out when my body found its ecstasy. With another hard thrust, his lips parted with a low groan as pleasure washed over him.

After a few minutes, he let my body slide against his until my feet met the ground as we both came down from our high, struggling to catch our breaths. He reached over, cutting off the icy shower water before stepping out and grabbing two towels from the closet.

Crawling into bed, I didn't bother dressing. I was too tired. I wanted to sleep and deal with reality tomorrow. Christian slid beside me, hooking an arm around me, pulling me back against his naked body, and pressing a kiss to my shoulder.

"We can talk in the morning," he whispered. I didn't even have the energy to give him an mm-hmm before I was asleep.

CHAPTER 39

Harper

It was late morning when I finally forced myself out of bed and stumbled down the stairs to the kitchen.

"Morning," Christian said, leaning shirtless against the countertop and holding a bottle of water. His skin was slick with sweat, and his dark hair damp, causing small curls. He'd just got done working out. My tongue swept over my bottom lip as my gaze raked over him, memories flashing back from last night in the shower. "Do you want breakfast?"

"Just some coffee right now," I said, placing a hand on his chest. He leaned down, pressing his lips to my forehead.

"Sit down," he ordered. "I'll get your coffee, and we need to talk before everyone gets back from the lake." I inwardly groaned as I sulked towards the table, sinking into the chair. His half-naked, sweaty body had distracted me from the seriousness in his eyes.

"So, what do you want to talk about?" I inhaled a deep breath, preparing myself for whatever was about to be sprung on me. He slid my coffee across the table before sliding into the chair across from me. "What is Noah up to now?"

"Harper," he said. His expression was serious, and my heart raced. "It's not Noah."

"What is it, Christian?" I narrowed my eyes on him. He

seemed to struggle to find the words, making my heart pound harder against my chest.

"It's your mom," he sighed after several long seconds.

My mom. I leaned forward in the chair. My body tensed as I sat a little straighter. "She's dead, isn't she?" I whispered.

"No," he said, shaking his head. "She's not dead." I exhaled harshly. I wasn't sure why he was acting like this if she wasn't dead. What could be worse than death?

"Is she in prison?" He shook his head. "Okay, what kept her from coming back to get me? Is she hurt?"

"Harper," he said.

"Christian." I shoved out of the chair. "Where is she?"

He paused for a long moment, and I could see the pity and pain softening his facial expression.

"She lives about fifteen minutes from here," he said, swallowing hard. "Just across the county line in Duval County."

"I don't understand," I said, pinching my brows together. I placed my palms flat on the table, leaning over toward him. "Like against her will?"

"Harper, she has a new home and a new family."

My chest tightened as I lost the ability to breathe. That couldn't be right. Maybe it wasn't my mom. Maybe he had the wrong person.

"Harper," Christian said, sounding far away. The room spun as I felt around blindly for a chair. Christian grabbed me around the waist, pulling me into him. "Harper." He pulled me tighter against him. The sound of his racing heart against my ear was oddly calming. "Long, slow breaths, Harper." I did as he said, pulling in deep breaths until my breathing was back to normal and the spinning stopped.

"Take me to her," I demanded, pushing off his chest.

"Harper," he started.

"Christian," I interrupted. "Please, take me to her."

"I will take you to her if that's what you want," he said. "But are you sure you don't want to take some time to let this settle before we go?"

"No." I shook my head. "I want to go now."

It was more than a want; it was a need. I needed to see if this woman was actually my mother. I needed to see if she abandoned me to start a whole new life without me; if the woman who brought me into this world decided she didn't want me anymore.

As far back as I remembered, my mother had been addicted to something. Even though I'd never had a normal childhood with a normal mother, in the beginning, she would still make sure I had my basic needs met, but over the years, that stopped. Most days, I wasn't even sure she knew she had a daughter; she was too high. She would disappear for weeks at a time, always coming back with some new boyfriend until Levi. Levi kept her so deeply out of it that I wasn't sure she was alive some days. See, Levi sold drugs, he didn't do drugs, and my mom was his best customer.

For the past few years, I always thought Levi had done something to her. Or that she'd overdosed, and he'd dumped her body somewhere.

I couldn't imagine my mother truly walking out our front door with the intention of never coming back for me and, even worse, leaving me with what she was running away from.

If it was her, there had to be some explanation. There had to be.

CHAPTER 40

Harper

By the time Christian steered his Jeep into the neighborhood, my initial shock had worn off, to be replaced by anger. Even though I was convinced that this was not my mother, I was still angry at the thought that it could be and that this could be my new reality—the reality where my mother left me for a new life I didn't fit into.

Christian slowed as he swerved his Jeep to the side of the road before stopping in front of a massive red brick home with a perfectly manicured lawn. It wasn't as big as Christian's house, but it was ten times the house I grew up in.

As I studied the property, I knew Christian was wrong. He'd made a mistake. The last time I saw my mom, she weighed about 90 pounds; the meth had eaten her face and teeth up, and track marks covered her arms. There was no way she ended up here.

Jumping out of the Jeep, a wave of confidence washed over me. Confidence that I wasn't going to find my mother here. That meant I still didn't know where she was, alive or dead, though.

Christian followed me up the long driveway, neither of us saying a word.

I knocked once before turning to lock eyes with Christian. The door creaked open, and when my head snapped to the open doorway, my heart sank.

My mother stood there.

She didn't look the same as the last time I saw her. Her dark hair was now long, with expensive streaks of blonde. She was still thin but not emaciated. She looked healthy and happy. An overwhelming wave of emotions washed over me as I stood frozen, eyes locked on her. Every part of my heart wanted to hug her, thankful she was alive, but my head knew the truth. She'd abandoned me.

"Harper?" my mother asked, a smile spreading across her face.

"Mom?"

The word mom must have jolted her back into whatever reality she lived in, because her smile disappeared as she stepped outside, quickly closing the door behind her.

"Harper," she whispered. "You can't be here." Those words cut deeper than I ever thought a word could do. "If you want to talk, we'll have to do it somewhere else later."

Was she serious? No, we were doing this now.

"I thought you were dead," I screamed, my fist balling at my side. Tears burned the back of my eyes as my chest heaved with hurt and anger. "You left me and never came back."

"Please keep your voice down," she hissed.

"How could you?" I yelled, ignoring her plea. The tears broke free, streaming down my face.

"Life isn't that black and white," she said. "I didn't have a choice."

She didn't have a choice? No, I didn't have a choice. I didn't have a choice about who my mother was or if she left me or not. She had so many choices and made the wrong one every time.

"It doesn't look like you're being held against your will." I pointed to the beautiful house behind her.

"What do you want me to say, Harper?" She threw her hands up.

"How about the truth," I said, feeling my heart shatter into a million pieces.

"Fine," she scowled. "You want the truth?" Her tone changed as her jaw flexed and her fist clenched at her side. She was angry. That only made me madder. She had no right to be angry. "Levi dumped me on the side of the road and told me never to come back. Alex found me. He helped me get clean. Paid for my rehab."

I almost snorted a laugh. She'd been to rehab so many times' and fallen back down the same hole every time. "Why didn't you come back for me?" I screamed so hard my chest burned.

"I couldn't," she cried. "Alex didn't want someone with children; he was my only chance to have a normal life. I needed him."

"I needed you," I sobbed, grabbing my chest.

"He had three small children, and they had just lost their mother," she said, ignoring me. My chest tightened. She could be their mother but not mine. She could clean up for them but not me. "I'm sorry, Harper, but not everything is about you." My head spun as I tried to catch my breath. "We could have a secret relationship, but Alex could never know about us. He doesn't want people like you around his kids."

"Go to hell," I growled. "You left me with Levi and Noah, who hurt me every day. They forced me to do things I didn't want to do just to eat. You left your own flesh and blood beaten and hungry so that you could play mommy to someone else's kids." I willed myself to walk away and never look back, but I couldn't. "He shouldn't be worried about people like me around his kids; he should be worried about mothers like you."

"Harper," she said, reaching out for me. She was trying to pacify me, so I'd be quiet.

"Don't," I ordered, pulling away from her. "I'm going to walk away, and I don't ever want to see you again." I spun to storm off, pushing past Christian but stopped. I had one more question before I left and never saw her again, and only she could answer it. "Wait." I turned back to face her. "There's one thing I want to know, and then you can return to your perfect life."

"What's that?"

"Who is my father?" You owe me this much. Tell me who he is."

"I was a stripper at Showgirls before you were born," she said. "I drank a lot but hadn't gotten too deep into drugs yet."

"Just spit out," I ordered. I didn't want to hear her played-out back story. I wanted to know and leave.

"There are two possibilities," she said. "I had a boyfriend at the time, and the other was married."

"Names," I said, wiping away my tears.

"Dylan West or AJ Elliott," she muttered.

"As in Adam James Elliott?" Christian spoke up for the first time. Her gaze flicked to him, widening as if she'd just realized we weren't alone.

"Yes," she said.

"Let's go," I said, tangling my fingers in Christian's and pulling him toward the Jeep.

Christian opened my door and shut it before running around and climbing in on the driver's side.

"Do you know him?" I asked after he shut his door.

"Yeah," he said, shaking his head. His gaze flashed to mine. Seriousness coated his expression. "It's Lincoln's dad."

My face dropped.

Lincoln could be my brother. The thought was oddly comforting. I'd never had any family, but I also knew the news could cause pain to others. Lincoln's mom and dad had been married for over twenty years.

"Are we going to tell Link?" My gaze scanning his facial expression, searching for any signs of what he was thinking. He shrugged. This was a shock for him, too. "And Dylan West, do you know him?"

"No, I have no idea who that is," Christian said, hitting the button to start the Jeep. "But we're going to find out."

CHAPTER 41

Harper

Staring aimlessly into the darkness, I shoved against the ground with my bare feet, forcing the large wooden swing back before pulling my feet out and letting it swing forward. A gust of wind wrapped around me, sending my hair flying off my shoulders and back as the swing fell back.

Christian was in the main house, running the day over with his mom. He was hoping she could help him figure out who Dylan West was. I sat outside in the silent darkness, letting the day process.

I was slowly making my way through the stages of grieving.

Even though she wasn't dead, she was dead to me. Today was probably the last time I would ever speak to her as my mother. If I ever saw her out in public, I would again see her in my eyes as my mother, just some woman I used to know. She had a new life, new children, and a new family, and she didn't want me to be a part of that.

"Hey," Lincoln said, strolling up his hands in his pocket. My chest tightened as my gaze flicked up to his. "Mind if I sit down?"

I dropped my feet to the ground, stopping the swing. I couldn't help but scan his face, looking for any feature that would give away that he was, in fact, my brother, but I saw nothing. Link dropped onto the swing beside me. I didn't say anything. I didn't know what to say.

"Christian said you found your mom today." My gaze blinked back out into the darkness as I aimlessly nodded. "Are you okay?"

"Yeah," I said, forcing a smile. "Did Christian send you out here?"

"No." He shook his head. "But he and his mom were discussing some man they think is your dad, and he said you were out here alone. So, I figured I would keep you company and let them talk." Whether Link realized it or not, that was Christian's way of sending Link out here. "I'm here if you need to talk."

"Why would she leave me?" I knew he couldn't answer the question, and I didn't really expect an answer. I needed to hear the words aloud.

"Because she's selfish," Link said, staring off into the darkness. "I'll never understand why some people get to be parents." I felt like this was the perfect opportunity to ask about his parents.

"How about your parents? Were they good parents?

"Yeah," he said after several long seconds. "My parents were great. They met in high school, and they've been married almost 25 years."

"Wow." I smiled. "Do you have any siblings?"

"No. Just me." He cleared his throat. "Something happened after my mom got pregnant with me, and she didn't want any more kids."

"What happened?" I shoved my hair out of my face.

"I don't know." He shrugged. "I always assumed he'd had some type of affair or something because my Aunt Charlotte said my father was a man-whore before I was born." He laughed. "But it's not something that is really ever talked about."

"Now we know where you got it from." I bumped his arm with mine, laughing.

"You're not flirting with my girl, are you?" Christian teased, appearing from the darkness. My eyes went wide, blinking up to meet his. He must have realized what he'd said because his lip pinched into a thin line.

"Funny." Lincoln huffed a laugh. "Does it look like I have a death wish?" He dropped his feet, forcing the swing to a stop before standing. "I'm headed back to the pool house to mix up some drinks." He turned to look at me. "You look like you could use a drink." He was right; I could use one or four.

"We'll be up in a minute," Christian said, taking Link's spot on the swing. "I need to talk to Harper."

Link nodded before strolling off.

"What's up?" I asked when I could no longer see Link.

"My parents have lived in this town for decades," Christian said. "And they've never heard the name Dylan West. So, there's a possibility he's not from here, or that's not his real name." He shoved his hand through his dark hair. "My mom is going to pass the info to her PI And see what we can find out."

"Are you going to tell Link?" I stared down at my fidgeting hands.

"I think we should eliminate all other possibilities before we stir up drama for Link and his family," he said. "I would hate to tell him, and then it not be true."

"I don't want to cause problems." I sighed.

"Harper," he said immediately, trying to retract what he'd said. "I didn't mean it like that."

"I know," I said, and I did know. I didn't know what this news would do to Lincoln or his family, and I didn't want to lose him as a friend. "But I mean it; I don't want to cause problems for Link and his family." I sucked in a deep breath, slowly releasing it. "Maybe we should drop it. I've lived eighteen years without knowing who my dad is. There's no reason to go digging up bones now." Especially when those bones could end up hurting someone I cared about.

Christian's gaze swept over mine before he finally threw an arm over my shoulder and pulled me into him. I laid my head on him as he shoved the swing back.

"You've got me," he whispered. "Always." I knew with every ounce of my being that he meant that.

CHAPTER 42

Christian

Early the next morning, I rushed down the stairs, half asleep, to the kitchen before fumbling with my phone and hitting the screen to accept the incoming call. Trying not to wake Harper, I kept my volume down.

"Did you get the package?" I whispered.

"Yes," Ace said, a friend of the family who worked with the local Sheriff's office and had access to resources I needed.

"Do you have everything you need?" I watched the staircase for any signs of Harper.

"Yes," Ace said. "I'll send it to the lab today."

"How long will it take?"

"Shouldn't take long," he answered. "I'll call as soon as I have the results."

"Thanks," I said and disconnected the phone.

While my mom and her PI hunted for Dylan West, I worked on my piece of the 'who's Harper's dad' puzzle.

"What are you up to?" Maverick said from behind me. Fuck! I didn't hear him come in. I shrugged like I didn't know what he was talking about. "Don't play dumb. You're up to something."

He wasn't going to let this go.

"You can't say anything right now," I whispered. He

nodded. "I think Harper's dad is AJ Elliott."

His eyes went wide. "As in Link's dad, AJ Elliott?" I nodded. "Holy shit!"

"Shhh..." I pointed up the stairwell to where Harper was still sleeping.

He shoved his hand through his thick dark hair. "I take it Link doesn't know." I shook my head. "Holy shit!"

"I stole D.N.A. from both of them," I said. "And I sent it to Ace. He should be able to use it to see if they are related."

"Link's mom is going to lose it," Maverick said, shaking his head. That was an understatement. Link's mom was extremely possessive of Link's dad, or at least she used to be when we were growing up. It had been years since we spent time with them.

"I know," I said. "I'm just getting the information, and it will be up to Harper what she wants to do with it, but if she decides to tell them, I will support her."

"You should tell Link, man," Maverick said. "He's your best friend, and he cares about Harper. We all do." I wasn't sure how Link would handle the news that his father cheated on his mother and Harper was the outcome of that affair. I knew he would do anything to protect her now, but I didn't know if that would change after finding out.

"I'm not saying anything to anyone until I know for sure," I said. "Harper doesn't know I'm running the test, either. There's no reason to cause problems when there isn't any yet."

"You know, if he is her father, he could put an end to Noah and Levi with his connections," Maverick said, leaning against the counter.

"He could also try to put an end to Harper with his connections," I added. "Mr. Elliott can be unpredictable when provoked, and I don't know how much he knows about Harper. Or what he would do to prevent Ms. Elliott from finding out." He pressed his lips into a thin line, nodding his head. It hadn't crossed his mind that it could go the other way.

Mr. Water's had unconventional ways of making his millions. There had been rumors growing up that Link's family was associated with the mafia, but it had never been confirmed. However, people who stood against him or his family always had a way of disappearing.

"For now, we keep this quiet," I said. "Once I get the results, we can figure this all out."

"Okay," he said, crossing his arms over his chest. He might not agree with me, but he respected my decision. "Party starts at noon today. You guys coming?"

"Yes, we'll be there," I said. "I'm letting Harper sleep in."

Today was senior skip day, an annual tradition in the Valley hosted by our parents and the Valleyview Country Club. The massive pool party during the day usually relocated to the Lake House after sunset.

"You know Link's parents will be there, right?" Maverick asked.

"I do. No one but Harper knows about the possibility of her being AJ Elliott's daughter. So, it shouldn't be an issue."

He nodded. "See you there." He turned to walk away but stopped, spinning back to me. "You know..."

"Don't," I said. I already knew what he was going to say, and he was wrong, or I hoped he was. I would make sure he was wrong. Harper was one of us now. Everyone had accepted and protected her, including my parents, but we didn't know how the other parents would receive her.

CHAPTER 43

Harper

Trying not to let my insecurities get the best of me, I forced a smile as everyone sat outside on the patio around the pool, talking and laughing. A perfect day for a pool party; the sun was bright and warm, with enough cloud coverage to stir a cool breeze occasionally. Christian, Aiden, and Chloe talked me into attending a Valley annual tradition for its senior skip day. I didn't fit in, but I was trying to for Christian.

Christian was trying so hard to fit me into his world that sometimes he forgot I was still from the Villas, even if the Valley had temporarily adopted me. Or at least some of the Valley. The occasional whispers and stares reminded me I was out of place.

For as far back as anyone could remember, the Valley and Villas had always been mortal enemies, and bringing me over to the Valley wouldn't change that, no matter how hard Christian tried.

"Not so bad, is it?" Chloe laughed, sinking into a seat beside me.

"No," I said, shifting in my seat to keep from fidgeting. So far, it wasn't that bad. None of my worst-case scenarios had happened yet, though the group of women and girls directly across from us hadn't stopped staring since I stepped outside as they whispered between themselves. It could be a complete coincidence, but I doubted it. I'm sure everyone wondered who brought the girl from the Villas into the Valley. "I need a drink." I pushed out of my chair. I needed a break from the stares. "Do you want anything?"

"No thanks," Chloe said. "I think everything is still inside." She pointed to the double doors leading into the clubhouse.

Pushing through the door leading into the country club, I searched the large room for any sign of where they served drinks. The room was full of proud parents mingling and discussing their children's successes. Jealousy bloomed in my chest, wishing I had a parent here swooning over me.

"Wow," a woman's voice said, stopping me. "You look just like your mother." I twisted to see a petite brunette woman standing to my left. Her eyes swept over my face like she was examining it.

"I'm sorry." I smiled politely. "Do I know you?" I knew I didn't, but she seemed to know my mother, and I would love to know how.

"Mom," Link interrupted, strolling up to us. Mom? She was Link's mom. The woman married to the man who could be my father. "I see you've met Harper." Link threw an arm across my shoulders, and her eyes went wide, locking on his arm.

"Is this—" she paused, swallowing hard; her entire body went ridged. She cleared her throat. "Um, is this your girlfriend?" And, at that moment, I knew she knew. I could see it in her eyes. The fear that her son could be fucking his sister. But what did she know? Did she know there was a possibility I was Link's half-sister, or did she know I was?

"No." Link laughed. "Harper and I are friends. She's Christian's girl." Her body visibly relaxed. There was a slim chance she was uptight because she didn't want her son dating a Villa girl, and if she knew my mother, then she knew where I was from, but I didn't think that was it. I was almost one hundred percent positive she knew who my father was.

I wanted to ask her, but I didn't want to do it in front of anyone, especially Link. Link was important to me, and I didn't want to hurt him unnecessarily.

"Well, you guys enjoy your day." She forced a smile before turning and walking away.

"Come on," Link said, guiding me towards the bar. "Let's grab some drinks." I nodded, my gaze following Ms. Elliott to her table.

I couldn't focus on anything but Link's mom for the rest of the day. The way she'd looked at Link and me when she thought we might be dating. There was no way she didn't know something, and I needed to find out what.

"Are you okay?" Christian asked, worry lines creasing his forehead. I'd tried to disguise how distracted I was, but apparently, I wasn't doing a good enough job.

"I'm good." I forced a smile. "I need to use the restroom."

"Do you want me to go with you?"

"No, thank you." I pushed out of my chair. I leaned over, placing a kiss on his lips before heading inside. I didn't want him to go with me because I wanted to find Link's mom alone and talk to her, but I knew that would be hard to do here.

As I walked through the crowd, I searched the room for Ms. Elliott, but she wasn't at her table or anywhere visible.

Sighing heavily, I pushed through the bathroom doors, deciding to use the restroom and then take a casual walk around the club. Maybe I'd get lucky and find Ms. Elliott alone. The clubhouse bathroom was bigger than my entire childhood trailer. Flipping on the hot water, I washed my hands. A toilet flushed behind me, and my eyes flashed to the mirror to see Ms. Elliott stepping out of the stall.

"Harper." She said, stepping beside me and flicking on the water. "I was hoping I'd run into you again." I wasn't sure what to say or how to respond. So, I let her do the talking. "Your mom was an old friend of mine." I somehow doubted that. My mom and Ms. Elliott were from two different worlds. "How is she?"

"I wouldn't know," I muttered. "She abandoned me a few years ago to start a new family." I bit down hard on the inside of my cheek. I had no idea why I'd just said that.

"You had a good childhood?" My brows furrowed as our eyes locked through the mirror. My mind raced. Why would she care? That was such a random question. Until it hit me, she was trying to make herself feel better. She needed to hear about my amazing childhood to feel better about Mr. Elliots abandoning me.

"You know," I said, more a statement than a question.

"Know what, dear?" she said, her gaze darted down to her hands still under the sink's running water.

"That your husband could be my father." I scoffed. I couldn't believe we were playing this game. She knew; I knew she did. She swallowed hard but made no effort to confirm my suspicion, which I took as confirmation. "Does Link or Mr. Elliott know?"

"No." she reached out for me. "Please, they can never know."

CHAPTER 44

Harper

How did she know if he didn't know?

My eyes locked with Mrs. Elliott, and I struggled to grasp what was happening.

How was it possible that she knew he was my father, but her husband didn't? I understood Link not knowing, but how could Mr. Elliott not know that he was going to have a baby? I couldn't imagine my mother telling Mrs. Elliott the news and not my father.

"Harper," she pleaded, her tone desperate. "I don't know what your mom has told you, but please, I'm begging you not to tell Lincoln."

"Mr. Elliott doesn't know?" I narrowed my eyes at her. "How do you know?

"We can't talk about this now," she said. "Not here. They'll be looking for me soon."

She side-stepped me, reaching for the door. What I did next was completely out of character, but I knew if I let her leave, I might never know the truth. She was willing to do whatever she needed to protect her family.

"No." I stepped into her path. "I want the truth now." I crossed my arms over my chest. "Please."

"I promise, Harper," she said. "We can meet tomorrow alone."

"Christian won't let me out of his sight," I said. "So, if you want to do this alone, it's now or never."

"Christian knows."

"He knows there is a possibility that Mr. Elliott is my father," I said. "Him or Dylan West."

"Dylan West." She chuckled, her eyes softening. "Leave it to your mom to make up a name. She was always a clever one."

"I'm sorry?"

"There is no Dylan West." She shook her head. "AJ Elliott is your father."

"How do you know that?" I dropped my arms.

"It's a long story, Harper," she said.

"Make it a short one," I demanded.

"Long story short," she shrugged, "AJ fell in love with your mom at summer camp at twelve years old. Back then, dating someone from the Villas was forbidden. So when we got to high school, our families arranged our life together, and I fell in love with him, but even though they tried to keep them apart, he always ran back to your mom." She pressed her lips into a thin line. "I found out your mom was pregnant, and my family paid her off, but she thought it was AJ."

"How?"

"I found the letter she'd left for him before he did, and I gave it to my parents. They'd been exchanging letters secretly. It said she was pregnant. My family left a wad of cash, and a letter she thought was from him saying he wasn't ready to be a father, and he never wanted to see her again."

My gaze darted around the room, not focusing on anything, as the room spun. It suddenly felt like there wasn't enough air in the room for both of us.

"Harper, are you okay?" She reached out for me, and I jerked out of her reach. My chest rose and fell as I struggled to catch my breath.

"So, when you asked me if I had a good life, you were trying to make yourself feel better about your decision to take my father away from me?"

"Harper," she started.

"No," I cut her off, throwing a hand out. "My mother turned to alcohol after I was born, and sometime after that, she needed something harder to numb her pain. I was in and out of foster care. Men she brought into the house beat me. I haven't lived in a house with running water since I lived with my grandma. But then, a few years ago, my mom took off, and I hadn't seen her since Christian found her. She started a new life without me. She left me with my stepbrother Noah, who beat me if I looked at him wrong, and now they want to kill me so I can't even live a normal life. So, if you need someone to make you feel better about yourself, look elsewhere." I jerked the door open and stormed out.

I was done with this place. I was finished with these people.

Ms. Elliott wasn't to blame for everything that happened to me, and I knew that, but I couldn't help but wonder what my life might have been like if I'd had a father. Would my mom have been different? Would he have gotten custody of me? Would he have even wanted me?

"Harper," Christian said as I passed him. I hadn't even seen him.

"I'm leaving," I demanded, fighting the tears threatening to fall. "I want to leave."

"Okay," he said, stepping in beside me. "Harper, what happened?" I shook my head. "Okay. We'll leave."

"No," I said, stopping him. "You stay. This is your party. I'm leaving."

He huffed out a laugh. "That's not happening." Sliding his hand into mine, he pulled me toward the door. "You want to leave? Then we are leaving together." He didn't give me a chance to argue. I didn't want to ruin his day, but I couldn't stay there anymore. I couldn't stay and listen to the parents doting on their children.

Part of me was glad he was leaving with me, but a major part of me wished I could have a minute to process all everything that happened today without Christian questioning me. I knew he meant well and only wanted to protect me, but I needed a little space.

CHAPTER 45

Christian

The sun was close to setting as I stared out the kitchen window, watching Harper, who was lost in her thought, swinging on the old wooden swing and staring aimlessly into the distance.

Harper hadn't said a single word the entire ride home. She was visibly upset, and I knew the moment I saw Link's mom walk out of the bathroom shortly after Harper that it had everything to do with her father. It took every part of my being not to go all psycho boyfriend and tear into Link's mom, but that wouldn't help right now.

Harper hadn't moved from that spot on the swing since we'd gotten home. She'd wanted to be alone, and I respected her wishes even though I hated it. She'd come in when she was ready and hopefully explain what the hell happened.

"What's up with Harper?" Aiden pushed through the front door to the pool house. "Maverick said you left in a hurry, and it seemed like Harper was upset."

Aiden was the only one who knew anything about what was going on with Harper's family, and only because we all lived together, and it would be hard to hide it from him.

"I'm not sure what happened, but Link's mom came out

of the bathroom behind Harper today," I twisted around to face him. He leaned over the island, balancing himself on his forearms. His black hat turned backward on his head. "I have no idea what happened or why she was so upset, and she doesn't want to talk to me."

"Have you talked to Link yet?" he asked, cocking an eyebrow.

"No." I sighed, shaking my head. "It's not my place."

"Christian." He scowled, pushing up with his hands. "I get it; Harper is one of us now, but you and Link go way back, and if he finds out about this from someone else, he's gonna be pissed." Aiden leaned forward, his gaze locked on mine. "You're risking a long-time friendship over this."

"I don't care." I crossed my arms over my chest. "If she wants time to process all this, that's her decision."

"Link cares about Harper, too," Aiden reminded me. "We all do. He'd put his life in danger to protect her. He's not going to be mad about this."

"It could destroy his family," I gritted out. "You don't know how he'll take that news." I dropped my arms to my side, curling my hands around the edge of the counter I was leaning against. "This is Harper's life. It's not my place."

He shook his head. "This is wrong." He shrugged. "And Harper is wrong for coming in between you and your family because Link is your family."

My jaw clenched, teeth gritted, and my nostrils flared as my knuckles went white, clenching the counter tighter. If Aiden weren't my brother, I'd split his face open for saying anything about Harper. I didn't know whether I was right or wrong because it didn't matter. Harper had no one. She had no one she could count on but us, and it was her decision if she wanted to tell Link. Whether Aiden believed it or not, Link would understand that. Maybe not to begin with, but eventually.

The front door pushed open, and I relaxed, expecting Harper to step through, but Maverick and Bash did.

"Someone going to tell us what the fuck is going on," Bash

asked, throwing the door shut. I shrugged, shaking my head. "What happened today?"

"Nothing," I muttered.

"Why is Harper leaving the Valley by herself?" Maverick asked, throwing his thumb over his shoulder.

My face fell flat as I whipped around, my gaze snapping to the empty swing.

"Where did you see her?" I hissed, raising up my gaze and darting around the yard, looking for her. They had to be wrong. It couldn't have been her, but she's not out there. "Did you talk to her?"

"She was headed out of the Valley," Maverick said, shrugging. A wave of panic washed over me, threatening to swallow me whole. "We stopped, but she kept walking."

"She seemed upset," Bash added.

"This doesn't make sense." I scowled, pushing past them as fear built in my chest, my heart pounding as I searched the property. Everyone followed. "Why would she leave? She knows Noah, and the entire Southside is looking for her."

"Maybe she heard you arguing about her." Bash shrugged. My eyes snapped up, meeting his. My heart squeezed at the thought of her hearing Aiden and knowing exactly how she would take it. "We could hear you outside."

"I'll get the truck," Aiden said, pushing past me. "She couldn't have gotten far. We'll find her."

"I'll get my truck, too," Bash said. "We'll split up and cover more ground."

I didn't wait; I took off on foot. Maverick stepped in beside me.

"I'm with you," Maverick said. "We'll find her."

CHAPTER 46

Harper

A chill slithered up my spine as I tucked myself into the darkness down by the lake. My plan had been to leave the Valley, but I had nowhere to go, and I feared what could be waiting for me on the other side of those gates.

Aiden had been right. It wasn't right of me to ask Christian to keep this secret from his best friend. I shouldn't have asked him to choose between the friend he'd known his whole life and me, the girl he just met, who only brought chaos into his life.

My only chance was to get out of this town and disappear forever, but tonight it was cold and dark, so it would have to wait until morning.

"Please be unlocked," I whispered, sucking in a deep breath as I turned the handle to the front door of Link's family's lake house, and when the door pushed open, I blew out a breath. "I'll just hang out here until morning."

Pulling the blanket off the back of the sofa, I wrapped it around myself. I needed heat. Running my hand along the electric fireplace, I searched for the button to turn it on when I heard tires crunching along the gravel road leading up to the house. "Shit!"

Dropping the blanket, I dipped into the first closet I found. The wood of the porch creaked, and the door handle jiggled. Someone was inside. My pulse raced as I sucked in a deep breath, holding it in.

"I know you're here, Harper," the deep voice said. Thank God, it was Link. "So, you can save us both some time and just come out."

Blowing out my breath, I pushed open the door and stepped out to find Link standing, fists on hips. "How did you find me?"

"The property and house are covered in camera." He pointed to a small black camera tucked into the corner.

"I never was very good at being bad," I mumbled, sinking onto the couch. Grabbing the throw pillow, I pulled it to me, hugging it to my chest. "Does Christian know?"

"No." He sighed, sinking into the couch beside me. "We've all been out searching, and I was right down the road when I got an alert that someone was at the lake house."

"You should just call him," I muttered. "I don't want to come between you two anymore."

"Anymore," he said, cocking a brow at me. "I won't call him unless you want me to, but I'm also not going to let you leave the Valley without protection. Noah and his pack of thugs are waiting for a moment of weakness to pounce." He shrugged. "So, if you want to leave, I will help you do it safely and never say a word to Christian."

"Why? Why would you go against your best friend?"

"Christian loves you, and he would want me to help you." He swept his tongue over his lip ring. "He might be upset, but he would understand. Why do you want to leave?"

"Because I feel stuck. I feel like the walls are caving in, and I can't breathe. I feel like this is all too much, and it's all because of me. I'm ruining everything for everyone."

"That's not true," he scoffed. "You are part of our family now, which is what family does. Is Christian smothering you?"

"No." I shook my head. "What would you do if you knew

a secret that could hurt others? If the secret came out, it could possibly hurt your friend's family."

"That's a tough one," he said, pursing his lips. "But honestly, everyone deserves the truth, even if it hurts."

"So, you would want to know? Even if that truth could possibly destroy your family?"

"Yeah," he said. "Wouldn't you?"

He was right! I'd been searching for the truth my entire life, and to find out that someone I knew purposely hid it from me, thinking they were protecting me, would be incredibly frustrating, but I didn't have the same perfect life Link had.

"I think I may be your half-sister," I mumbled.

"What?" he narrowed his eyes.

"I think I may be your half-sister," I said, this time louder. He stared past me as his facial expression went from processing my words to disbelief to something I couldn't quite read. "Link? Are you mad?"

"No." He half smiled. "Truth?" I nodded. "I overheard my mother and grandmother talking a few months ago about a baby girl my father had. I didn't know it was you, though." He sucked in a deep breath before slowly blowing it out. "I questioned my father about it, and he had no idea what I was talking about."

"Your mother and grandmother paid my mom to leave your father alone," I said. "Your mom told me at the senior skip day event."

"That's why you left so upset," he said.

I nodded. "You don't seem surprised," I said.

"I love my mother, but sometimes she does stupid things," he scoffed.

"She asked me not to tell you."

"You shouldn't have had to tell me," he said. "None of this should have gone down the way it did."

"Christian knew," I added. "I asked him not to tell you until I had time to process everything, so please don't be mad at him. So, what do we do now?"

"I guess that's up to you." He shrugged. "What do you

want?"

"I have no idea."

CHAPTER 47

Christian

Three days... It had been three days since Harper disappeared without a word.

Pacing the kitchen floor in the main house, I searched my memories for where Harper could have disappeared.

"This doesn't make sense." Chloe scowled. "Harper knows Noah is looking for her. So why would she leave?" We hadn't had the chance to explain to her that it was our fault. That she'd heard Aiden talking to me, and she'd left.

Twisting to look at her, it hit me. Harper should be able to leave without me worrying about her safety. She should be able to go for a walk and not worry that someone would hurt her. I wanted to find Harper more than anything in the world to fix this, but right now, I was worried about the wrong thing.

I knew what I needed to do.

Snatching my keys off the counter, I stormed towards the door.

"Where are you going?" Aiden followed behind me.

"To do what I should have done a long time ago," I said dryly, pushing through the front door and storming down the driveway.

"Christian," Aiden pleaded. "Think about this."

"I have," I said, beeping the Jeep unlocked. "If I can't find

Harper to bring her back, then at least she will be safe out there without me."

"This is insane," Aiden barked. "You have no idea what you're walking into." I threw the door open and jumped into the Jeep, and Aiden did the same on the passenger side. "If you're not going to listen to me, I'm going with you."

"Christian," Chloe shouted. "Aiden." Aiden flashed her a look, and she gave a slight nod. He'd told her something with a look, but I didn't have time to figure out what. It didn't matter. Flicking on the headlights, I threw the Jeep into drive.

I'd burned the single-wide dump 'where they'd lived to the ground, but I'd heard rumors that Noah had moved his dirty business into a bar on the south side. A bar that Levi owned. Moving in on their turf was a death wish, and I knew it. Who knew how many would be there or what weapons they had available? I had to be smart about this.

"If something happens to you, Harper has no one," Aiden hissed, grabbing the dash as I whipped the Jeep around a corner. He was wrong. She had an entire family in the Valley. Aiden, Link, Chloe, Ryder, Bash, Maverick, and Julian would ensure she was taken care of, not to mention my family. I had to do this. I had to end this for her, even if it meant I died, too.

It took fifteen minutes to get to the old run-down bar. Pulling the Jeep into a dark back corner of the bar, I killed the lights and engine.

"Now what?" Aiden asked. I didn't answer. I didn't know yet. The bar was eerily dark and quiet, even though several cars were in the parking lot. I wasn't even sure if it was a functioning business or a drug house.

"We wait," I muttered. We would wait for the perfect moment to end this.

"We don't even know if Noah is in there." Aiden groaned, slumping back in his seat.

I opened my mouth to respond but immediately snapped it shut when the back entrance door flew open, and Noah strolled out with a phone to his ear. My gaze flashed to Aiden.

Game on!

"You have about 30 seconds," Aiden warned before you'll have the entire south side out here." He swallowed hard. "You can't fight them all."

"Guess I'll have to be quick," I said, the corners of my lips curving up into a smirk.

"And quiet," he warned.

Before he could say anything else, I silently slid out of the Jeep, stalking toward my prey.

Noah's back was turned to me. Distracted by his phone call, he never saw me coming. Tapping his shoulder, he whipped around, and I sunk my fist into his jaw. His phone went flying, and everything went white with rage. I knew he'd gotten a punch in, but I couldn't feel them. The adrenaline pumping overpowered any pain. I threw another hard fast punch that landed square in his face, sending him flying back to the ground.

"This is for Harper." I climbed over him to finish this. The fight would draw a crowd soon. My fist connected with his jaw. The sound of cracking bones echoed over the commotion behind me—another punch and then another. Using every ounce of body weight to pin him in place, I curled my hands tightly around his throat, squeezing. His eyes widened as he struggled beneath me, desperately fighting for air. His dirty hands scratched and clawed at my hands, tightening. This was it. Noah would never be a problem for Harper again.

"Stop, now," a muffled voice demanded, but I could barely hear through my rage. I didn't know if it was Aiden or someone else, but it didn't matter. I wouldn't stop unless they pulled me off.

I jolted, ducking, when the sound of a gun boomed, cracking through the night from behind me. I twisted around, my gaze flashing up. Red and blue flashing strobe lights filled the night, and men in uniforms surrounded us with guns drawn and pointed directly at us.

Who called the cops? My gaze flashed around the parking lot, trying to see through all the flashing lights. Noah and his gang weren't the types to involve the law, especially bringing it to their place of dirty business. They would let one of their own die and still wouldn't get law enforcement involved.

CHAPTER 48

Christian

"Noah Beckham," an officer announced as they surrounded him with weapons drawn. "You are under arrest for drug distribution." The officers passed me, moving quickly to Noah. "You have the right to remain silent. Anything you say can and will be used against you in a court of law. If you cannot afford an attorney, one will be provided."

Jumping to my feet, I brushed myself off; my gaze focused on the officers cuffing Noah.

"Christian," Link said from behind me. "What the fuck are you doing here?" I twisted around, eyes locked on his. The more important question was, why was he here? My gaze flicked over his shoulder, my face falling flat when my gaze locked with Mr. Elliott. And why was his dad here?

"What's going on?" I narrowed my eyes, flicking my gaze between them.

"Harper no longer needs to worry about anyone from the Villas," Mr. Water said, his gaze focused on what was happening behind me. "She's free to live her life now."

"Yeah, until they're released," I growled, my tone laced with anger and irritation. AJ Elliott knew nothing about the Villas or how this worked. He just made things worse because when they got out, and they would get out, they would come straight for Harper. If they ever waited that long. They could hire someone from the inside to take care of her.

"They'll never be released," Link whispered.

I snorted a laugh. Link knew better than that. We'd seen how the judicial system worked in this town. "Link," I started.

"They won't make it to the jail, son," AJ whispered in a low, deadly tone that only I could hear, and everything sank in. It all made sense now. AJ Elliott had nothing to do with the judicial system, but he had a lot of pull in this town, and his methods were always unconventional. I wanted to know exact details, but I knew he wouldn't give them, and more than likely, Link was only on need-to-know information as well, but I'd hear about whatever he'd planned tomorrow morning on the news.

My gaze met AJ's, and I gave the slightest of nods, relaying the message that I heard him loud and clear. AJ returned the nod before strolling back towards all the flashing lights.

"So, it's over," Aiden said, stepping in beside Link and me as we watched them load Noah into a squad car.

"This part is," Link sighed. "Harper is free from the Villa Boys."

Those words hit me hard for some reason. Harper was free. She was free from the Villas and would no longer be in danger, but she would never be completely free from her past.

"Wait," I paused. Bumping Link's shoulder, I twisted around to face him. "Do you know where Harper is?"

"Don't kill me," he exclaimed, holding his hands out. "But yes. She is safe."

"How long?" I said, stepping into him.

"I found her at the lake house the day she went missing." Anger simmered low in my stomach as I tried to steady my breathing. He'd known the whole time she was safe. My fist clenched at my sides. "Christian, she asked me not to tell you." He paused. His throat flexed on a hard swallow. "The same way she asked you not to tell me."

"She told you?" He nodded. "Everything?" He nodded again. My entire body relaxed with a sigh. I couldn't be angry with him or Harper, even if they hurt me. I was relieved she was safe.

"I—" I started, but my eyes widened as Aiden's fist slammed into Link's face shoving him back to the ground. "What the..." I surged forward, grabbing Aiden's arm and jerking him back.

"Did she ask you not to tell me, too?" Aiden hissed. My eyes flashed from Link, who was wiping the blood off his lip with the pad of his thumb, to Aiden, who was heaving with anger.

Aiden had taken all of this personally. He'd beaten himself up every night over Harper leaving because she'd heard him talking. She'd gone and put herself in danger because of him, or at least that's what he thought, and if something had happened to her, he never would have been able to forgive himself.

"I deserved that," Link said, pushing up to his feet. "But yes, she did." He dusted himself off. "She didn't want either of you to deal with her problems. She wanted to handle it, but this was over all of our heads, so I got my dad involved."

"Does he know?" I asked, releasing Aiden's arm.

"Yeah." He nodded. "With her permission, I told him." I wanted to know more. I wanted to know everything, but at that moment, I needed to talk to Harper. I had to see her, to see that she was okay.

"Where is she?"

"She's at the lake house." I didn't wait for any more explanations or excuses. I needed to see Harper. I needed to explain that whatever she heard didn't matter; she was important to me, my family, and Aiden, and I couldn't imagine my life without her. I needed her to come back home.

CHAPTER 49

Harper

The soft rumble of a truck had me on alert. Only Link knew where I was. Cracking the curtains, I exhaled as I watched Link's truck swerve up the driveway.

Throwing open the front, I stepped out on the porch, pulling my thin jacket around me. Glancing up, I froze. It wasn't Link, but Christian. My chest swelled at the sight of him. I'd missed him.

I'd practiced what I would say the next time I saw him a hundred times, yet nothing came to mind standing here frozen, unable to speak.

"I'm sorry." I sighed after several long minutes. "I—"

He didn't let me finish. Instead, he grabbed my waist, pulling me flush against him. "Don't ever. Do that. Again." I could hear the relief in his tone as guilt wrapped tightly around me at whatever I'd put him through.

"I'm sorry," I muttered, pushing off his chest. My gaze flashed up to meet his. "Aiden was right. I need to handle this myself."

"No, I wasn't," Aiden's voice called out from behind Christian. We both twisted around to see Aiden strolling up the porch. "I was wrong, and I'm sorry."

"No one was wrong or right," Link chimed in. We all

turned to see Link strolling up with his dad. My dad. That was a weird thought. My gaze flashed between Link and his dad. What was he doing here?

"What's going on?" I narrowed my eyes at Link.

"Link's right," Mr. Elliott said. "This was a fucked up situation, and everyone did their best."

I nodded, understanding what he was saying. He was right.

"Mom," Christian asked. Following his line of sight, I see Christian's mom and Mrs. Elliott.

"Wait," I said. "What's going on?"

"She doesn't know," Link said.

"I don't know what?"

"After I left here the other day," Link started. "I knew you were going to try to handle Noah and Levi yourself, and I knew we were in over our heads. So, I went to my dad for help. If anyone knew how to deal with Noah and Levi, it would be him." His tongue swept out, wetting his dry lips. "I wasn't going to tell him who you were, but he already knew."

"How?" I asked, my gaze flashing from Link to Mr. Elliott.

"I told him." Link's mom said. "I'm sorry, Harper. There's no excuse for what I did to you and your mother back then, but I hope you'll give me a chance to make it up to you." Overwhelmed, I didn't know what else to do, so I nodded. "When we discovered you were in danger, we called Christian's mom."

"Wait," Christian said, his eyes narrowed on his mother. "You knew where she was?"

"I did," his mom said. "I found out yesterday. Link asked us not to say anything until after Noah and Levi were taken care of. He wanted her to have a safe place to stay and was scared she'd leave if anyone knew."

"Taken care of," I muttered, repeating her words.

"Noah was arrested today along with Levi and everyone affiliated with them and their illegal business," Christian said. "I was there. I was going to kill him, but the cops showed up."

"What?" I snapped. When I'd left, I wanted to protect

Christian and his family to keep them out of this mess I'd caused, but I should have known Christian wouldn't let it go that easily.

"There was an accident on Laurel Dr. near the annex," Christian's mom said, and my heart caught in my throat. "Noah and Levi were both pronounced DOA."

"DOA?" I asked.

"Dead on arrival," she said, her lip twitching into a smile as her eyes flashed from AJ to Christian and back to me. Noah and Levi were gone. It was over.

"So, it's over then," I muttered. My eyes flashed to each of them as they all nodded.

"They can't hurt you anymore." Christian's mom said. "No more hiding."

A wave of emotions washed over me all at once. Tears burned the back of my eyes. I swallowed the lump forming in my throat. "Thank you," I whispered to everyone.

"What happens now?" Christian asked, throwing an arm across my shoulder.

"Well," Mr. Elliott said, nodding toward me. "That all depends on Harper." He offered a soft smile. "I would love a chance to get to know my daughter if she's interested. We have an extra room in the house. We could make it yours."

As much as I would love that, I knew Mrs. Elliott would be uncomfortable with me being there.

"We would all love it," Mrs. Elliott smiled, looping an arm around Lincoln's waist.

CHAPTER 50

Harper

Days turned into weeks, and I stayed in the pool house at Christian's. I liked having my own space even if Christian was always there. I'd agreed to dinners at the Elliott house twice a week and attend all family functions in the future.

Scanning the room, a flood of emotions washed over me: joy, gratitude, sadness, excitement, and most of all, love.

Three hours ago, Christian, Lincoln, Aiden, Chloe, Julius, Sebastian, Maverick, and I walked across the stage with all our classmates for graduation.

"I would like to make a toast," Mr. Elliott said, clanking a fork against his champagne glass. Quiet rolled over the room, and all eyes focused on Mr. Elliott. A room filled with everyone's families and friends. I'd always felt out of place in these situations. I didn't have any family, or at least none that cared enough to show up for me, but now I did, not just Mr. Elliott and Lincoln, but everyone. They'd all gone out of their way to make today as special for me as they did for everyone else. Even Chloe's parents, who I thought hated me.

"It doesn't feel like it was that long ago that we were dropping you all off for your first day of kindergarten, but now two blinks later, here we are, watching all of you graduate." My chest tightened. No one had dropped me off on my first day of kindergarten. No one had been there to pick me up either. Forcing a smile, I shoved those memories back. The past didn't matter anymore. It was time to look forward to my future. "I know I am beyond proud of each of your accomplishments, and I can't wait to see what your futures hold. Cheers to the graduating class of 2019."

Everyone shouted 'cheers' holding their glasses high before finally taking a sip.

"Harper," Christian's mom said, stepping in beside me. My gaze flicked up, meeting hers. "Can I borrow you for a minute?"

"Yes, of course." I smiled, setting my glass on the table behind me. The room was loud with excitement and music, making it hard to hear. Christian's mom threw her thumb over her shoulder towards the back door. I nodded.

Pushing through the door, I sucked in a deep breath of fresh air, letting the quiet sink in for a moment. I enjoyed the quiet, probably more than I should, but so much chaos had always filled my life that I learned to appreciate silence.

"I have something for you." Christian's mom said, pulling a long, thick white envelope out of her bag and handing it to me. Taking the envelope, I narrowed my eyes at the black printed writing with my name on it. Nothing good ever came for me in an envelope this large. "Open it."

Forcing a smile, I nodded only because she seemed excited about the envelope. I paused when the back door flew open, and Christian stepped out, holding the same white envelope. My gaze flashed between them.

"Go on, Harper," Christian urged, a large grin covering his handsome face. "Open it."

I tore the envelope open and pulled out the contents.

Dear Harper Brooks,
Congratulations on your acceptance
into Brigham University!

My eyes widened. I stopped reading as my gaze shot up to

meet Christian's mom.

"Congratulations!"

"This is real?" I asked, holding up the letter. They both nodded. "I'm going to a real university?" They nodded again. "How? I missed all the deadlines."

"I have a friend, and she pulled some strings," Christian's mom said. "We did miss all the deadlines for financial aid, though." My entire body sank. No way I could afford to pay for college without a scholarship or grant, even with two jobs. Brigham was an out-of-state private university. Their tuition alone would be astronomical, which didn't include books, supplies, or fees. It also didn't include living expenses, which I would need because Brigham University was close to a thousand miles away from here.

"I've already taken care of all the tuition," Mr. Elliott said from the doorway. I hadn't even noticed him. "I will cover everything financially." I couldn't fight the uncontrollable tears as they started streaming. "We can discuss living arrangements and everything over dinner tomorrow since Christian will also be going..."

"You're going too?" I interrupted, my gaze snapping up to his.

He nodded. "If you're going, I'm going."

"Perhaps we can all have dinner together tomorrow," Mr. Elliott said to Christian's mom. "We can fine-tune all the details then."

Mr. Elliott and Christian's mom disappeared inside after a few more 'thank you's and a hug.

"I thought you didn't want to go to college."

"I don't." He laughed, stepping into my personal space. His fingers curled around my hips as he pulled me into him. "I want to be with you, and if that means I go to college to be with you, then that's what I'll do." Dropping his head, his mouth captured mine in a kiss that made my knees buckle. "I want to take you home," he breathed against my lips.

With finishing school and all the chaos tied to both our

lives, we hadn't gotten a lot of alone time unless we were passed out.

"What about the party?"

"What about it?"

"Let's get out of here," I laughed. His arms slid around my waist as he hoisted me up against him, carrying me to his Jeep.

I didn't know exactly what the future held, but I knew he would be a part of it, and to think it all started with a tiny bag of weed. If Lincoln hadn't stolen that bag of weed, and I'd never gone into the Valley to get it, who knows where my life would be right now?

"What the..." Christian hissed, stopping halfway to his Jeep, freezing in the driveway. He dropped me to my feet. I twisted around, and my eyes widened.

"Mom?"

CHAPTER 51

Harper

"What are you doing here?" I asked, anger illuminating my face. Staring at the woman who'd left one morning and never returned, I realized I didn't even recognize her. When she'd left, she'd been wearing a pair of faded, ripped jeans and a stained light pink tank she'd gotten from a church during a free clothing drive. She was too thin for her height, her teeth rotted from years of neglect and drug abuse, and her skin crawled with puncture wounds. This woman was healthy and drug-free. She wore expensive clothing and drove a fancy car.

"I know you're upset with me," she started.

"Upset," I repeated, cutting her off. Anger colored my tone. "You abandoned me and started a whole new life without me." Gritting my teeth together, I stepped forward, feeling Christian's presence directly behind me. "Leaving me to fend for myself with Noah and Levi."

"Harper, please," she pleaded. "I know I don't deserve it, but I only want a minute to talk to you."

What could she possibly have to say now, and would it really make a difference in how I felt about her?

"Do you want her to leave?" Christian asked, and I knew what he was asking. He wanted to know if he should remove her himself. Twisting around to face him, I realized we weren't alone. Everyone from the party had started to migrate outside.

"AJ," my mother muttered, blinking in surprise. "What are you doing here?"

"I'm here for my son and daughter's graduation," AJ said, stepping in beside me. "What are you doing here?"

"I need to talk to Harper," she sighed. "But I probably need to talk to you too." AJ's gaze flicked down to me. His dark eyes searched my face, but I couldn't figure out what he was searching for until he spoke. He was searching for permission to step up and be my father.

"No," he said, his gaze flashing back to meet hers. His tone was not angry but harsh and dripping with disappointment. "I know why you left and didn't tell me about Harper, but I will never understand how you abandoned her as a child. I never had the opportunity to be a parent to her then, but I do now." My chest tightened with a weird mixture of pain and rage, but also gratitude. I was so angry with my mother but thankful for AJ, who was here to stand up for me—something I'd never experienced from a parent before. "So get in your fancy car and leave. Don't ever come back. Don't call her. Don't follow her. Don't even do a Google search on her. You forfeited all your rights to know anything about her the day you walked out, started a new family, and left your child to fend for herself against grown men hurting her."

A tear streamed down my mother's face, and a wave of rage surged through me. She didn't get to be sad. She didn't get to be upset now. This was all her fault.

"Save the tears. You have no right to be upset." Tears prickled at my throat, but I forced them back, swallowing them. I wouldn't shed a tear for her. She didn't deserve my tears. "If some time in the future Harper decides she wants to talk to you, she'll contact you, but until then, don't attempt to contact her, or I'll see to you myself." The threat came through loud and clear.

"You don't understand," my mother cried.

"There's nothing left to understand," AJ muttered, sadness twisting his facial features. "What my wife and her family did to you and Harper was wrong, and I'm hoping to have the chance to fix it with Harper." His gaze flicked over to where his wife stood with Lincoln and then back to my mother. "But what you did to your own daughter is unforgivable." His gaze blinked down at me as a sad smile spread across his face.

"It's sad," Christian said, throwing an arm over my shoulder. "You missed out on being a part of Harper's life, and she's pretty amazing." His gaze flicked down to me. "Harper has a family now." His gaze flicked back to her. "And you aren't part of it."

"We will all make sure Harper has everything she needs," AJ said, holding his arms out and gesturing to everyone huddled around me. "We will make sure she's safe."

"We will make sure she's not hungry," Christian's mom spoke up.

"We will make sure she has a roof over her head," Lincoln's mom smiled.

"We will make sure she has electricity and running water," Chloe shouted.

"We will make sure she has clean clothes," Ryder said.

"We will make sure she has a clean bed to sleep in," Aiden snarled.

"We will make sure no one ever hurts her again," Maverick said.

"Because that's what families do," AJ said. The tears streamed down my face uncontrollably, but not for her. For them. For everyone who didn't have to be but chose to be. For the family, I'd always dreamed about, and now I had. "They don't abandon each other when times get tough."

"They take care of each other," Christian finished his sentence. "So, you should leave, and if Harper decides she wants to talk to you, she'll let you know."

"She's only here because her husband found out," Chloe's mother spoke up from the back of the crowd. Everyone twisted around, glaring at Chloe's mom. "I'm friends with her husband's sister. We had drinks yesterday, and she was venting about her brother's wife. I didn't know it was you until I just called her and asked her the wife's name. He kicked you out because he found out you abandoned Harper."

Spinning back around to face her, my eyes widened. "So, you're only back to ask me to help you fix it, aren't you?" I choked out as a wave of pain washed over me. This all made sense now why she would show up out of the blue. "Did you come back to ask me to cover for you? Or to lie about something else?"

"Harper," she pleaded. "I have nowhere to go, and my girls need me." I exhaled sharply as if I'd been punched in the gut. My knees felt weak, and suddenly I struggled to breathe. Why would I think she'd come back because she wanted to apologize or felt bad for what she'd done? She didn't. She only cared about herself.

"Leave," I hissed, pointing toward her car.

"Harper."

"She said leave." Christian's tone was low and threatening. His entire body tensed as his fist clenched at his side. When she didn't move fast enough, he jerked forward, sending her flying backward so fast and hard that she tripped over her feet, falling back. Lincoln, Maverick, Aiden, and Sebastian moved in quickly, each grabbing a limb.

"What are you doing?" my mother asked. They didn't answer as they lifted her off the ground. "Get your hands off me. Harper, please don't do this. Please talk to me." Christian was fast. So fast, I didn't realize he'd moved until he was already leaning down in her face.

A low growl tore out of him. "Don't. Ever. Say her name. Again." Her eyes widened with fear, shock, or both, but she got the message.

AJ opened her car door, and they shoved her in. AJ leaned into the car, saying something only she could hear, but I had a pretty good idea what it was.

Watching my mother's expensive car back out and pull away, I decided that would be the last time I saw her. She would never be the person I wanted her to be, the mother I'd longed for. At that moment, I made peace with the fact that she was gone forever.

CHAPTER 53

Christian

Shoving the last brown moving box into the back of my Jeep, I slammed the door shut. This was it. We were all packed and ready to leave for college.

That was something I never thought I'd say.

We'd said most of our goodbyes yesterday, but Chloe, Ryder, and my mom came to see us off today. Chloe and my mom struggled the most with our departure.

"Are you guys sure you want to leave so early?" my mom sighed, pulling me in for a quick hug. "College doesn't start for another six weeks."

"Yeah." I pulled out of the hug, throwing an arm across Harper's shoulder. "I think we are both ready for a fresh start."

"Okay," she said before sucking in a deep breath. "I'm coming to visit before school starts, though." I smiled and nodded.

"It's not going to be the same without you guys here," Aiden said, smiling sadly.

"We'll be back for Thanksgiving and Christmas," I said." And you guys can come to visit anytime." I glanced at my watch. "We really need to get on the road if we are going to make it before dark."

"You promise you'll call me once a day?" Chloe asked.

"I promise," Harper laughed. "And once you're settled in your new dorm, I'll come to visit."

"Don't forget about me," Ryder said, holding out his arms for a hug. Harper leaned in for a hug before pulling Chloe into the hug. "You take care of her." Ryder's eyes flicked to me. I nodded.

Some goodbyes were harder than others. Saying goodbye to Chloe and Ryder was hard for Harper. They'd been her only life source for many years, but she'd see them both soon. Chloe was accepted to a college only an hour away, and Ryder to an Art School only forty-five minutes away, but we all knew it wouldn't be the same.

"Wait," AJ called out, jogging up the driveway as I opened Harper's door. "Sorry, I'm late. The bank took forever." He reached into his pocket and pulled out a credit card. "Here." He held it out to Harper. "I wanted to make sure you got this before you left."

"Thank you." She smiled politely. "But I'm going to get a job once we get there and get settled."

"Please," AJ said. "Just take it, and if you don't need it, that's fine, but I'll feel better knowing you have it if you need it." She nodded. "Not that I don't trust Christian; I just want to make sure you have your own money." She nodded again, taking the card and leaning in for a hug. "Be safe and let me know when you make it." She nodded. "We'll be up to visit before school starts."

"Thank you." Harper said, hopping into the Jeep.

"If you need anything, call me," AJ said. "Seriously, anything."

Jumping into the driver's side, I started the Jeep and waved goodbye as we pulled away.

"You okay?" I asked once we were out of the Valley.

"Oddly." She sighed, staring out the window, "I feel a huge sense of relief leaving this town and all the bad memories. Of course, I'm sad to leave everyone behind, but saying goodbye to the past feels pretty good." A smile spread across my face. "I'm excited to see what the future holds."

I didn't know what the future had planned for us, but I knew no matter what, she was free. Free from the Villas. Free to live her own life. Free to be who she wanted to be, and I could live with that.

EPILOGUE

Harper

"I have to go," Sophia called out, her dark falling into her face as she leaned forward to grab her bag. "I have to get to work."

"I'll see you tomorrow. Same time, same place."

"Of course," she said, brushing her hair out of her hazel eyes.

"Oh wait, you're still coming for dinner this weekend, right?"

"Yes." She narrowed her eyes, tossing her bag over her shoulder. "As long as you swear it's not a setup."

Pursing my lips, I shrugged innocently. "I don't know what you're talking about."

"Well, then I can't wait to meet your family and friends." She opened the front door at the same time Christian was attempting to do the same.

"Oh." He laughed. "Hey, Soph."

"What's up, Christian. Do me a favor and remind your girlfriend this weekend is not a setup." His gaze flashed to me.

"What?" I shrugged. "It's not a setup."

"See you later." Sophia laughed, and Christian closed the door behind him.

"Is it a setup?" He dropped his gym bag by the door before his long fingers curled around my hips, pulling me into him.

"No." I smirked, looking up at him. "But I mean, she's single, and Link's single, so..." I shrugged dramatically. "Who knows what will happen?"

He rolled his eyes, leaning in to kiss my forehead.

Sinking onto the couch, I blew out a heavy breath as a smile spread across my face. We'd officially been in our new place for a year. School was great. I'd made new friends and gotten my first job offer at a local bar waitressing at night. Christian wasn't super thrilled, but he acted excited for me.

Christian stayed busy with school and his daily workouts and worked full-time remotely with Aiden for Chandler Enterprises.

My phone chimed.

"Hey." A smile spread across my face at the screen when Link's face appeared.

"Hey, What's up? You ready to party this weekend?"

"Of course."

"What's up, Link?" Christian said, stepping into view from over my shoulder.

"What's up?" he squealed in the bromance tone I'd gotten used to.

"My flight lands Friday at three p.m.," he said. "I'll text you my flight info tonight."

"Be warned," Christian chuckled. "Harper is planning to set you up with her new bestie."

"Harper," Link scolded. "Does Chloe know you have a new bestie?"

I laughed. "Chloe will always be my number one ride or die. And Chloe and Aiden will be here this weekend too."

"No shit," Link chuckled. "Hey, is your friend hot?"

"Yes," I said, my lips curling into a mischievous grin. Sophia was hot. She was tall, with long dark hair and big hazel eyes. She had flawless tanned skin and was smart and funny, and I knew that if she and Link met, they'd hit it off.

"Christian," Link called out. "Is her friend hot?"

"No way, man." Christian laughed. "I'm not going down that rabbit hole."

"Oh shit," Link said, his gaze flicking to the side. "I gotta go.

See you guys Friday."

"See you Friday," I said.

"Oh, Harper," he interrupted. "Call Dad, or he will show up at your house."

"I'll call him tonight."

We disconnected, and I tossed my phone on the coffee table in front of me.

Things were so different now. I had people who cared enough to worry about me.

I tried to make a habit of calling my father once a week, but that usually wasn't enough for him. Chloe and I talked at least once a day, but we hadn't seen each other in over six months. I sometimes found myself missing parts of my old life, which was crazy because I would never go back and relive them, especially the days before Christian. I mostly missed my old friends, school, and the new friends I'd made after Christian. I missed crawling through Chloe's window and staying up all night talking. I missed hiding out in the bathroom with Ryder when I didn't want to go to class.

I knew once everyone showed up this weekend, those feelings would fade. I missed my friends and family.

"What do you want for dinner tonight?" Christian asked from the kitchen. "Do you want to go out, or do you want me to cook?"

The question was so easy, yet so complicated. Did I want to go out with Christian for dinner, or did I want him to cook something and stay home?

Pushing off the couch, I strolled into the kitchen. I licked my lips, my gaze raking over his tight and toned torso, and I realized I wasn't hungry for food.

His eyes locked on mine, and I knew he was reading my mind. Wrapping his fingers around my hips, he jerked me into him, pulling my body flush against his. His mouth collided with mine in an all-consuming kiss that stole the air from my lungs. Slipping my hand inside the waistband of his boxers, he groaned into my mouth as I gripped him.